THE CONQUEST

THE CONQUEST

THE STORY OF
A NEGRO PIONEER

OSCAR MICHEAUX

Introduction by
Professor Jayna J. Brown

WASHINGTON SQUARE PRESS
New York London Toronto Sydney Singapore

This book is a work of fiction. Names, characters, places and
incidents are products of the author's imagination or are used
fictitiously. Any resemblance to actual events or locales or persons,
living or dead, is entirely coincidental.

A Washington Square Press Publication of
POCKET BOOKS, a division of Simon & Schuster, Inc.
1230 Avenue of the Americas, New York, NY 10020

Introduction copyright (c) 2003 by Simon & Schuster, Inc.

ISBN: 0-7434-6058-8

First Washington Square Press trade paperback printing April 2003

10   9   8   7   6   5   4   3   2   1

WASHINGTON SQUARE PRESS and colophon are
registered trademarks of Simon & Schuster, Inc.

For information regarding special discounts for bulk purchases,
please contact Simon & Schuster Special Sales at 1-800-456-6798
or business@simonandschuster.com

Printed in the U.S.A.

To the

HONORABLE BOOKER T. WASHINGTON

INTRODUCTORY

*This is a true story of a negro who was discontented
and the circumstances that were the outcome of that discontent.*

Introduction

THE CONQUEST, written in 1913, is the first of seven novels Oscar Micheaux (1884–1951) would write over the course of his career. He is best remembered though as a driven and prolific filmmaker. From his first film, *The Homesteader*, finished in 1919, to his last, *The Betrayal*, released in 1947, Micheaux wrote, produced, and directed approximately forty films. Most of his films remain missing—including his first effort—yet Micheaux is responsible for the largest number of "race films" extant today by a single director. Two of his previously missing, early silent films have been found: *Within Our Gates*, produced in 1919, and *Symbol of the Unconquered*, produced in 1920. Fortunately, both films have been restored and are now readily available to the public. But Micheaux began his career by writing a novel. Inspired by Tuskegee educator Booker T. Washington's autobiographical opines, his fictional autobiography is the *bildungsroman* of a self-made man. The "biographical legend" Micheaux begins to develop here would inform the rest of his novels and films.[1] His signature textual strategy is the reuse and revision of semiautobiographical material; beginning with Oscar Devereaux of *The Conquest*, Micheaux's narrator/central protagonists are all fictional versions of himself.

Tales of lone men conquering the wild distinguished American popular literature in the first decades of the twentieth century. In this respect *The Conquest* is a useful document of its time, reflecting turn-of-the-century ideologies of manhood and empire, rugged individualism, and capitalist competition. In a literary context, we can understand *The Conquest* as influenced by early twentieth-century American popular literature—western romances and frontier survival stories—like those by Jack London. *The Conquest* confounds our understanding, however, by openly appropriating a version of the ideology of Manifest Destiny, seemingly ignoring its openly white supremacist agenda.

The Conquest sits in interesting contrast to the autobiography of another black frontiersman, Nat Love. Born in 1854 in Tennessee, Love self-published his autobiography in 1907. In 1869, Love struck out for Kansas, preceding the Exodusters, ex-slaves who migrated to Kansas after the Civil War, the largest number leaving en masse in the spring of 1879.[2] Locating first to Dodge City, he becomes a hard-drinking cowboy, leading the "wild life of the plains . . . courting death in fights with Indians and Mexicans and daredevil riding on the range."[3] Love was one of "several colored cowboys" driving cattle and horses across the western plains.[4] Carousing with rough and tough outlaws such as Billy the Kid, Love had a very different relationship to the West than did Micheaux. Micheaux/Devereaux has scathing words for the same western towns that so captivated Love, filled as they were with "pick pockets, con men, lewd women and their consorts . . . idle sports [and] ragtime music" (p. 128). Yet there are interesting similarities in the ways each man constructs himself. Both are equally quick to deride North American native populations, the "blood thirsty red skins" as Love calls them,[5] as well as the cattle rustlers, "the outlaws and mixed bloods" who defy the will of the U.S. government (p. 120).

Both men also worked the Pullman trains. After the closing of the frontier in 1890, Love becomes a Pullman porter on trains running mostly out of Colorado, but at some point he also worked the same Portland to Chicago route as did Micheaux/Devereaux in *The Conquest*.

Unlike Nat Love's adventure tale, *The Conquest* is a funny combination of adventure story and black uplift polemic. Bidding farewell to "Chicago's black belt with its beer cans, drunken men and women," Devereaux states, "I turned my face westward with the spirit of Horace Greeley before his words 'go west, young man,' ringing in my ears. So westward I journeyed, to the land of real beginning, and where I was soon to learn more than a mere observer ever could by living in the realm of a big city" (p. 36). In response to the black people migrating from the rural South to midwestern, southern and northern indus-trial cities in the first decades of the century, factions of the black urban middle class organized as reformers, dedicated to the moral education of these migrants. Throughout his career Micheaux laced his works with ethical catechisms for the migrants, criticizing them for the lack of an appropriate work ethic and for their participation in alternative economies, such as numbers running, bootlegging, and welfare fraud.

Micheaux's fervent belief in the strategies for racial uplift developed and promoted by Booker T. Washington helps us to understand *The Conquest*'s polemical narrative. Micheaux dedi-cates *The Conquest* to the educator, whose own life story was published in 1901, and Washington's ideological presence can be felt throughout all of Micheaux's works.[6] Key elements from Washington's autobiography appear in the plot of Micheaux's 1920 film *The Symbol of the Unconquered;* his photograph appears on the walls of houses and cabins in most of Micheaux's films.

First developed in *The Conquest,* all of his novels feature

Micheaux personae, "race men," modeled on Booker T. Washington, whose work ethic and moral fortitude provide a much-needed example of his fellow black people. Devereaux is frugal, hardworking and sober. He describes himself in contrast to the other young men in Metropolis. "I didn't shoot craps nor drink, neither did I belong to church," he states (p. 12). As was Washington, Micheaux's personae are consistently critical of what they deem the profligate and materialistic tendencies of black working and middle classes in the cities. Devereaux finds his own brother, who had gone to Chicago, a disappointing example of such tendencies. When Devereaux decides also to make the journey to Chicago, he finds his brother, "broke, but with a lot of fine clothes and a diamond or two . . . I was greatly disappointed for I had anticipated that my big brother would have accumulated some property or become master of a bank account during those five or six years he had been away from home" (p. 16). In contrast with his brother, "economy, frugality became fixed habits of my life," he explains (p. 32).

Following Washington's criticism of a liberal arts education, and his belief in vocational training, Devereaux considers other members of the growing middle-class community in suburban Chicago "overeducated Negroes," whose "sole object in life was obviously nothing, but who dressed up and aped the white people" (p. 177). Like Washington also, he rails against ministers and other members of the black Christian church leadership, whom he considers to be opportunistic and manipulative of their mostly female congregations. As we will discuss below, the conflict between the Reverend and the young entrepreneur is the central theme in many of his works.

Throughout his career, Micheaux maintained a dogged loyalty to Washington's model for the appropriate cultivation of black manliness and the uplifting of the black race, even after black urban migration and industrial development had rendered Washington's racially accommodationist platform outdated. By the seventh novel, Micheaux's scolding words and scalding disapproval of both "ignorant and envious" country folk and the "overeducated Negroes" of the cities becomes a tedious and self-righteous harangue. Micheaux's personae are unrelentingly self-promoting, absurdly grandiose, and often shockingly reactionary in their racial politics. But in *The Conquest* (despite overt racialisms, particularly against native North Americans), the narrative voice retains a certain humility, a sense of humor and a willingness to admit failure that disappears in his later novels. After placing *The Conquest* in relation to Micheaux's later works as well as to his early biography, we will take a closer look at how the strategies by which Micheaux imagines himself in this first novel are shaped by contemporaneous discourses of manhood and masculinity then structuring social mores.

Micheaux wrote his novels in two stints, both before and toward the end of his filmmaking career. He wrote his first three semiautobiographies while a young man, fresh from his experience homesteading in South Dakota: *The Conquest* in 1913, *The Forged Note* in 1915 and *The Homesteader* in 1917. Micheaux published these novels himself, raising money to set up the Western Book and Supply Company by selling shares to his neighboring homesteaders in South Dakota.

The Conquest is the story of a brave black homesteader, Oscar Devereaux, whose dream is to tame 1,000 acres of land, and establish himself as an example of success for his wayward people. As a restless young man Devereaux leaves his hometown and, after attempting a number of different jobs, takes up as a Pullman porter. While on the job he hears of the opening of the Rosebud Reservation—the U.S. government making land in South Dakota, previously reserved for Native Americans, available to settlers. In 1904, Devereaux decides to try his hand at a claim, and purchases a relinquishment. While on the plains, he encounters many difficulties: drought, loneliness and a frustrated romance with a Scottish woman, Agnes Stewart, the daughter of a neighboring settler. His homesteading endeavor ends in failure, compounded by an early marriage fraught with domestic conflict. His wife is Orleans McCraline, the daughter of a Chicago preacher, the Reverend McCraline. Devereaux's nemesis, McCraline is the prototype for the corrupt preachers found in Micheaux's next two novels as well as in his silent films.

In *The Forged Note*, as in Micheaux's first novel, hard work and self-sacrifice are the keys to success. Although a sequel to *The Conquest*, in this second book the pioneer protagonist is named Sydney Wyeth. Wyeth has decided to take up writing as a career, and writes his autobiography. He leaves the Rosebud territory for the southern city of Attalia (read Atlanta) to peddle his book. Having failed at his agricultural endeavor, it is now time for him to stake his claim in the city. Book in hand, he prepares to "spread intelligence among people who greatly needed it."[7] Micheaux's third novel, *The Homesteader*, is perhaps his most well-known. Micheaux made *The Homesteader* into his first feature film in 1919, which unfortunately remains lost. *The Homesteader* is virtually the same tale of a Negro pioneer as told in *The Conquest*, with some important and telling revisions. The central protagonist has been renamed Jean Baptiste (after the founding father of the city of Chicago), and Micheaux gives this novel a tidy resolution, compensating for the somewhat melancholy ending of *The Conquest*. Unlike Oscar Devereaux, Jean Baptiste emerges victorious over his trying circumstances, marrying his true love, the Scottish Agnes Stewart. Baptiste discovers that Agnes's mother was mulatto, making Agnes herself black and therefore free to marry Baptiste without violating what he calls "the custom of the country and its law," or threatening his status as a race man and leader of his people.[8]

Micheaux wrote his last four novels after retiring from filmmaking in 1940. His fourth was another semiautobiography: *The Wind from Nowhere*, published in 1944. The novel's hero, Martin Eden, starts out as a prosperous landowner. Micheaux uses this character to again elaborate on his earlier experience writing *The Conquest*, and it is clear that his initial inspiration was partly influenced by Jack London's semiautobiographical work *Martin Eden*. This was followed by two murder mysteries: *The Case of Mrs. Wingate* in 1945 and *The Story of Dorothy Stanfield* in 1946. The protagonists here are not homesteaders but successful entrepreneurs and brave black detectives; the narrative strain in each of them remains consistently and transparently self-referential. None of Micheaux's material was ever original, for his constantly reused and revised material. Corey Creekmur suggests we think about his "incessant refashioning" of material as *"radically* unoriginal."[9] His last effort, *The Masquerade*, published in 1947, is a revision of Charles Chesnutt's novel *The House Behind the Cedars*, which Micheaux had already adapted into his 1932 film *Veiled Aristocrats*.

Despite his Washingtonian ideology, Micheaux's story is of the Midwest—not of the Deep South. As Micheaux was from a town on the Ohio River in Illinois, Devereaux's decision to try his hand at a claim in South Dakota is not that far afield. "I knew more about the mode of farming employed in that section of the country, it being somewhat similar to that in southern Illinois," he explains (p. 44). In fact, the history of the Exodusters fits more accurately as a model for Micheaux's homesteaders than does Washington's plan for rural industry in the Deep South. Micheaux has high regard for this first generation out of slavery who, with hard work and frugality, managed to reach a level of success as farmers, many owning their own land and freeing themselves from systems of sharecropping and peonage.[10] "During my visit to Kansas . . . I had found many prosperous colored families, most of whom had settled in Kansas in the seventies and eighties and were mostly ex-slaves, [who] made their farms pay by careful methods," he remarks (p. 176). Earlier in *The Conquest* Micheaux is nostalgic for this class of newly freed, industrious ex-slaves, and critical of the consumerist ways of their children:

> In the neighborhood and throughout the country there had at one time been many colored farmers, or ex-slaves, who had settled there after the war. Many of them had built up nice homes. . . . But as time wore on and the older generation died, the younger were attracted to the towns and cities in quest of occupations that were more suitable to their increasing desires for society and good times. Leaving the farms to care for themselves until the inevitable German immigrant came along and bought them up at his own price, tilled the land, improved the farm and roads, straightened out the streams by digging canals, and grew prosperous (pp. 3–4).

This polemic, calling black people not to Kansas but to the task of empire building in the South Dakota plains, follows throughout the text, with Micheaux cast as the only man with enough vision to attempt such innovation.

Curiously, what Micheaux does not underscore is that members of his own family were themselves prosperous Exodusters, or that most of his immediate family in fact relocated to Kansas as a result. In the late 1870s Micheaux's paternal grandmother, Melvina Michaux (alternate spelling), with three of her children—William (1849–1900), Edward (1857–1910), and Andrew

Jackson (1859–1942)—migrated to Kansas, as part of the Exoduster movement. They became prosperous homesteaders—his uncle William called by many the "richest black man in Kansas." Micheaux's family's experience as Kansas homesteaders, and the success of his uncle, remains understated in his works, even though his family's success there seems an obvious primary inspiration for his own vision for settlement in South Dakota.

Despite the obsessively self-referential nature of his novels, they give surprisingly little biographical information about Micheaux, fictional or otherwise, or about his family. Oscar Micheaux was born the fifth of eleven children to Bell and Calvin Swan Micheaux, both former slaves.[11] Melvina Michaux was born in 1832 and was a slave in Calloway County, Kentucky. After the Civil War she and her family moved north across the Ohio River to Massac County, Illinois. After migrating to Kansas, William and Andrew bought land in Barton and Stafford counties, which they farmed. They were quite successful; William also purchased a lot in the town of Great Bend, which later became the Micheaux family's primary hometown.

While his grandmother and three uncles moved to Kansas, Micheaux's parents stayed in Massac County. They stayed there until 1900, when his father inherited his brother's land in Kansas. In *The Conquest*, Devereaux mentions casually and without elaboration that his father inherits "part of the estate of a brother which came as a great relief to his ever increasing burden of debt" (p. 6). From Micheaux's family records we now know that, upon his death in 1900, Oscar Micheaux's uncle William left his land to Oscar's father, Calvin. The family then resettled in Great Bend, Kansas. Oscar Micheaux did not go with them, however, but left instead for Chicago. Although not part of what Micheaux chooses to tell about himself, we also know that his other uncle, Andrew Jackson Micheaux, grown rich from his enterprises in Kansas, was one of the primary backers of Micheaux's film corporation. Micheaux's younger brother Swan (1895–1975) worked for Micheaux's film company from 1919 to 1927 and after disagreements he left his brother's employ, but stayed in the film industry.

In *The Conquest*, Devereaux brings his sister and grandmother out to the Rosebud Reservation to claim territory. However, he relates very little about them, and we hear nothing directly from them in the narrative. In Micheaux's family it was his maternal grandmother, Louisa Gough, and his sister Olive who joined him, briefly taking up homesteads in South Dakota. Micheaux's maternal grandparents Louisa and John Gough were also from Kentucky and also migrated to Massac County, Illinois. In 1911, Louisa Gough joined Micheaux in South Dakota, and homesteaded on a section of Tripp County (Tipp County, in *The Conquest*). She stayed two years or so, and then went back to Great Bend. His younger sister Olive (1889–1957) graduated from Great Bend High School in 1909 and then joined Micheaux, purchasing 160 acres of Tripp County. She soon returned to Great Bend, before moving to Los Angeles.

Micheaux has more to say about his brothers than about any other members of his family. As in *The Conquest*, Micheaux's oldest brother, William Owen (1878–1924), quit school and moved to Chicago. Micheaux includes his other two older brothers in Devereaux's narrative:

> *When the Spanish-American War broke out the two brothers above me enlisted with a company of other patriotic young fellows and were taken to Springfield to go into camp. At Springfield their company was disbanded and those of the company that wished to go on were accepted into other com-*

panies, and those that desired to go home were permitted to do so. The younger of the two brothers returned home by freight; the other joined a Chicago company and was sent to Santiago and later to San Louis de Cuba, where he died of typhoid pneumonia (pp. 4–5).

Micheaux's second oldest brother, Lawrence (1879–1898) did indeed enlist as a private in Company C, 8th Infantry, and died as Micheaux/Devereaux reports, on October 14, 1898 in San Louis de Cuba of typhoid pneumonia. Finis (1882–1948) his third eldest brother, did go home when the company disbanded, later serving in the U.S. Army. The U.S. conquest of an overseas empire, seizing and annexing Hawaii, colonizing the Philippines, Guam, Puerto Rico and Cuba, coincided with the effective conquest of North America. Micheaux's dream of building an empire in the plains was his claim as a son of U.S. soil.

Devereaux's impetus to build an empire in the prairie is not based on a love of the soil, a talent for farming, or even an interest in agricultural technique. Farming per se is not Devereaux's true commitment, nor is a desire for African-American civic enfranchisement, the long-beleaguered struggle of African Americans for equal participation in the United States' electoral political system. Capitalist entrepreneurship is what interests him. Washington's Tuskegee model for industrial education provided a template for Micheaux. Tuskegee furnished its students with practical knowledge, not so much to go out and farm themselves, but to be able to train others in appropriate economic and social behavior, to guide less fortunate brethren out of ignorant darkness. Micheaux hungers for such managerial authority.

Throughout *The Conquest* the majority of his reportage is to the development of the towns of Megory and Calias and the competition between their respective founding fathers, as they vie for prime sites as the railroad lays its tracks. "Before I had any colored people to discourage me with their ignorance of business or what is required for success, I was stimulated to effort by the example of my white neighbors and friends who were doing what I admired, building an empire; to me that was the big idea" (p. 221). Devereaux expresses unveiled admiration for these empire builders, particularly Ernest Nicholson, a character based on a man named Ernest Jackson, whose family were South Dakota boosters, related to the head of the railroad. "Ernest Nicholson had a pleasing personality and forceful as well. He was a king of reasoning . . . [his] walls profusely decorated with the pictures of prominent capitalists and financiers of the middle west, some of whom were financing the schemes of the fine looking young men who were trying to show these struggling waifs of the prairie in the inevitable result" (p. 191). Micheaux adapts a version of Social Darwinism, popularly known as the "survival of the fittest." In spite of this doctrine's structural racism, Devereaux includes himself as one of the "fine looking young men of the prairie." At first an outsider and oddity, racially ridiculed and taken advantage of for his lack of experience, Devereaux becomes a committed member of the town of Calias, and quite involved in the heated competition. As he gradually succeeds in breaking the tough South Dakota soil, he gains the respect of the community of white homesteaders. "At first I was regarded as an object of curiosity, which changed to appreciation and late admiration," he writes. "I was not called a free-and-easy coon, but a genuine booster for Calias and Little Crow" (p. 87).

Ideologies of racial uplift were often linked to and articulated as projects of empire building.[12] The ideal of black manhood was realized through success as a model of individualism, of the conquest over environment and adversity. Acting as a leader of his people, the black man by example offered direction and guidance to others. Devereaux retains his "race loyalty," taking on his responsibility to his people, as a good "race man" should. But Devereaux/Micheaux is a race man of a certain kind, conflicted about his people and their capabilities. Although he refuses an interracial marriage (unlike other colored home-steaders) it is with a heavy sigh, for he admires the hardworking thrift of Agnes Stewart and her Scottish homesteading family.

A young Devereaux explains his impetus for leaving his hometown, expressing his disdain for black community members. "I became very anxious to get away," he writes. "In fact I didn't like M—pls or its surroundings . . . the colored people were in most part wretchedly poor, ignorant and envious. They were set in the ways of their localisms . . . the social life centered in the two churches where praying, singing and shouting on Sundays, to back-biting, stealing, fighting and getting drunk during the week was common among the men" (pp. 6-7). He places himself apart, especially from the church. He explains he was "regarded by the Elders as being worldly, a free thinker," unpopular for his "persistent declarations that there were not enough competent colored people to grasp the many opportunities that presented themselves." Describing the years coming into his manhood, he sets up what will be the central arguments for the rest of his story. "In the following chapters I hope to show that what I believed fourteen years ago was true" (p. 8).

Devereaux sets out to define himself as a man, against the model of male leadership he finds dominating the black community, the black preacher. Micheaux constructs his fictional self as a model of Victorian manhood, his character distinguished by "honesty, piety, self-control, and a commitment to the producer values of industry, thrift, punctuality and sobriety."[13]

Preachers may seem to provide moral guidance, but as

dramatized in Micheaux's works they more often lie, cheat, and take advantage of their female congregations. His mother, he explains, was a "shouting Methodist," one of the women of the church who did domestic work for white families, and "fed the preachers. When we lived in the country we fed so many of the Elders, with their long tailed coats and assuming and authoritative airs, that I grew to almost dislike the sight of a colored man in a Prince Albert coat and clerical vest. At sixteen I was fairly disgusted with it all and took no pains to keep my disgust concealed" (p. 7).

Throughout Micheaux's early works looms the presence of the lecherous and parasitic black preacher, invariably philandering, dishonest and lazy. Devereaux's outspoken anticlerical opinion reflects Booker T. Washington's conflict with members of ministry. According to Washingtonian producerist values, the biggest bone of contention is that church leaders contribute nothing practical, they produce nothing. "I was becoming more and more convinced that he belonged to the class of the negro race that desires ease, privilege, freedom, position and luxury without any great material effort on their part to acquire it," Devereaux says of his father-in-law, the Reverend McCraline (p. 226). Throughout Micheaux's early works (including his silent films *Within Our Gates, Symbol of the Unconquered* and *Body and Soul*), the conflicts Between the two types of male leadership take on epic proportions. The de-crowning of the father and the mantling of the son are key elements in the construction of Micheaux's self-made American man.

Micheaux borrows and adapts from a European immigrant paradigm its central conflict—the struggle to assimilate traditional ways of the old country while adopting new ways of life in America. This process mirrors the struggle of second generation European Americans to separate themselves from old loyalties, associated with the homeland, and is gendered as the struggle between patriarchal leaders. What distinguishes Micheaux's narrative vision from a European paradigm is an arrogant nativism. "We were never immigrants," Dr. Vivian assures Sylvia Landry in *Within Our Gates*. Yet this is not a citizenship based solely on claims of proper residence. Devereaux describes Native Americans as "easily flattered spendthrifts" who sell their government land allotments to the European immigrants only to spend the money "as quickly as they get it" (p. 162). What the black soldiers, like Micheaux/Devereaux's brother, did under Roosevelt in Cuba during the Spanish-American War was to claim an Americanness over the second-wave immigrants, an Americanness legitimized by prior enlistment in imperialist conquest.

Micheaux recasts this conflict between the old and the new. The preacher represents the old, or traditional, African-American way of life, while the rugged, individualistic, hardworking, young black man symbolizes the possibilities for a prosperous future. In *The Conquest*, Devereaux attributes his ultimate failure in South Dakota to the conniving manipulation of his father-in-law. The relationship between the two of them is doomed from the start, as their differences are explicitly political. "We got along fine until he and I got to arguing the race question, which brought about friction," Devereaux explains (p. 225). "I had always approved of Booker T. Washington, his life and his work in the uplift of the negro. . . . He was bitterly opposed to the educator" (p. 226). As the conflict intensifies Devereaux insists, "I am being persecuted on account of my ideas" (p. 278). Two chapters in particular are openly polemical. In Chapter 23, "Where the Negro Fails," Micheaux/Devereaux comments specifically on young thinker W. E. B. Du Bois, who, early in his career, was known for his criticism of Booker T. Washington's ideas (p. 130). Du Bois first voiced criticism of Washington in his collection of essays *Souls of Black Folk,* published in 1903. Du Bois continued to oppose Washington's apologist and increasingly defensive posture into the 1920s, publishing editorial essays in *The Crisis,* the NAACP journal of which he was the editor. Du Bois led a growing number of the members of the emerging black middle class in challenging Washington's Tuskegee platform. One of Du Bois's early ideas was his call for the development of a leading elite, composed of a highly educated, ten percent of the black population. This Talented Tenth—urbane, sophisticated, and well-heeled—continue to come under fire throughout Micheaux's works. In Chapter 37, "The Progressives and the Reactionaries," he refers to Du Bois as a "certain professor of a colored university" (p. 228) and to his publication, and comments on the "thousands of anti-Booker T.s" rallying around it. Although he agrees that black schools were vastly underfunded, he insists that "industrial education was the first means of lifting the ignorant masses to a state of good citizenship." He and the Reverend McCraline argue heatedly about education. "The Reverend and I could not in any way agree, he was so bitter against industrial education and the educator's name" (p. 229). As a result of this conflict, *The Conquest* ends rather abruptly. It would seem also that the brave black homesteader fails according to the terms that he himself set.

Micheaux left the plains and left homesteading, turning instead back to the city and the forms of production possible there. Filmmaking provided a ready forum for Micheaux to represent the race. Perhaps Micheaux's tenacity, the reason for his prolific output, is part and parcel with an obsessive obstinacy, why throughout his works he would return again and again to the homestead, and to the producerist values set so early on in his career. Whatever the reason for his dedication, and however we may feel about his often troubling, often laughable politics, Micheaux has left us invaluable material through which we can more fully understand the range of self-defining strategies developed in early twentieth-century African-American discourse.

—Jayna J. Brown

1. Pearl Bowser and Louise Spence, *Writing Himself into History: Oscar Micheaux, His Silent Films, and His Audiences* (New Brunswick: Rutgers University Press, 2000), 5.
2. Nell Irvin Painter, *Exodusters: Black Migration to Kansas after Reconstruction* (New York: Alfred A. Knopf, 1971).
3. Nat Love, *The Life and Adventures of Nat Love* (New York: Arno Press, 1968), 127.
4. Ibid., 41.
5. Ibid., 95.
6. According to the leading African-American historian David Levering Lewis, Washington's autobiography was actually ghostwritten by a white man, Max Bennett Thrasher, a newspaper journalist from Vermont. *W. E. B. Du Bois: Biography of a Race, 1865–1919* (New York: Henry Holt, 1993), 262–264.
7. Oscar Micheaux, *The Forged Note: A Romance of the Darker Races* (Lincoln: Western Book Supply Company, 1915), 168.
8. Oscar Micheaux, *The Homesteader: A Novel* (Lincoln: University of Nebraska Press, 1994), 138.
9. Corey K. Creekmur, "Telling White Lies: Oscar Micheaux and Charles Chesnutt," *Oscar Micheaux and His Circle: African-American Filmmaking and Race Cinema of the Silent Era*, Pearl Bowser, Jane Gaines, and Charles Musser, eds. (Bloomington: Indiana University Press, 2001), 147–158.
10. Manning Marable, "The Politics of Land Tenure: 1877–1915," *A Question of Manhood: A Reader in U.S. Black Men's History and Masculinity*, Vol. 2, Earnestine Jenkins and Darlene Clark Hine, eds. (Bloomington: Indiana University Press, 2001), 129–138.
11. For a thorough genealogy of Oscar Micheaux, see Karen P. Neuforth, "Generations: The Family and Ancestry of Oscar Micheaux," shorock.com/arts/micheaux/papersO.html.
12. I would like to thank Anthony Foy for his insights on ideologies of black masculinity and class formation, and particularly for his work on Nat Love, Matthew Henson, and Booker T. Washington.
13. Martin Summers, *Manliness and its Discontents: The Transformation of Masculinity Among the Black Middle Class 1900–1930* (Chapel Hill: University of North Carolina Press, 2003).

LIST OF CHAPTERS

THE CONQUEST

CHAPTER I

DISCONTENT—SPIRIT OF THE PIONEER

OOD GRACIOUS, has it been that long? It does not seem possible; but it was this very day nine years ago when a fellow handed me this little what-would-you-call-it, Ingalls called it "Opportunity." I've a notion to burn it, but I won't—not this time, instead, I'll put it down here and you may call it what you like.

> *Master of human destinies am I.*
> *Fame, love, and fortune on my footsteps wait.*
> *Cities and fields I walk. I penetrate*
> *Deserts and seas remote, and passing by*
> *Hovel, and mart, and palace—soon or late*
> *I knock unbidden once at every gate.*
> *If sleeping, wake—if feasting, rise before*
> *I turn away. It is the hour of fate,*
> *And they who follow me reach every state*
> *Mortals desire, and conquer every foe*
> *Save death; but those who doubt or hesitate,*
> *Condemned to failure, penury, and woe*
> *Seek me in vain and uselessly implore,*
> *I answer not, and I return no more.*

Yes, it was that little poem that led me to this land and some-times I wonder well, I just wonder, that's all. Again, I think it would be somewhat different if it wasn't for the wind. It blows and blows until it makes me feel lonesome and so far away from that little place and the country in southern Illinois.

I was born twenty-nine years ago near the Ohio River, about forty miles above Cairo, the fourth son and fifth child of a family of thirteen, by the name of Devereaux—which, of course, is not my name but we will call it that for this sketch. It is a peculiar name that ends with an "eaux," however, and is considered an odd name for a colored man to have, unless he is from Louisiana where the French crossed with the Indians and slaves, causing many Louisiana negroes to have the French names and many speak the French language also. My father, however, came from Kentucky and inherited the name from his father who was sold off into Texas during the slavery period and is said to be living there today.

He was a farmer and owned eighty acres of land and was, therefore, considered fairly "well-to-do," that is, for a colored man. The county in which we lived bordered on the river some twenty miles, and took its name from an old fort that used to do a little cannonading for the Federal forces back in the Civil War.

The farming in this section was hindered by various disad-vantages and at best was slow, hard work. Along the valleys of the numerous creeks and bayous that empty their waters into the Ohio, the soil was of a rich alluvium, where in the early Spring the back waters from the Ohio covered thousands of acres of farm and timber lands, and in receding left the land plastered with a coat of river sand and clay which greatly added to the soil's productivity. One who owned a farm on these bot-toms was considered quite fortunate. Here the corn stalks grew like saplings, with ears dangling one and two to a stalk, and as sound and heavy as green blocks of wood.

The heavy rains washed the loam from the hills and deposited it on these bottoms. Years ago, when the rolling lands were cleared, and before the excessive rainfall had washed away the loose surface, the highlands were considered most valuable for agricultural purposes, equally as valuable as the bottoms now are. Farther back from the river the more rolling the land became, until some sixteen miles away it was known as the hills, and here, long before I was born, the land had been very valuable. Large barns and fine stately houses—now gone to wreck and deserted—stood behind beautiful groves of chestnut, locust and stately old oaks, where rabbits, quail and wood-peckers made their homes, and sometimes a raccoon or opossum founded its den during the cold, bleak winter days. The orchards, formerly the pride of their owners, now dropped their neglected fruit which rotted and mulched with the leaves. The fields, where formerly had grown great crops of wheat, corn, oats, timothy and clover, were now grown over and enmeshed in a tangled mass of weeds and dew-berry vines; while along the branches and where the old rail fences had stood, black-berry vines had grown up, twisting their thorny stems and forming a veritable hedge fence. These places I promised mother to avoid as I begged her to allow me to follow the big boys and carry their game when they went hunting.

In the neighborhood and throughout the country there had at one time been many colored farmers, or ex-slaves, who had settled there after the war. Many of them having built up nice homes and cleared the valley of tough-rooted hickory, gum, pecan and water-oak trees, and the highlands of the black, white, red or post oak, sassafras and dogwood. They later grubbed the stumps and hauled the rocks into the roads, or dammed treacherous little streams that were continually breaking out and threatening the land with more ditches. But as time wore on and the older generation died, the younger were attracted to the towns and cities in quest of occupations that were more suitable to their increasing desires for society and good times. Leaving the farms to care for themselves until the inevitable German immigrant came along and bought them up at his own price, tilled the land, improved the farm and roads, straightened out the streams by digging canals, and grew prosperous.

As for me, I was called the lazy member of the family; a shirker who complained that it was too cold to work in the winter, and too warm in the summer. About the only thing for which I was given credit was in learning readily. I always received good grades in my studies, but was continually criticised for talking too much and being too inquisitive. We finally moved into the nearby town of M—pls. Not so much to get off the farm, or to be near more colored people (as most of the younger negro farmers did) as to give the children better educational facilities.

The local colored school was held in an old building made of plain boards standing straight up and down with batten on the cracks. It was inadequate in many respects; the teachers very often inefficient, and besides, it was far from home. After my oldest sister graduated she went away to teach, and about the same time my oldest brother quit school and went to a nearby town and became a table waiter, much to the dissatisfaction of my mother, who always declared emphatically that she wanted none of her sons to become lackeys.

When the Spanish-American War broke out the two brothers above me enlisted with a company of other patriotic young fellows and were taken to Springfield to go into camp. At Springfield their company was disbanded and those of the company that wished to go on were accepted into other companies, and those that desired to go home were permitted to do so. The younger of the two brothers returned home by freight; the other joined a Chicago company and was sent to Santiago and later to San Luis DeCuba, where he died with typhoid pneumonia.

M—pls was an old town with a few factories, two flour mills, two or three saw mills, box factories and another concern where veneering was peeled from wood blocks softened with steam. The timber came from up the Tennessee River, which emptied into the Ohio a few miles up the river. There was also the market house, such as are to be seen in towns of the Southern states—and parts of the Northern. This market house, or place, as it is often called, was an open building, except one end enclosed by a meat-market, and was about forty by one hundred feet with benches on either side and one through the center for the convenience of those who walked, carrying their produce in a home-made basket. Those in vehicles backed to a line guarded by the city marshall, forming an alleyway the width of the market house for perhaps half a block, depending on how many farmers were on hand. There was always a rush to get nearest the market house; a case of the early bird getting the worm. The towns people who came to buy, women mostly with baskets, would file leisurely between the rows of vehicles, hacks and spring wagons of various descriptions, looking here and there at the vegetables displayed.

We moved back to the country after a time where my father complained of my poor service in the field and in disgust I was sent off to do the marketing—which pleased me, for it was not only easy but gave me a chance to meet and talk with many people—and I always sold the goods and engaged more for the afternoon delivery. This was my first experience in real business and from that time ever afterward I could always do better business for myself than for anyone else. I was not given much credit for my ability to sell, however, until my brother, who complained that I was given all the easy work while he had to labor and do all the heavier farm work, was sent to do the marketing. He was not a salesman and lacked the aggressiveness to approach people with a basket, and never talked much; was timid and when spoken to or approached plainly showed it.

On the other hand, I met and became acquainted with people quite readily. I soon noticed that many people enjoy being flattered, and how pleased even the prosperous men's wives would seem if bowed to with a pleasant "Good Morning, Mrs. Quante, nice morning and would you care to look at some fresh roasting ears—ten cents a dozen; or some nice ripe strawberries, two boxes for fifteen cents?" "Yes Maam, Thank you! and O, Mrs. Quante, would you care for some radishes, cucumbers or lettuce for tomorrow? I could deliver late this afternoon, you see, for maybe you haven't the time to come to market every day." From this association I soon learned to give to each and every prospective customer a different greeting or suggestion, which usually brought a smile and a nod of appreciation as well as a purchase.

Before the debts swamped my father, and while my brothers were still at home, our truck gardening, the small herd of milkers and the chickens paid as well as the farm itself. About this time father fell heir to a part of the estate of a brother which came as a great relief to his ever increasing burden of debt.

While this seeming relief to father was on I became very anxious to get away. In fact I didn't like M—pls nor its surroundings. It was a river town and gradually losing its usefulness by the invasion of railroads up and down the river; besides, the colored people were in the most part wretchedly poor, ignorant and envious. They were set in the ways of their localisms, and it was quite useless to talk to them of anything that would better oneself. The social life centered in the two churches where praying, singing and shouting on Sundays, to back-biting, stealing, fighting and getting drunk during the week was common among the men. They remained members in good standing at the churches, however, as long as they paid their dues, contributed to the numerous rallies, or helped along in camp meetings and festivals. Others were regularly turned out, mostly for not paying their dues, only to warm up at the next revival on the mourners bench and come through converted and be again accepted into the church and, for awhile at least, live a near-righteous life. There were many good Christians in the church, however, who were patient with all this conduct, while there were and still are those who will not sanction such carrying-on by staying in a church that permits of such sham-ming and hypocrisy. These latter often left the church and were then branded either as infidels or human devils who had forsaken the house of God and were condemned to eternal damnation.

My mother was a shouting Methodist and many times we children would slip quietly out of the church when she began to get happy. The old and less religious men hauled slop to feed a few pigs, cut cord-wood at fifty cents per cord, and did any odd jobs, or kept steady ones when such could be found. The women took in washing, cooked for the white folks, and fed the preach-ers. When we lived in the country we fed so many of the Elders, with their long tailed coats and assuming and authoritative airs, that I grew to almost dislike the sight of a colored man in a Prince Albert coat and clerical vest. At sixteen I was fairly disgusted with it all and took no pains to keep my disgust concealed.

This didn't have the effect of burdening me with many friends in M—pls and I was regarded by many of the boys and girls, who led in the whirlpool of the local colored society, as being of the "too-slow-to-catch-cold" variety, and by some of the Elders as being worldly, a free thinker, and a dangerous associate for young Christian folks. Another thing that added to my unpopularity, perhaps, was my persistent declarations that there were not enough competent colored people to grasp the many opportunities that presented themselves, and that if white people could possess such nice homes, wealth and luxuries, so in time, could the colored people. "You're a fool", I would be told, and then would follow a lecture describing the time-worn long and cruel slavery, and after the emancipation, the prejudice and hatred of the white race, whose chief object was to prevent the progress and betterment of the negro. This excuse for the negro's lack of ambition was constantly dinned into my ears from the Kagle corner loafer to the minister in the pulpit, and I became so tired of it all that I declared that if I could ever leave M—pls I would never return. More, I would disprove such a theory and in the following chapters I hope to show that what I believed fourteen years ago was true.

CHAPTER II

LEAVING HOME—A MAIDEN

I WAS seventeen when I at last left M—pls. I accepted a rough job at a dollar and a quarter a day in a car manufacturing concern in a town of eight thousand population, about eight hundred being colored. I was unable to save very much, for work was dull that summer, and I was only averaging about four days' work a week. Besides, I had an attack of malaria at intervals for a period of two months, but by going to work at five o'clock A. M. when I was well I could get in two extra hours, making a dollar-fifty. The concern employed about twelve hundred men and paid their wages every two weeks, holding back one week's pay. I came there in June and it was some time in September that I drew my fullest pay envelope which contained sixteen dollars and fifty cents.

About this time a "fire eating" colored evangelist, who apparently possessed great converting powers and unusual eloquence, came to town. These qualities, however, usually became very uninteresting toward the end of a stay. He had been to M—pls the year before I left and at that place his popularity greatly diminished before he left. The greater part of the colored people in this town were of the emotional kind and to these he was as attractive as he had been at M—pls in the beginning.

Coincident with the commencement of Rev. McIntyre's soul stirring sermons a big revival was inaugurated, and although the little church was filled nightly to its capacity, the aisles were kept clear in order to give those that were "steeping in Hell's fire" (as the evangelist characterized those who were not members of some church) an open road to enter into the field of the righteous; also to give the mourners sufficient room in which to exhaust their emotions when the spirit struck them—and it is needless to say that they were used. At times they virtually converted the entire floor into an active gymnasium, regardless of the rights of other persons or of the chairs they occupied. I had seen and heard people shout at long intervals in church, but here, after a few soul stirring sermons, they began to run outside where there was more room to give vent to the hallucination and this wandering of the mind. It could be called nothing else, for after the first few sermons the evangelist would hardly be started before some mourner would begin to "come through." This revival warmed up to such proportions that preaching and shouting began in the afternoon instead of evening. Men working in the yards of the foundry two block away could hear the shouting above the roaring furnaces and the deafening noise of machinery of a great car manufacturing concern. The church stood on a corner where two streets, or avenues, intersected and for a block in either direction the influence of fanaticism became so intense that the converts began running about like wild creatures, tearing their hair and uttering prayers and supplications in discordant tones.

At the evening services the sisters would gather around a mourner that showed signs of weakening and sing and babble until he or she became so befuddled they would jump up, throw their arms wildly into the air, kick, strike, then cry out like a dying soul, fall limp and exhausted into the many arms outstretched to catch them. This was always conclusive evidence of a contrite heart and a thoroughly penitent soul. Far into the night this performance would continue, and when the mourners' bench became empty the audience would be searched for sinners. I would sit through it all quite unemotional, and nightly I would be approached with "aren't you ready?" To which I would make no answer. I noticed that several boys, who were not in good standing with the parents of girls they wished to court, found the mourners' bench a convenient vehicle to the homes of these girls—all of whom belonged to church. Girls over eighteen who did not belong were subjects of much gossip and abuse.

A report, in some inconceivable manner, soon became spread that Oscar Devereaux had said that he wanted to die and go to hell. Such a sensation! I was approached on all sides by men and women, regardless of the time of day or night, by the young men who gloried in their conversion and who urged me to "get right" with Jesus before it was too late. I do not remember how long these meetings lasted but they suddenly came to an end when notice was served on the church trustees by the city council, which irreverently declared that so many converts every afternoon and night was disturbing the white neighborhood's rest as well as their nerves. It ordered windows and doors to be kept closed during services, and as the church was small it was impossible to house the congregation and all the converts, so the revival ended and the community was restored to normal and calm once more prevailed.

That was in September. One Sunday afternoon in October, as I was walking along the railroad track, I chanced to overhear voices coming from under a water tank, where a space of some eight or ten feet enclosed by four huge timbers made a small, secluded place. I stopped, listened and was sure I recognized the voices of Douglas Brock, his brother Melvin, and two other well known colored boys. Douglas was betting a quarter with one of the other boys that he couldn't pass. (You who know the dice and its vagaries will know what he meant.) This was mingled with words and commands from Melvin to the dice in trying to make some point. It must have been four. He would let out a sort of yowl: "Little Joe, can't you do it?" I went my way. I didn't shoot craps nor drink neither did I belong to church but was called a dreadful sinner while three of the boys under the tank had, not less than six weeks before, joined church and were now full-fledged members in good standing. Of course I did not consider that all people who belonged to church were not Christians, but was quite sure that many were not.

The following January a relative of mine got a job for me bailing water in a coal mine in a little town inhabited entirely by negroes. I worked from six o'clock P.M. to six A.M., and received two dollars and twenty-five cents therefor. The work was rough and hard and the mine very dark. The smoke hung like a cloud near the top of the tunnel-like room during all the night. This was because the fans were all but shut off at night, and just enough air was pumped in to prevent the formation of black damp. The smoke made my head ache until I felt stupid and the dampness made me ill, but the two dollars and twenty-five cents per day looked good to me. After six weeks, however, I was forced to quit, and with sixty-five dollars—more money than I had ever had—I went to see my older sister who was teaching in a nearby town.

I had grown into a strong, husky youth of eighteen and my sister was surprised to see that I was working and taking care of myself so well. She shared the thought of nearly all of my acquaintances that I was too lazy to leave home and do hard work, especially in the winter time. After awhile she suddenly looked at me and spoke as though afraid she would forget it, "O,

Oscar! I've got a girl for you; what do you think of that?" smiling so pleasantly, I was afraid she was joking. You see, I had never been very successful with the girls and when she mentioned having a girl for me my heart was all a flutter and when she hesitated I put in eagerly.

"Aw go on—quit your kidding. On the level now, or are you just chiding me?" But she took on a serious expression and speaking thoughtfully, she went on.

"Yes, she lives next door and is a nice little girl, and pretty. The prettiest colored girl in town."

Here I lost interest for I remembered my sister was foolish about beauty and I said that I didn't care to meet her. I was suspicious when it came to the pretty type of girls, and had observed that the prettiest girl in town was oft times petted and spoiled and a mere butterfly.

"O why?" She spoke like one hurt. Then I confessed my suspicions. "O, You're foolish," she exclaimed softly, appearing relieved. "Besides," she went on brightly "Jessie isn't a spoiled girl, you wait until you meet her." And in spite of my protests she sent the landlady's little girl off for Miss Rooks. She came over in about an hour and I found her to be demure and thoughtful, as well as pretty. She was small of stature, had dark eyes and beautiful wavy, black hair, and an olive complexion. She wouldn't allow me to look into her eyes but continued to cast them downward, sitting with folded hands and answering when spoken to in a tiny voice quite in keeping with her small person.

During the afternoon I mentioned that I was going to Chicago, "Now Oscar, you've got no business in Chicago," my sister spoke up with a touch of authority. "You're too young, and besides," she asked "do you know whether W. O. wants you?" W. O. was our oldest brother and was then making Chicago his home.

"Huh!" I snorted "I'm going on my own hook," and drawing up to my full six feet I tried to look brave, which seemed to have the desired effect on my sister.

"Well" she said resignedly, "you must be careful and not get into bad company—be good and try to make a man of yourself."

CHAPTER III

CHICAGO, CHASING A WILL-O-THE-WISP

HAT was on Sunday morning three hundred miles south of Chicago, and at nine-forty that night I stepped off the New Orleans and Chicago fast mail into a different world. It was, I believe, the coldest night that I had ever experienced. The city was new and strange to me and I wandered here and there for hours before I finally found my brother's address on Armour Avenue. But the wandering and anxiety mattered little, for I was in the great city where I intended beginning my career, and felt that bigger things were in store for me.

The next day my brother's landlady appeared to take a good deal of interest in me and encouraged me so that I became quite confidential, and told her of my ambitions for the future and that it was my intention to work, save my money and eventually become a property owner. I was rather chagrined later, however, to find that she had repeated all this to my brother and he gave me a good round scolding, accompanied by the unsolicited advice that if I would keep my mouth shut people wouldn't know I was so green. He had been traveling as a waiter on an eastern railroad dining car, but in a fit of independence—which had always been characteristic of him—had quit, and now in mid-winter, was out of a job. He was not enthusiastic concerning my presence in the city and I had found him broke, but with a lot of fine clothes and a diamond or two. Most folks from the country don't value good clothes and diamonds in the way city folks do and I, for one, didn't think much of his finery.

I was greatly disappointed, for I had anticipated that my big brother would have accumulated some property or become master of a bank account during these five or six years he had been away from home. He seemed to sense this disappointment and became more irritated at my presence and finally wrote home to my parents—who had recently moved to Kansas—charging me with the crime of being a big, awkward, ignorant kid, unsophisticated in the ways of the world, and especially of the city; that I was likely to end my "career" by running over a street car and permitting the city to irretrievably lose me, or something equally as bad. When I heard from my mother she was worried and begged me to come home. I knew the folks at home shared my brother's opinion of me and believed all he had told them, so I had a good laugh all to myself in spite of the depressing effect it had on me. However, there was the reaction, and when it set in I became heartsick and discouraged and then and there became personally acquainted with the "blues", who gave me their undivided attention for some time after that.

The following Sunday I expected him to take me to church with him, but he didn't. He went alone, wearing his five dollar hat, fifteen dollar made-to-measure shoes, forty-five dollar coat and vest, eleven dollar trousers, fifty dollar tweed overcoat and his diamonds. I found my way to church alone and when I saw him sitting reservedly in an opposite pew, I felt snubbed and my heart sank. However, only momentarily, for a new light dawned upon me and I saw the snobbery and folly of it all and resolved that some day I would rise head and shoulders above that foolish, four-flushing brother of mine in real and material success.

I finally secured irregular employment at the Union Stock Yards. The wages at that time were not the best. Common labor a dollar-fifty per day and the hours very irregular. Some days I was called for duty at five in the morning and laid off at three in the afternoon or called again at eight in the evening to work until nine the same evening. I soon found the mere getting of jobs to be quite easy. It was getting a desirable one that gave me trouble. However, when I first went to the yards and looked at the crowds waiting before the office in quest of employment, I must confess I felt rather discouraged, but my new surroundings and that indefinable interesting feature about these crowds with their diversity of nationalities and ambitions, made me forget my own little disappointments. Most all new arrivals, whether skilled or unskilled workmen, seeking "jobs" in the city find their way to the yards. Thousands of unskilled laborers are employed here and it seems to be the Mecca for the down-and-out who wander thither in a last effort to obtain employment.

The people with whom I stopped belonged to the servant class and lived neatly in their Armour Avenue flat. The different classes of people who make up the population of a great city are segregated more by their occupations than anything else. The laborers usually live in a laborer's neighborhood. Tradesmen find it more agreeable among their fellow workmen and the same is true of the servants and others. I found that employment which soiled the clothes and face and hands was out of keeping among the people with whom I lived, so after trying first one job, then another, I went to Joliet, Illinois, to work out my fortune in the steel mills of that town. I was told that at that place was an excellent opportunity to learn a trade, but after getting only the very roughest kind of work to do around the mills, such as wrecking and carrying all kinds of broken iron and digging in a canal along with a lot of jabbering foreigners whose English vocabulary consisted of but one word—their laborer's number. It is needless to say that I saw little chance of learning a trade at any very early date.

Pay day "happened" every two weeks with two weeks held back. If I quit it would be three weeks before I could get my wages, but was informed of a scheme by which I could get my money, by telling the foreman that I was going to leave the state. Accordingly, I approached the renowned imbecile and told him that I was going to California and would have to quit, and would like to get my pay. "Pay day is every two weeks, so be sure to get back in time," he answered in that officious manner so peculiar to foremen. I had only four dollars coming, so I quit anyway.

That evening I became the recipient of the illuminating information that if I would apply at the coal chutes I would find better employment as well as receive better wages. I sought out the fellow in charge, a big colored man weighing about two hundred pounds, who gave me work cracking and heaving coal into the chute at a dollar-fifty per twenty-five tons.

"Gracious," I expostulated. "A man can't do all of that in a day."

"Pooh", and he waved his big hands depreciatingly, "I have heaved forty tons with small effort."

I decided to go to work that day, but with many misgivings as to cracking and shoveling twenty-five tons of coal. The first day I managed, by dint of hard labor, to crack and heave eighteen tons out of a box car, for which I received the munificent sum of one dollar, and the next day I fell to sixteen tons and likewise to eighty-nine cents. The contractor who superintended the coal business bought me a drink in a nearby saloon, and as I drank it with a gulp he patted me on the shoulder, saying, "Now, after the third day, son, you begin to improve and at the end of a week you can heave thirty tons a day as easily as a clock ticking the time." I thought he was going to add that I would be shoveling forty tons like Big Jim, the fellow who gave me the job, but I cut him off by telling him that I'd resign before I became so proficient.

I had to send for more money to pay my board. My brother, being my banker, sent a statement of my account, showing that I had to date just twenty-five dollars, and the statement seemed to read coldly between the lines that I would soon be broke, out of a job, and what then? I felt very serious about the matter and when I returned to Chicago I had lost some of my confidence regarding my future. Mrs. Nelson, the landlady, boasted that her husband made twenty dollars per week; showed me her diamonds and spoke so very highly of my brother, that I suspicioned that she admired him a great deal, and that he was in no immediate danger of losing his room even when he was out of work and unable to meet his obligations.

My next step was to let an employment agency swindle me out of two dollars. Their system was quite unique, and, I presume, legitimate. They persuaded the applicant to deposit three dollars as a guarantee of good faith, after which they were to find a position for him. A given percentage was also to be taken from the wages for a certain length of time. Some of these agencies may have been all right, but my old friend, the hoodoo, led me to one that was an open fraud. After the person seeking employment has been sent to several places for imaginary positions that prove to be only myths, the agency offers to give back a dollar and the disgusted applicant is usually glad to get it. I, myself, being one of many of these unfortunates.

I then tried the newspaper ads. There is usually some particular paper in any large city that makes a specialty of want advertisements. I was told, as was necessary, to stand at the door when the paper came from the press, grab a copy, choose an ad that seemed promising and run like wild for the address given. I had no trade, so turned to the miscellaneous column, and as I had no references I looked for a place where none were required. If the address was near I would run as fast as the crowded street and the speed laws would permit, but always found upon arrival that someone had just either been accepted ahead of me, or had been there a week. I having run down an old ad that had been permitted to run for that time. About the only difference I found between the newspapers and the employment agencies was that I didn't have to pay three dollars for the experience.

I now realized the disadvantages of being an unskilled laborer, and had grown weary of chasing a "will-o-the-wisp" and one day while talking to a small Indian-looking negro I remarked that I wished I could find a job in some suburb shining shoes in a barber shop or something that would take me away from Chicago and its dilly-dally jobs for awhile.

"I know where you can get a job like that," he answered, thoughtfully.

"Where?" I asked eagerly.

"Why, out at Eaton," he went on, "a suburb about twenty-five miles west. A fellow wanted me to go but I don't want to leave Chicago."

I found that most of the colored people with whom I had become acquainted who lived in Chicago very long were similarly reluctant about leaving, but I was ready to go anywhere. So my new friend took me over to a barber supply house on Clark street, where a man gave me the name of the barber at Eaton and told me to come by in the morning and he'd give me a ticket to the place. When I got on the street again I felt so happy and grateful to my friend for the information, that I gave the little mulatto a half dollar, all the money I had with me, and had to walk the forty blocks to my room. Here I filled my old grip and the next morning "beat it" for Eaton, arriving there on the first of May, and a cold, bleak, spring morning it was. I found the shop without any trouble—a dingy little place with two chairs. The proprietor, a drawn, unhappy looking creature, and a hawkish looking German assistant welcomed me cordially. They seemed to need company. The proprietor led me upstairs to a room that I could have free with an oil stove and table where I could cook—so I made arrangements to "bach".

I received no wages, but was allowed to retain all I made "shining". I had acquired some experience shining shoes on the streets of M—pls with a home-made box—getting on my knees whenever I got a customer. "Shining shoes" is not usually considered an advanced or technical occupation requiring skill. However, if properly conducted it can be the making of a good solicitor. While Eaton was a suburb it was also a country town and this shop was never patronized by any of the metropolitan class who made their homes there, but principally by the country class who do not evidence their city pride by the polish of their shoes. Few city people allow their shoes to go unpolished and I wasn't long in finding it out, and when I did I had something to say to the men who went by, well dressed but with dirty shoes. If I could argue them into stopping, if only for a moment, I could nearly always succeed in getting them into the chair.

Business, however, was dull and I began taking jobs in the country from the farmers, working through the day and getting back to the shop for the evening. This, however, was short lived, for I was unaccustomed to farm work since leaving home and found it extremely difficult. My first work in the country was pitching timothy hay side-by-side with a girl of sixteen, who knew how to pitch hay. I thought it would be quite romantic before I started, but before night came I had changed my mind. The man on the wagon would drive alongside a big cock of sweet smelling hay and the girl would stick her fork partly to one side of the hay cock and show me how to put my fork into the other. I was left-handed while she was right, and with our backs to the wagon we could make a heavy lift and when the hay was directly overhead we'd turn and face each other and over the load would go onto the wagon. Toward evening the loads thus balanced seemed to me as heavy as the load of Atlas bearing the earth. I am sure my face disclosed the fatigue and strain under which I labored, for it was clearly reflected in the knowing grin of my companion. I drew my pay that night on the excuse of having to get an overall suit, promising to be back at a quarter to seven the next morning.

Then I tried shocking oats along with a boy of about twelve, a girl of fourteen and the farmer's wife. The way those two children did work—Whew! I was so glad when a shower came up about noon that I refrained from shouting with difficulty. I drew my pay this time to get some gloves, and promised to be back as soon as it dried. The next morning I felt so sore and stiff as the result of my two days' experience in the harvest fields, that I forgot all about my promise to return and decided to stay in Eaton.

It was in Eaton that I started my first bank account. The little twenty-dollar certificate of deposit opened my mind to different things entirely. I would look at it until I had day dreams. During the three months I spent in Eaton I laid the foundation of a future. Simple as it was, it led me into channels which carried me away from my race and into a life fraught with excitement; a life that gave experiences and other things I had never dreamed of. I had started a bank account of twenty dollars and I found myself wanting one of thirty, and to my surprise the desire seemed to increase. This desire fathered my plans to become a porter on a P———n car. A position I diligently sought and applied for between such odd jobs about town as mowing lawns, washing windows, scrubbing floors and a variety of others that kept me quite busy. Taking the work, if I could, by contract, thus permitting me to use my own time and to work as hard as I desired to finish. I found that by this plan I could make money faster and easier than by working in the country.

I was finally rewarded by being given a run on a parlor car by a road that reached many summer resorts in southern Wisconsin. Here I skimped along on a run that went out every Friday and Saturday, returning on Monday morning. The regular salary was forty dollars per month, but as I never put in more than half the time I barely made twenty dollars, and altho' I made a little "on the side" in the way of tips I had to draw on the money I had saved in Eaton.

CHAPTER IV

THE P———N COMPANY

THE P———n Company is a big palace, dining and sleeping car company that most American people know a great deal about. I had long desired to have a run on one of the magnificent sleepers that originated out of Chicago to every part of North America, that I might have an opportunity to see the country and make money at the same time, and from Monday to Friday I had nothing to do but report at one of the three P———n offices in my effort to get such a position. One office where I was particularly attentive, operated cars on four roads, so I called on this office about twice a week, but a long, slim chief clerk whose chair guarded the entrance to the Superintendent's office would drawl out lazily: "We don't need any men today." I had been to the office a number of times before I left Eaton and had heard his drawl so often that I grew nervous whenever he looked at me. That district employed over a thousand porters and there was no doubt that they hired them every day. One day I was telling troubles to a friendly porter whom I later learned to be George Cole (former husband of the present wife of Bert Williams, the comedian). He advised me to see Mr. Miltzow, the Superintendent.

"But I can never see him," I said despairingly, "for that long imbecile of a clerk."

"Jump him some day when he is on the way from luncheon, talk fast, tell him how you have been trying all summer to 'get on', the old man" he said, referring to the superintendent, "likes big, stout youngsters like you, so try it." The next day I watched him from the street and when he started to descend the long stairway to his office, I gathered my courage and stepped to his side. I told him how I had fairly haunted his office, only to be turned away regularly by the same words; that I would like a position if he would at any time need any men. He went into his office, leaving me standing at the railing, where I held my grounds in defiance of the chief clerk's insolent stare. After a few minutes he looked up and called out "Come in here, you." As I stood before him he looked me over searchingly and inquired as to whether I had any references.

"No Sir," I answered quickly, "but I can get them." I was beside myself with nervous excitement and watched him eagerly for fear he might turn me away at the physicological moment, and that I would fail to get what I had wanted so long.

"Well," he said in a decisive tone, "get good references, showing what you have been doing for the last five years, bring them around and I'll talk to you."

"Thank you Sir," I blurted out and with hopes soaring I hurried out and down the steps. Going to my room, I wrote for references to people in M—pls who had known me all my life. Of course they sent me the best of letters, which I took immediately to Mr. Miltzow's office. After looking them over carelessly he handed them to his secretary asking me whether I was able to buy a uniform. When I answered in the affirmative he gave me a letter to the company's tailor, and one to the instructor, who the next day gave me my first lessons in a car called the "school" in a nearby railroad yard placed there for that purpose. I learned all that was required in a day, although he had some pupils who had been with him five days before I started and who graduated with me. I now thought I was a full-fledged porter and was given an order for equipment, combs, brushes, etc., a letter from the instructor to the man that signed out the runs, a very apt appearing young man with a gift for remembering names and faces, who instructed me to report on the morrow. The thought of my first trip the next day, perhaps to some distant city I had never seen, caused me to lie awake the greater part of the night.

When I went into the porter's room the next day, or "down in the hole," as the basement was called, and looked into the place, I found it crowded with men, and mostly old men at that and I felt sure it would be a long time before I was sent out. However, I soon learned that the most of them were "emergency men" or emergies, men who had been discharged and who appeared regularly in hopes of getting a car that could not be supplied with a regular man.

There was one by the name of Knight, a pitiable and forlorn character in whose breast "hope sprang eternal," who came to the "hole" every day, and in an entire year he had made one lone trip. He lived by "mooching" a dime, quarter or fifty cents from first one porter then another and by helping some porters make down beds in cars that went out on midnight trains. It was said that he had been discharged on account of too strict adherence to duty. Every member of a train crew, whether porter, brakeman or conductor, must carry a book of rules; more as a matter of form than to show to passengers as Knight had done. A trainman should, and does, depend more on his judgment than on any set of rules, and permits the rule to be stretched now and then to fit circumstances. Knight, however, courted his rule book and when a passenger requested some service that the rules prohibited, such for instance as an extra pillow to a berth, and if the passenger insisted or showed dissatisfaction Knight would get his book of rules, turn to the chapter which dwelt on the subject and read it aloud to the already disgruntled passenger, thereby making more or less of a nuisance to the traveling public.

But I am digressing. Fred, the "sign-out-clerk" came along and the many voices indulging in loud and raucous conversation so characteristic of porters off duty, gave way to respectful silence. He looked favorably on the regular men but seemed to pass up the emergies as he entered. The poor fellows didn't expect to be sent out but it seemed to fascinate them to hear the clerk assign the regular men their cars to some distant cities in his cheerful language such as: "Hello! Brooks, where did you come from?—From San Antonio? Well take the car 'Litchfield' to Oakland; leaves on Number Three at eleven o'clock to-night over the B. & R. N.; have the car all ready, eight lowers made down." And from one to the other he would go, signing one to go east and another west. Respectfully silent and attentive the men's eyes would follow him as he moved on, each and every man eager to know where he would be sent.

Finally he got to me. He had an excellent memory and seemed to know all men by name. "Well Devereaux," he said, "do you think that you can run a car? "

"Yes Sir!" I answered quickly. He fumbled his pencil thoughtfully while I waited nervously then went on:

"And you feel quite capable of running a car, do you?"

"Yes Sir" I replied with emphasis, "I learned thoroughly yesterday."

"Well," he spoke as one who has weighed the matter and is not quite certain but willing to risk, and taking his pad and pencil he wrote, speaking at the same time, "You go out to the Ft. Wayne yards and get on the car 'Altata', goes extra to

Washington D.C. at three o'clock; put away the linen, put out combs, brushes and have the car in order when the train backs down."

"Yes Sir," and I hurried out of the room, up the steps and onto the street where I could give vent to my elation. To Washington, first of all places. O Glory! and I fairly flew out to Sixteenth street where the P. F. & W. passenger yards were located. Here not less than seven hundred passenger and P————n cars are cleaned and put in readiness for each trip daily, and standing among them I found the Altata. O wonderful name! She was a brand new observation car just out of the shops. I dared not believe my eyes, and felt that there must be some mistake; surely the company didn't expect to send me out with such a fine car on my first trip. But I should have known better, for among the many thousands of P————n cars with their picturesque names, there was not another "Altata." I looked around the yards and finally inquired of a cleaner as to where the Altata was.

"Right there," he said, pointing to the car I had been look-ing at and I boarded her nervously; found the linen and lockers but was at a loss to know how and where to start getting the car in order. I was more than confused and what I had learned so quickly the day before had vanished like smoke. I was afraid too, that if I didn't have the car in order I'd be taken off when the train backed down and become an "emergie" myself. This shocked me so it brought me to my senses and I got busy put-ting the linen somewhere and when the train stopped in the shed the car, as well as myself, was fairly presentable and ready to receive.

Then came the rush of passengers with all their attending requests for attention. "Ah Poiter, put my grip in Thoiteen," and "Ah Poiter, will you raise my window and put in a deflector?"

Holy Smitherines! I rushed back and forth like a lost calf, trying to recall what a deflector was, and I couldn't distinguish thoiteen from three. Then—"Ah, Poiter, will you tell me when we get to Valparaiso?" called a little blonde lady, "You see, I have a son who is attending the Univoisity theah—now Poiter don't don't forget please" she asked winsomely.

"Oh! No, Maam," I assured her confidently that I never forgot anything. My confusion became so intense had I gotten off the car I'd probably not have known which way to get on again.

The clerk seemed to sense my embarrassment and helped me seat the passengers in their proper places, as well as to answer the numerous questions directed at me. The G. A. R. encampment was on in Washington and the rush was greater than usual on that account. By the time the train reached Valparaiso I had gotten somewhat accustomed to the situation and recalled my promise to the little blonde lady and filled it. She had been asleep and it was raining to beat-the-band. With a sigh she looked out of the window and then turned on her side and fell asleep again. At Pittsburg I was chagrined to be turned back and sent over the P. H. & D. to Chicago.

At Columbus, Ohio, we took on a colored preacher who had a ticket for an upper berth over a Southerner who had the lower. The Southern gentleman in that "holier than thou" attitude made a vigorous kick to the conductor to have the colored "Sky-pilot," as he termed him, removed. I heard the conductor tell him gently but firmly, that he couldn't do it. Then after a few characteristic haughty remarks the Southerner went forward to the chair car and sat up all night. When I got the shoes shined and lavatory ready for the morning rush I slipped into the Southerner's berth and had a good snooze. However, longer than it should have been, for the conductor found me the next morning as the train was pulling into Chicago. He threatened to report me but when I told him that it was my first trip out, that I hadn't had any sleep the night before and none the night before that on account of my restlessnes in anticipation of the trip, he relented and helped me to make up the beds.

I barely got to my room before I was called to go out again. This time going through to Washington. The P. F. & W. tracks pass right through Washington's "black belt" and it might be interesting to the reader to know that Washington has more colored people than any other American city. I had never seen so many colored people. In fact, the entire population seemed to be negroes. There was an old lady from South Dakota on my car who seemed surprised at the many colored people and after looking quite intently for some time she touched me on the sleeve, whispering, "Porter, aren't there anything but colored people here?" I replied that it seemed so.

At the station a near-mob of colored boys huddled before the steps and I thought they would fairly take the passengers off their feet by the way they crowded around them. However, they were harmless and only wanted to earn a dime by carrying grips. Two of them got a jui jitsu grip on that of the old lady from South Dakota, and to say that she became frightened would be putting it mildly. Just then a policeman came along and the boys scattered like flies and the old lady seemed much relieved. Having since taken up my abode in that state myself, and knowing that there were but few negroes inhabiting it, I have often wondered since how she must have felt on that memorable trip of hers, as well as mine.

After working some four months on various and irregular runs that took me to all the important cities of the United States east of the Mississippi River, I was put on a regular run to Portland, Oregon. This was along in February and about the same time that I banked my first one hundred dollars. If my former bank account had stirred my ambition and become an incentive to economy and a life of modest habits, the larger one put everything foolish and impractical entirely out of my mind, and economy, modesty and frugality became fixed habits of my life.

At a point in Wyoming on my run to Portland my car left the main line and went over another through Idaho and Oregon. From there no berth tickets were sold by the station agents and the conductors collected the cash fares, and had for many years mixed the company's money with their own. I soon found myself in the mire along with the conductors. "Getting in" was easy and tips were good for a hundred dollars a month and sometimes more. "Good Conductors," a name applied to "color blind" cons, were worth seventy-five, and with the twenty-five dollar salary from the company, I averaged two hundred dollars a month for eighteen months.

There is something fascinating about railroading, and few men really tire of it. In fact, most men, like myself, rather enjoy it. I never tired of hearing the t-clack of the trucks and the general roar of the train as it thundered over streams and crossings throughout the days and nights across the continent to the Pacific coast. The scenery never grew old, as it was quite varied between Chicago and North Platte. During the summer it is one large garden farm, dotted with numerous cities, thriving hamlets and towns, fine country homes so characteristic of the great middle west, and is always pleasing to the eye.

Between North Platte and Julesburg, Colorado, is the heart of the semi-arid region, where the yearly rainfall is insufficient to mature crops, but where the short buffalo grass feeds the rancher's herds winter and summer. As the car continues westward, climbing higher and higher as it approaches the Rockies, the air becomes quite rare. At Cheyenne the air is so light it blows a gale almost steadily, and the eye can discern objects for miles away while the ear cannot hear sounds over twenty rods. I shall not soon forget how I was wont to gaze at the herds of cattle ten to thirty miles away grazing peacefully on the great Laramie plains to the south, while beyond that lay the great American Rockies, their ragged peaks towering above in great sepulchral forms, filling me alternately with a feeling of romance or adventure, depending somewhat on whether it was a story of the "Roundup," or some other article typical of the west, I was reading.

Nearing the Continental divide the car pulls into Rawlins, which is about the highest, driest and most uninviting place on the line. From here the stage lines radiate for a hundred miles to the north and south. Near here is Medicine Bow, where Owen Wister lays the beginning scenes of the "Virginian"; and beyond lies Rock Springs, the home of the famous coal that bears its name and which commands the highest price of any bituminous coal. The coal lies in wide veins, the shafts run horizontally and there are no deep shafts as there are in the coal fields of Illinois and other Central states.

From here the train descends a gentle slope to Green River, Wyoming, a division point in the U. P. South on the D. & R. G. is Green River, Utah. Arriving at Granger one feels as though he had arrived at the jumping off place of creation. Like most all desert stations it contains nothing of interest and time becomes a bore. Here the traffic is divided and the O. S. L. takes the Portland and Butte section into Idaho where the scenery suddenly begins to get brighter. Indeed, the country seems to take on a beautiful and cheerful appearance; civilization and beautiful farms take the place of the wilderness, sage brush and skulking coyotes. Thanks to the irrigation ditch.

After crossing the picturesque American Falls of Snake

River, the train soon arrives at Minidoka. This is the seat of the great Minidoka project, in which the United States Government has taken such an active interest and constructed a canal over seventy miles in length. This has converted about a quarter of a million acres of Idaho's volcanic ash soil into productive lands that bloom as the rose. It was the beautiful valley of the Snake River, with its indescribable scenery and its many beautiful little cities, that attracted my attention and looked as though it had a promising future. I had contemplated investing in some of its lands and locating, if I should happen to be compelled by stress of circumstances to change my occupation. This came to pass shortly thereafter.

The end came after a trip between Granger and Portland, in company with a shrewd Irish conductor by the name of Wright, who not only "knocked down" the company's money, but drank a good deal more whiskey than was good for him. On this last trip, when Wright took charge of the car at Granger, he began telling about his newly acquired "dear little wifey." Also confiding to me that he had quit drinking and was going to quit "knocking down"—after that trip. Oh, yes! Wright was always going to dispense with all things dishonest and dishonorable— at some future date. Another bad thing about Wright was that he would steal, not only from the company, but from the porter as well, by virtue of the rule that required the porter to take a duplicate receipt from the conductor for each and every passenger riding on his car, whether the passenger has a ticket or pays cash fare. These receipts are forwarded to the Auditor of the company at the end of each run.

Wright's method of stealing from the porter was not to turn over any duplicates or receipts until arriving at the terminus. Then he would choose a time when the porter was very busy brushing the passengers' clothes and getting the tips, and would then have no time to count up or tell just how many people had ridden. I had received information from others concerning him and was cautioned to watch. So on our first trip I quietly checked up all the passengers as they got on and where they got off, as well as the berth or seat they occupied. Arriving at Granger going east he gave me the wink and taking me into the smoking room he proceeded to give me the duplicates and divide the spoils. He gave me six dollars, saying he had cut such and such a passenger's fare and that was my part. I summed up and the amount "knocked down" was thirty-one dollars. I showed him my figures and at the same time told him to hand over nine-fifty more. How he did rage and swear about the responsibilities being all on him, that he did all the collecting and the "dirty work" in connection therewith, that the company didn't fire the porter. He said before he would concede to my demands he would turn all the money in to the company and report me for insolence. I sat calmly through it all and when he had exhausted his vituperations I calmly said "nine-fifty, please." I had no fear of his doing any of the things threatened for I had dealt with grafting conductors long enough to know that when they determined on keeping a fare they weren't likely to turn in their portion to spite the porter, and Wright was no exception.

But getting back to the last trip. An old lady had given me a quart of Old Crow Whiskey bottled in bond. There had been perhaps a half pint taken out. I thanked her profusely and put it in the locker, and since Wright found that he could not keep any of my share of the "knocked down" fares he was running straight—that is with me, and we were quite friendly, so I told him of the gift and where to find it if he wanted a "smile." In one end of the P———n where the drawing room cuts off the main portion of the car, and at the beginning of the curved aisle and opposite to the drawing room, is the locker. When its door is open it completely closes the aisle, thus hiding a person from view behind it. Before long I saw Wright open the door and a little later could hear him ease the bottle down after taking a drink.

When we got to Portland, Wright was feeling "about right" and the bottle was empty. As he divided the money with me he cried: "Let her run on three wheels." It was the last time he divided any of the company's money with a porter. When he stepped into the office at the end of that trip he was told that they "had a message from Ager" the assistant general superintendent, concerning him. Every employee knew that a message from this individual meant "off goes the bean." I never saw Wright afterwards, for they "got" me too that trip.

The little Irish conductor, who was considered the shrewdest of the shrewd, had run a long time and "knocked down" a great amount of the company's money but the system of "spotting" eventually got him as it does the best of them.

I now had two thousand, three hundred and forty dollars in the bank. The odd forty I drew out, and left the remainder on deposit, packed my trunk and bid farewell to Armour Avenue and Chicago's Black Belt with its beer cans, drunken men and women, and turned my face westward with the spirit of Horace Greeley before and his words "Go west, young man, and grow up with the country" ringing in my ears. So westward I journeyed to the land of raw material, which my dreams had pictured to me as the land of real beginning, and where I was soon to learn more than a mere observer ever could by living in the realm of a great city.

CHAPTER V

"GO WEST YOUNG MAN AND GROW UP WITH THE COUNTRY"

I N justice to the many thousands of P———n porters, as well as many conductors, who were in the habit of retaining the company's money, let it be said that they are not the hungry thieves and dishonest rogues the general public might think them to be, dishonest as their conduct may seem to be. They were victims of a vicious system built up by and winked at by the company itself.

Before the day of the Inter-State Commerce Commission and anti-pass and two-cent-per-mile legislation, and when passengers paid cash fares, it was a matter of tradition with the conductors to knockdown, and nothing was said, although the conductors, as now, were fairly well paid and the company fully expected to lose some of the cash fares.

In the case of the porters, however, the circumstances are far more mitigating. At the time I was with the company there were, in round numbers, eight thousand porters in the service on tourist and standard sleepers who were receiving from a minimum of twenty-five dollars to not to exceed forty dollars per month, depending on length and desirability of service. Out of this he must furnish, for the first ten years, his own uniforms and cap, consisting of summer and winter suits at twenty and twenty-two dollars respectively. After ten years of continuous service these things are furnished by the company. Then there is the board, lodging and laundry expense. Trainmen are allowed from fifty to sixty per cent off of the regular bill of fare, and at this price most any kind of a meal in an a-la-carte diner comes to forty and fifty cents. Besides, the waiters expect tips from the crew as well as from the passengers and make it more uncomfortable for them if they do not receive it than they usually do for the passenger.

I kept an accurate itemized account of my living expenses, including six dollars per month for a room in Chicago, and economize as I would, making one uniform and cap last a whole year, I could not get the monthly expense below forty dollars—fifteen dollars more than my salary, and surely the company must have known it and condoned any reasonable amount of "knock down" on the side to make up the deficiency in salary. The porter's "knock down" usually coming through the sympathy, good will and unwritten law of "knocking down"—that the conductor divide equally with the porter. All of which, however, is now fast becoming a thing of the past, owing to recent legislation, investigations and strict regulation of common carriers by Congress and the various laws of the states of the Union, with the added result that conductors' wages have increased accordingly. Few conductors today are foolish enough to jeopardize their positions by indulging in the old practice, and it leaves the porters in a sorry plight indeed.

All in all, the system, while deceptive and dishonest on its face, was for a time a tolerated evil, apparently sanctioned by the company and became a veritable disease among the colored employees who, without exception, received and kept the company's money without a single qualm of conscience. It was a part of their duty to make the job pay something more than a part of their living expenses.

Ignorant as many of the porters were, most of them knew that from the enormous profits made that the company could and should have paid them better wages, and I am sure that if they received living wages for their services it would have a great moralizing effect on that feature of the service, and greatly add to the comfort of the traveling public.

However, the greedy and inhuman attitude of this monoply toward its colored employees has just the opposite effect, and is demoralizing indeed. Thousands of black porters continue to give their services in return for starvation wages and are compelled to graft the company and the people for a living.

Shortly before my cessation of activities in connection with the P———n company it had a capitalization of ninety-five million dollars, paying eight per cent dividend annually, and about two years after I was compelled to quit, it paid its stockholders a thirty-five million dollar surplus which had accumulated in five years. Just recently a "melon was cut" of about a like amount and over eight thousand colored porters helped to accumulate it, at from twenty-five to forty dollars per month. A wonder it is that their condition does not breed such actual dishonesty and deception that society would be forced to take notice of it, and the traveling public should be thankful for the attentive services given under these near-slave conditions. As for myself, the reader has seen how I made it "pay" and I have no apologies or regrets to offer. When that final reckoning comes, I am sure the angel clerk will pass all porters against whom nothing more serious appears than what I have heretofore related.

While I was considered very fortunate by my fellow employees, the whole thing filled me with disgust. I suffered from a nervous worry and fear of losing my position all the time, and really felt relieved when the end came and I was free to pursue a more commendable occupation.

In going out of the Superintendent's office on my farewell leave, the several opportunities I had seen during my experience with the P———n company loomed up and marched in dress parade before me; the conditions of the Snake River valley and the constructiveness of the people who had turned the alkali desert into valuable farms worth from fifty to five hundred dollars an acre, thrilled me so that I had no misgivings for the future. But Destiny had other fields in view for me and did not send me to that land of Eden of which I had become so fond, in quest of fortune. Such a variety of scenes was surely an incentive to serious thought.

What was termed inquisitiveness at home brought me a world of information abroad. This inquisitiveness, combined with the observation afforded by such runs as those to Portland and around the circle and, perhaps, coming back by Washington D.C., gave practical knowledge. Often western sheepmen, who were ready talkers, returning on my car from taking a shipment to Chicago, gave me some idea of farming and sheepraising. I remember thinking that Iowa would be a fine place to own a farm, but quickly gave up any further thought of owning one there myself. A farmer from Tama, that state, gave me the information. He was a beautiful decoration for a P———n berth and a neatly made bed with three sheets, and I do not know what possessed him to ever take a sleeper, for he slept little that night, I am sure. The next morning about five o'clock, while gathering and shining shoes, I could not find his, and being curious, I peeped into his berth. What I saw made me laugh, indeed. There he lay, all bundled into his bed in his big fur overcoat and shoes on, just as he came into the car the evening before. He was awake and looked so uncomfortable that I suggested that he get up if he wasn't sleepy. "What say?" he answered, leaning over and sticking his head out of the berth as though afraid someone would grab him.

As this class of farmers like to talk, and usually in loud tones, I led him into the smoking room as soon as he jumped out of his berth, to keep him from annoying other passengers. Here he washed his face, still keeping his coat on.

"Remove your coat," I suggested, "and you will be more comfortable."

"You bet," he said taking his coat off and sitting on it. Lighting his pipe, he began talking and I immediately inquired of him how much land he owned.

He answered that he owned a section. "Gee! but that is a lot of land," I exclaimed, getting interested, "and what is it worth an acre?"

"The last quarter I bought I paid eighty dollars an acre," he returned. That is over thirteen thousand and I could plainly see that my little two thousand dollar bank account wouldn't go very far in Iowa when it came to buying land. That was nine years ago and the same land today will sell around one hundred and fifty dollars an acre, and the "end is not yet."

I concluded on one thing, and that was, if one whose capital was under eight or ten thousand dollars, desired to own a good farm in the great central west he must go where the land was new or raw and undeveloped. He must begin with the beginning and develop with the development of the country. By the proper and accepted methods of conservation of the natural resources and close application to his work, his chances for success are good.

When I finally reached this conclusion I began searching for a suitable location in which to try my fortune in the harrowing of the soil.

CHAPTER VI

"AND WHERE IS ORISTOWN?"
THE TOWN ON THE MISSOURI

I T CAME a few days later in a restaurant in Council Bluffs, Iowa, when I heard the waiters, one white man and the other colored, saying, "I'm going to Oristown." "And where is Oristown?" I inquired, taking a stool and scrutinizing the bill of fare. "Oristown," the white man spoke up, drawing away at a pipe which gave him the appearance of being anything from a rover to a freight brakeman, "is about two hundred and fifty miles northwest of here in southern South Dakota, on the edge of the Little Crow Reservation, to be opened this summer." This is not the right name, but the name of an Indian chief living near where this is written.

"Oristown is the present terminus of the C. & R. W. Ry," and he went on to tell me that the land in part was valuable, while some portions were no better than Western Nebraska. A part of the Reservation was to be opened to settlement by lottery that summer and the registration was to take place in July. It was now April. "And the registration is to come off at Oristown?" I finished for him with a question. "Yes," he assented.

At Omaha the following day I chanced to meet two surveyors who had been sent out to the reservation from Washington,

D.C. and who told me to write to the Department of the Interior for information regarding the opening, the lay of the land, quality of the soil, rainfall, etc. I did as they suggested and the pamphlets received stated that the land to be opened was a deep black loam, with clay subsoil, and the rainfall in this section averaged twenty-eight inches the last five years. I knew that Iowa had about thirty inches and most of the time was too wet, so concluded here at last was the place to go. This suited me better than any of the states or projects I had previously looked into, besides, I knew more about the mode of farming employed in that section of the country, it being somewhat similar to that in Southern Illinois.

On the morning of July fifth, at U. P. Transfer, Iowa, I took a train over the C. P. & St. L., which carried me to a certain town on the Missouri in South Dakota. I did not go to Oristown to register as I had intended but went to the town referred to, which had been designated as a registration point also. I was told by people who were "hitting" in the same direction and for the same purpose, that Oristown was crowded and lawless, with no place to sleep, and was overrun with tin-horn gamblers. It would be much better to go to the larger town on the Missouri, where better hotel accommodation and other conveniences could be had. So I bought a ticket to Johnstown, where I arrived late in the afternoon of the same day. There was a large crowd, which soon found its way to the main street, where numerous booths and offices were set up, with a notary in each to accept applications for the drawing. This consisted of taking oath that one was a citizen of the United States, twenty-one years of age or over. The head of a family, a widow, or any woman upon whom fell the support of a family, was also accepted. No person, however, owning over one hundred and sixty acres of land, or who had ever had a homestead before, could apply. The application was then enclosed in an envelope and directed to the Superintendent of the opening.

After all the applications had been taken, they were thoroughly mixed and shuffled together. Then a blindfolded child was directed to draw one from the pile, which became number one in the opening. The lucky person whose oath was contained in such envelope was given the choice of all the land thrown open for settlement. Then another envelope was drawn and that person was given the second choice, and so on until they were all drawn.

This system was an out and out lottery, but gave each and every applicant an equal chance to draw a claim, but guaranteed none. Years before, land openings were conducted in a different manner. The applicants were held back of a line until a signal was given and then a general rush was made for the locations and settlement rights on the land. This worked fairly well at first but there grew to be more applicants than land, and two or more persons often located on the same piece of land and this brought about expensive litigation and annoying disputes and sometimes even murder, over the settlement. This was finally abolished in favor of the lottery system, which was at least safer and more profitable to the railroads that were fortunate enough to have a line to one or more of the registration points.

At Johnstown, people from every part of the United States, of all ages and descriptions, gathered in crowded masses, the greater part of them being from Illinois, Iowa, Missouri, Minnesota, North Dakota, Kansas and Nebraska. When I started for the registration I was under the impression that only a few people would register, probably four or five thousand, and as there were twenty-four hundred homesteads I had no other thought than I would draw and later file on a quarter section. Imagine my consternation when at the end of the first day the registration numbered ten thousand. A colored farmer in Kansas had asked me to keep him posted in regard to the opening. He also thought of coming up and registering when he had completed his harvest. When the throngs of people began pouring in from the three railroads into Johnstown (and there were two other points of registration besides) I saw my chances of drawing a claim dwindling, from one to two, to one to ten, fifteen and twenty and maybe more. After three days in Johnstown I wrote my friend and told him I believed there would be fully thirty thousand people apply for the twenty-four hundred claims. The fifth day I wrote there would be fifty thousand. After a week I wrote there would be seventy-five thousand register, that it was useless to expect to draw and I was leaving for Kansas to visit my parents. When the registration was over I read in a Kansas City paper that one hundred and seven thousand persons had registered, making the chance of drawing one to forty-four.

Received a card soon after from the Superintendent of the opening, which read that my number was 6504, and as the number of claims was approximately twenty-four hundred, my number was too high to be reached before the land should all be taken. I think it was the same day I lost fifty-five dollars out of my pocket. This, combined with my disappointment in not drawing a piece of land, gave me a grouch and I lit out for the Louisiana Purchase Exposition at St. Louis with the intention of again getting into the P———n service for a time.

Ofttimes porters who had been discharged went to another city, changed their names, furnished a different set of references and got back to work for the same company. Now if they happened to be on a car that took them into the district from which they were discharged, and before the same officials, who of course recognized them, they were promptly reported and again discharged. I pondered over the situation and came to the conclusion that I would not attempt such deception, but avoid being sent back to the Chicago Western District. I was at a greater disadvantage than Johnson, Smith, Jackson, or a number of other common names, by having the odd French name that had always to be spelled slowly to a conductor, or any one else who had occasion to know me. Out of curiosity I had once looked in a Chicago Directory. Of some two million names there were just two others with the same name. But on the other hand it was much easier to avoid the Chicago Western District, or at least Mr. Miltzow's office and by keeping my own name, assume that I had never been discharged, than it was to go into a half a dozen other districts with a new name and avoid being recognized. Arriving at this decision, I approached the St. Louis office, presented my references which had been furnished by other M—pls business men, and was accepted. After I had been sent out with a porter, who had been running three months, to show me how to run a car, I was immediately put to work. I learned in two trips, according to the report my tutor handed to the chief clerk, and by chance fell into one of the best runs to New York on one of the limited trains during the fair. There was not much knocking down on this run, but the tips, including the salary, were good for three hundred dollars per month. I ran on this from September first to October fourth and saved three hundred dollars. I had not given up getting a Dakota Homestead, for while I was there during the summer I learned if I did not draw a number I could buy a relinquishment.

This relates to the purchasing of a relinquishment:

An entryman has the right at any time to relinquish back to the United States all his right, title, and interest to and in the land covered by his filing. The land is then open to entry.

A claimholder who has filed on a quarter of land will have

plenty of opportunity to relinquish his claim, for a cash consideration, so that another party may get a filing on it. This is called buying or selling a relinquishment. The amount of the consideration varies with quality of the land, and the eagerness of the buyer or seller, as the case may be.

Relinquishments are the largest stock in trade of all the real estate dealers, in a new country. Besides, everybody from the bank president down to the humble dish washer in the hotel, or the chore boy in the livery, the ministers not omitted, would, with guarded secrecy, confide in you of some choice relinquishment that could be had at a very low figure compared with what it was really worth.

CHAPTER VII

ORISTOWN, THE "LITTLE CROW" RESERVATION

WHEN I left St. Louis on the night of October fourth I headed for Oristown to buy someone's relinquishment. I had two thousand, five hundred dollars. From Omaha the journey was made on the C. & R. W.'s one train a day that during these times was loaded from end to end, with everybody discussing the Little Crow and the buying of relinquishments. I was the only negro on the train and an object of many inquiries as to where I was going. Some of those whom I told that I was going to buy a relinquishment seemingly regarded it as a joke, judging from the meaning glances cast at those nearest them.

An incident occurred when I arrived at Oristown which is yet considered a good joke on a real estate man then located there, by the name of Keeler, who was also the United States Commissioner. He could not only sell me a relinquishment, but could also take my filing. I had a talk with Keeler, but as he did not encourage me in my plan to make a purchase I went to another firm, a young lawyer and a fellow by the name of Slater, who ran a livery barn, around the corner. Watkins, the lawyer, impressed me as having more ambition than practical business qualities. However, Slater took the matter up and agreed to take me over the reservation and show me some good claims. If I bought, the drive was gratis, if not four dollars per day, and I accepted his proposition.

After we had driven a few miles he told me Keeler had said to him that he was a fool to waste his time hauling a d— nigger around over the reservation; that I didn't have any money and was just "stalling." I flushed angrily, and said "Show me what I want and I will produce the money. What I want is something near the west end of the county. You say the relinquishments are cheaper there and the soil is richer. I don't want big hills or rocks nor anything I can't farm, but I want a nice level or gently rolling quarter section of prairie near some town to be, that has prospects of getting the railroad when it is extended west from Oristown." By this time we had covered the three miles between Oristown and the reservation line, and had entered the newly opened section which stretched for thirty miles to the west. As we drove on I became attracted by the long grass, now dead, which was of a brownish hue and as I gazed over the miles of it lying like a mighty carpet I could seem to feel the magnitude of the development and industry that would some day replace this state of wildness. To the Northeast the Missouri River wound its way, into which empties the Whetstone Creek, the breaks of which resembled miniature mountains, falling abruptly, then rising to a point where the dark shale sides glistened in the sunlight. It was my longest drive in a buggy. We could go for perhaps three or four miles on a table-like plateau, then drop suddenly into small canyon-like ditches and rise abruptly to the other side. After driving about fifteen miles we came to the town, as they called it, but I would have said village of Hedrick—a collection of frame shacks with one or two houses, many roughly constructed sod buildings, the long brown grass hanging from between the sod, giving it a frizzled appearance. Here we listened to a few boosters and mountebanks whose rustic eloquence was no doubt intended to give the unwary the impression that they were on the site of the coming metropolis of the west. A county-seat battle was to be fought the next month and the few citizens of the sixty days declared they would wrest it from Fairview, the present county seat situated in the extreme east end of the county, if it cost them a million dollars, or one-half of all they were worth. They boasted of Hedrick's prospects, sweeping their arms around in eloquent gestures in alluding to the territory tributary to the town, as though half the universe were Hedrick territory.

Nine miles northwest, where the land was very sandy and full of pits, into which the buggy wheels dropped with a grinding sound, and where magnesia rock cropped out of the soil, was another budding town by the name of Kirk. The few prospective citizens of this burg were not so enthusiastic as those in Hedrick and when I asked one why they located the town in such a sandy country he opened up with a snort about some pinheaded engineer for the "guvment" who didn't know enough to jump straight up "a locating the town in such an all fired sandy place"; but he concluded with a compliment, that plenty of good water could be found at from fifteen to fifty feet.

This sandy land continued some three miles west and we often found springs along the streams. After ascending an unusually steep hill, we came upon a plateau where the grass, the soil, and the lay of the land, were entirely different from any we had as yet seen. I was struck by the beauty of the scenery and it seemed to charm and bring me out of the spirit of depression the sandy stretch brought upon me. Stretching for miles to the northwest and to the south, the land would rise in a gentle slope to a hog back, and as gently slope away to a draw, which drained to the south. Here the small streams emptied into a larger one, winding along like a snake's track, and thickly wooded with a growth of small hardwood timber. It was beautiful. From each side the land rose gently like huge wings, and spread away as far as the eye could reach. The driver brought me back to earth, after a mile of such fascinating observations, and pointing to the north, said: "There lays one of the claims." I was carried away by the first sight of it. The land appeared to slope from a point, or table, and to the north of that was a small draw, with water. We rode along the south side and on coming upon a slight raise, which he informed me was the highest part of the place, we found a square white stone set equally distant from four small holes, four or five feet apart. On one side of the stone was inscribed a row of letters which ran like this, SWC, SWQ, Sec. 29-97-72 W. 5th P. M., and on the other sides were some other letters similar to these. "What does all that mean?" I asked. He said the letters were initials describing the land and reading from the side next to the place we had come to see it, read: "The southwest corner of the southwest quarter of section twenty-nine, township ninety-seven, and range seventy-two, west of the fifth principal meridian."

When we got back to Oristown I concluded I wanted the place and dreamed of it that night. It had been drawn by a girl who lived with her parents across the Missouri. To see her, we had to drive to their home, and here a disagreement arose, which for a time threatened to cause a split. I had been so enthusiastic over the place, that Slater figured on a handsome commission, but I had been making inquiries in Oristown, and found I could buy relinquishments much cheaper than I had anticipated. I had expected the price to be about one thousand, eight hundred dollars and came prepared to pay that much, but was advised to pay not over five hundred dollars for land as far west as the town of Megory, which was only four miles northwest of the place I was now dickering to buy. We had agreed to give the girl three hundred and seventy-five dollars, and I had partly agreed to give Slater two hundred dollars commission. However, I decided this was too much, and told him I would give him only seventy-five dollars. He was in for going right back to Oristown and calling the deal off, but when he figured up that two and a half day's driving would amount to only ten dollars, he offered to take one hundred dollars. But I was obstinate and held out for seventy-five dollars, finally giving him eighty dollars, and in due time became the proud owner of a Little Crow homestead.

All this time I had been writing to Jessie. I had written first while I was in Eaton, and she had answered in the same demure manner in which she had received me at our first meeting, and had continued answering the letters I had written from all parts of the continent, in much the same way. For a time I had quit writing, for I felt that she was really too young and not taking me seriously enough, but after a month, my sister wrote me, asking why I did not write to Jessie; that she asked about me every day. This inspired me with a new interest and I began writing again.

I wrote her in glowing terms all about my advent in Dakota, and as she was of a reserved disposition, I always asked her opinion as to whether she thought it a sensible move. I wanted to hear her say something more than: "I was at a cantata last evening and had a nice time", and so on. Furthermore, I was skeptical. I knew that a great many colored people considered farming a deprivation of all things essential to a good time. In fact, to have a good time, was the first thing to be considered, and everything else was secondary. Jessie, however, was not of this kind. She wrote me a letter that surprised me, stating, among other things, that she was seventeen and in her senior year high school. That she thought I was grand and noble, as well as practical, and was sorry she couldn't find words to tell me all she felt, but that which satisfied me suited her also. I was delighted with her answer and wrote a cheerful letter in return, saying I would come to see her, Christmas.

CHAPTER VIII

FAR DOWN THE PACIFIC—THE PROPOSAL

AFTER the presidential election of that year I went to South America with a special party, consisting mostly of New York capitalists and millionaires. We traveled through the southwest, crossing the Rio Grand at Eagle Pass, and on south by the way of Toreon, Zacatecas, Aguas Calientes, Guadalajara, Puebla, Tehauntepec and to the southwest coast, sailing from Salina Cruz down the Pacific to Valparaiso, Chile, going inland to Santiago, thence over the Trans-Andean railway across the Andes, and onward to the western plateau of Argentina.

Arriving at the new city of Mendoza, we visited the ruins of the ancient city of the same name. Here, in the early part of the fifteenth century, on a Sunday morning, when a large part of the people were at church, an earthquake shook the city. When it passed, it left bitter ruin in its wake, the only part that stood intact being one wall of the church. Of a population of thirteen thousand, only sixteen hundred persons escaped alive. The city was rebuilt later, and at the time we were there it was beautiful place of about twenty-five thousand population. At this place a report of bubonic plague, in Brazil, reached us. The party became frightened and beat it in post haste back to Valparaiso, setting sail immediately for Salina Cruz, and spent the time that was scheduled for a tour of Argentina, in snoopin' around the land of the Montezumas. This is the American center of Catholic Churches; the home of many gaudy Spanish women and begging peons; where the people, the laws, and the customs, are two hundred years behind those of the United States. Still, I thought Mexico very beautiful, as well as of historical interest.

One day we journeyed far into the highlands, where lay the ancient Mexican city of Cuernavaca, the one-time summer home of America's only Emperor, Maximilian. From there we went to Puebla, where we saw the old Cathedral which was begun in 1518, and which at that time was said to be the second largest in the world. We saw San Louis Potosí, and Monterey, and returned by the way of Laredo, Texas. I became well enough acquainted with the liberal millionaires and so useful in serving their families that I made five hundred and seventy-five dollars on the trip, besides bringing back so many gifts and curiosities of all kinds that I had enough to divide up with a good many of my friends.

Flushed with prosperity and success in my undertakings since leaving Southern Illinois less than three years before, I went to M—boro to see my sister and to see whether Miss Rooks had grown any. I was received as a personage of much importance among the colored people of the town, who were about the same kind that lived in M—pls; not very progressive, excepting with their tongues when it came to curiosity and gossip. I arrived in the evening too late to call on Miss Rooks and having become quite anxious to see her again, the night dragged slowly away, and I thought the conventional afternoon would never come again. Her father, who was an important figure among the colored people, was a mail carrier and brought the mail to the house that morning where I stopped. He looked me over searchingly, and I tried to appear unaffected by his scrutinizing glances.

By and by two o'clock finally arrived, and with my sister I went to make my first call in three years. I had grown quite tall and rugged, and I was anxious to see how she looked. We were received by her mother who said: "Jessie saw you coming and will be out shortly." After a while she entered and how she had changed. She, too, had grown much taller and was a little stooped in the shoulders. She was neatly dressed and wore her hair done up in a small knot, in keeping with the style of that time. She came straight to me, extended her hand and seemed delighted to see me after the years of separation.

After awhile her mother and my sister accommodatingly found an excuse to go up town, and a few minutes later with her on the settee beside me, I was telling of my big plans and the air castles I was building on the great plains of the west. Finally, drawing her hand into mine and finding that she offered no resistance, I put my arm around her waist, drew her close and declared I loved her. Then I caught myself and dared not go farther with so serious a subject when I recalled the wild, rough, and lonely place out on the plains that I had selected as a home, and finally asked that we defer anything further until the claim on the Little Crow should develop into something more like an Illinois home.

"O, we don't know what will happen before that time," she spoke for the first time, with a blush as I squeezed her hand.

"But nothing can happen," I defended, nonplused, "can there?"

"Well, no," she answered hesitatingly, leaning away.

"Then we will, won't we?" I urged.

"Well, yes", she answered, looking down and appearing a trifle doubtful. I admired her the more. Love is something I had longed for more than anything else, but my ambition to over-come the vagaries of my race by accomplishing something wor-thy of note, hadn't given me much time to seek love.

I went to my old occupation of the road for awhile and spent most of the winter on a run to Florida, where the tipping was as good as it had been on the run from St. Louis to New York. However, about a month before I quit I was assigned to a run to Boston. By this time I had seen nearly all the important cities in the United States and of them all none interested me so much as Boston.

What always appeared odd to me, however, was the fact that the passenger yards were right at the door of the fashionable Back Bay district on Huntington Avenue, near the Hotel Nottingham, not three blocks from where the intersection of Huntington Avenue and Boylston Street form an acute angle in which stands the Public Library, and in the opposite angle stands Trinity Church, so thickly purpled with aristocracy and the memory big with the tradition of Philip Brooks, the last of that group of mighty American pulpit orators, of whom I had read so much. A little farther on stands the Massachusetts Institute of Technology.

The mornings I spent wandering around the city, visiting Faneuil Hall, the old State House, Boston commons, Bunker Hill, and a thousand other reminders of the early heroism, rugged courage, and far seeing greatness of Boston's early citi-zens. Afternoons generally found me on Tremont or Washington Street attending a matinee or hearing music. There once I heard Caruso, Melba, and two or three other grand opera stars in the popular Rigeletto Quartette, and another time I wit-nessed "Siberia" and the gorgeous and blood-curdling reproduc-tion of the Kishneff Massacre, with two hundred people on the stage. On my last trip to Boston I saw Chauncy Olcott in

"Terrence the Coach Boy," a romance of old Ireland with the scene laid in Valley Bay, which seemed to correspond to the Back Bay a few blocks away.

Dear old Boston, when will I see you again, was my thought as the train pulled out through the most fashionable part of America, so stately and so grand. Even now I recall the last trip with a sigh. If the Little Crow, with Oristown as its gateway, was a land of hope; through Massachusetts; Worcester, with the Polytechnic Institute arising in the back ground; Springfield, and Smith School for girls, Pittsfield, Brookfield, and on to Albany on the Hudson, is a memory never to be forgotten, which evolved in my mind many long years afterward, in my shack on the homestead.

CHAPTER IX

THE RETURN—ERNEST NICHOLSON

I LEFT St. Louis around April first with about three thousand dollars in the bank and started again for Oristown, this time to stay. I had just paid Jessie a visit and I felt a little lonely. With the grim reality of the situation facing me, I now began to steel my nerves for a lot of new experience which soon came thick and fast.

Slater met the train at Oristown, and as soon as he spied me informed me that I was a lucky man. That a town had been started adjoining my land and was being promoted by his brother and the sons of a former Iowa Governor, and gave every promise of making a good town, also, if I cared to sell, he had a buyer who was willing to pay me a neat advance over what I had paid. However, I had no idea of parting with the land, but I was delighted over the news, and the next morning found me among Dad Durpee's through stage coach passengers, for Calias, the new town joining my homestead, via Hedrick and Kirk. As we passed through Hedrick I noticed that several frame shacks had been put up and some better buildings were under way. The ground had been frozen for five months, so sod-house building had been temporarily abandoned.

It was a long ride, but I was beside myself with enthusiasm.

Calias finally loomed up, conspicuously perched on a hill, and could be seen long before the stage arrived, and was the scene of much activity. It had been reported that a colored man had a claim adjoining the town on the north, so when I stepped from the stage before the post office, the many knowing glances informed me that I was being looked for. A fellow who had a claim near and whom I met in Oristown, introduced me to the Postmaster whose name was Billinger, an individual with dry complexion and thin, light hair. Then to the president of the Townsite Company, second of three sons of the Iowa Governor.

My long experience with all classes of humanity had made me somewhat of a student of human nature, and I could see at a glance that here was a person of unusual agressiveness and great capacity for doing things. As he looked at me his eyes seemed to bore clear through, and as he asked a few questions his searching look would make a person tell the truth whether he would or no. This was Ernest Nicholson, and in the following years he had much to do with the development of the Little Crow.

CHAPTER X

THE OKLAHOMA GRAFTER

HAT evening at the hotel he asked me whether I wished to double my money by selling my relinquishment. "No," I answered, "but I tell you what I do want to do," I replied firmly. "I am not here to sell; I am here to make good or die trying; I am here to grow up with this country and prosper with the growth, if possible. I have a little coin back in old "Chi." (my money was still in the Chicago bank) "and when these people begin to commute and want to sell, I am ready to buy another place." I admired the fellow. He reminded me of "the richest man in the world" in "The Lion and the Mouse," Otis Skinner as Colonel Phillippi Bridau, an officer on the staff of Napoleon's Army in "The Honor of the Family," and other characters in plays that I greatly admired, where great courage, strength of character, and firm decision were displayed. He seemed to have a commanding way that one found himself feeling honored and willing to obey.

But getting back to the homestead. I looked over my claim and found it just as I had left it the fall before, excepting that a prairie fire during the winter had burned the grass. The next morning I returned to Oristown and announced my intentions of buying a team. The same day I drew a draft for five hundred dollars with which to start.

Now if there is anywhere an inexperienced man is sure to go wrong in starting up on a homestead, it is in buying horses. Most prospective homesteaders make the same mistake I did in buying horses, unless they are experienced. The inefficient man reasons thus: "Well, I will start off economically by buying a cheap team"—and he usually gets what he thought he wanted, "a cheap team."

If I had gone into the country and bought a team of young mares for say three hundred dollars, which would have been a very high price at that time, I would have them yet, and the increase would have kept me fairly well supplied with young horses, instead of scouting around town looking for something cheaper, in the "skate" line, as I did. I looked at so many teams around Oristown that all of them began to look alike. I am sure I must have looked at five hundred different horses, more in an effort to appear as a conservative buyer than to buy the best team. Finally I ran onto an "Oklahoma" grafter by the name of Numemaker.

He was a deceiving and unscrupulous rascal, but nevertheless possessed a pleasing personality, which stood him in good in his schemes of deception, and we became quite chummy. He professed to know all about horses—no doubt he did, but he didn't put his knowledge at my disposal in the way I thought he should, being a friend, as he claimed. He finally persuaded me to buy a team of big plugs, one of which was so awkward he looked as though he would fall down if he tried to trot. The other was a powerful four-year-old gelding, that would have never been for sale around Oristown if it hadn't been that he had two feet badly wire cut. One was so very large that it must have been quite burdensome for the horse to pick it up, swing it forward and put it down, as I look back and see him now in my mind.

When I was paying the man for them I wondered why Nunemaker led him into the private office of the bank, but I was not left long in doubt. When I crossed the street one of the men who had tried to sell me a team jumped me with: "Well, they got you, did they?" his voice mingled with sarcasm and a sneer.

"Got who?" I returned questioningly.

"Does a man have to knock you down to take a hint?" he went on in a tone of disappointment and anger. "Don't you know that man Nunemaker is the biggest grafter in Oristown? I would have sold you that team of mine for twenty-five dollars less'n I offered 'em, if the goldarn grafter hadn't of come to me'n said, 'give me twenty-five dollars and I will see that the coon buys the team.' I would have knocked him down with a club if I'd had one, the low life bum." He finished with a snort and off he went.

"Stung, by cracky," was all I could say, and feeling rather blue I went to the barn where the team was, stroked them and hoped for the best.

I then bought lumber to build a small house and barn, an old wagon for twenty dollars, one wheel of which the blacksmith had forgotten to grease, worked hard all day getting loaded, and wearied, sick and discouraged, I started at five o'clock P.M. to drive the thirty miles to Calias. When I was out two miles the big old horse was wobbling along like a broken-legged cow, hobbling, stumbling, and making such a burdensome job of walking, that I felt like doing something desperate. When I looked back the wheel that had not been greased was smoking like a hot box on the Twentieth Century Limited.

The sun was nearly down and a cold east wind was whooping it up at about sixty miles an hour, chilling me to the marrow. The fact that I was a stranger in a strange land, inhabited wholly by people not my own race, did not tend to cheer my gloomy spirits. I decided it might be all right in July but never in April. I pulled my wagon to the side of the road, got down and unhitched and jumped on the young horse, and such a commotion as he did make. I am quite sure he would have bucked me off, had it not for his big foot being so heavy, he couldn't raise it quick enough to leap. Evidently he had never been ridden. When I got back to Oristown and put the team in the barn and warmed up, I resolved to do one thing and do it that night. I would sell the old horse, and I did, for twenty-two-fifty. I considered myself lucky, too. I had paid one hundred and ninety dollars for the team and harness the day before.

I sat down and wrote Jessie a long letter, telling her of my troubles and that I was awfully, awfully, lonesome. There was only one other colored person in the town, a barber who was married to a white woman, and I didn't like him.

The next day I hired a horse, started early and arrived at Calias in good time. At Hedrick I hired a sod mason, who was also a carpenter, at three dollars a day and we soon put up a frame barn large enough for three horses; a sod house sixteen by fourteen with a hip roof made of two by fours for rafters, and plain boards with tar paper and sod with the grass turned downward and laid side by side, the cracks being filled with sand. The house had two small windows and one door, that was a little short on account of my getting tired carrying sod. I ordered the "contractor" to put the roof on as soon as I felt it was high enough to be comfortable inside.

The fifth day I moved in. There was no floor, but the thick, short buffalo grass made a neat carpet. In one corner I put the bed, while in another I set the table, the one next the door I placed the stove, a little two-hole burner gasoline, and in the other corner I made a bin for the horse's grain.

CHAPTER XI

DEALIN' IN MULES

IT MUST have been about the twentieth of April when I finished building. I started to "batch" and prepared to break out my claim. Having only one horse, it became necessary to buy another team. I decided to buy mules this time. I remembered that back on our farm in southern Illinois, mules were thought to be capable of doing more work than horses and eat less grain. So when some boys living west of me came one Sunday afternoon, and said they could sell me a team of mules, I agreed to go and see them the next day. I thought I was getting wise. As proof of such wisdom I determined to view the mules in the field. I followed them around the field a few times and although they were not fine looking, they seemed to work very well. Another great advantage was, they were cheap, only one hundred and thirty-five dollars for the team and a fourteen-inch-rod breaking plow. This looked to me like a bargain. I wrote him a check and took the mules home with me. Jack and Jenny were their names, and I hadn't owned Jack two days before I began to hate him. He was lazy, and when he went down hill, instead of holding his head up and stepping his front feet out, he would lower the bean and perform a sort of crow-hop. It was too exasperating for words and I used to strike him viciously for it, but that didn't seem to help matters any.

I shall not soon forget my first effort to break prairie. There are different kinds of plows made for breaking the sod. Some kind that are good for one kind of soil cannot be used in another. In the gummy soils of the Dakotas, a long slant cut is the best. In fact, about the only kind that can be used successfully, while in the more sandy lands found in parts of Kansas and Nebraska, a kind is used which is called the square cut. The share being almost at right angles with the beam instead of slanting back from point to heel. Now in sandy soils this pulls much easier for the grit scours off any roots, grass, or whatever else would hang over the share. To attempt to use this kind in wet, sticky land, such as was on my claim, would find the soil adhering to the plow share, causing it to drag, gather roots and grass, until it is impossible to keep the plow in the ground. When it is dry, this kind of plow can be used with success in the gummy land; but it was not dry when I invaded my homestead soil with my big horse, Jenny and Jack, that first day of May, but very wet indeed,

To make matters worse, Doc, the big horse, believed in "speeding." Jenny was fair but Jack, on the landside, was affected with "hook-worm hustle," and believed in taking his time. I tried to help him along with a yell that grew louder as I hopped, skipped, and jumped across the prairie, and that plow began hitting and missing, mostly missing. It would gouge into the soil up to the beam, and the big horse would get down and make a mighty pull, while old Jack would swing back like the heavy end of a ball bat when a player draws to strike, and out would come the plow with a skip, skip, skip; the big horse nearly trotting and dragging the two little mules, that looked like two goats beside an elephant. Well, I sat down and gave up to a fit of the blues; for it looked bad, mighty bad for me.

I had left St. Louis with two hundred dollars in cash, and

had drawn a draft for five hundred dollars more on the Chicago bank, where my money was on deposit, and what did I have for it? One big horse, tall as a giraffe; two little mules, one of which was a torment to me; a sod house; and old wagon. As I faced the situation there seemed nothing to do but to fight it out, and I turned wearily to another attempt, this time with more success. Before I had started breaking I had invited criticism. Now I was getting it on all sides. I was the only colored homesteader on the reservation, and as an agriculturist it began to look mighty bad for the colored race on the Little Crow.

Finally, with the assistance of dry weather, I got the plow so I could go two or three rods without stopping, throw it out of the ground and clear the share of roots and grass. Sometimes I managed to go farther, but never over forty rods, the entire summer.

I took another course in horse trading or mule trading, which almost came to be my undoing. I determined to get rid of Jack. I decided that I would not be aggravated with his laziness and crow-hopping any longer than it took me to find a trade. So on a Sunday, about two weeks after I bought the team, a horse trader pulled into Calias, drew his prairie schooner to a level spot, hobbled his horses—mostly old plugs of diverse descriptions, and made preparation to stay awhile. He had only one animal, according to my horse-sense (?), that was any good, and that was a mule that he kept blanketed. His camp was so situated that I could watch the mule, from my east window, and the more I looked at the mule, the better he looked to me. It was Wednesday noon the following week and old Jack had become almost unbearable. My continuing to watch a good mule do nothing, while I continued to fret my life away trying to be patient with a lazy brute, only added to my restlessness and eagerness to trade. At noon I entered the barn and told old Jack I would get rid of him. I would swap him to that horse trader for his good mule as soon as I watered him. He was looking pretty thin and I thought it would be to my advantage to fill him up.

During the three days the trader camped near my house he never approached me with an offer to sell or trade, and it was with many misgivings that I called out in a loud, breezy voice and David Harum manner; "Hello, Governor, how will you trade mules?" "How'll I trade mules? did you say how'll I trade mules? Huh, do you suppose I want your old mule?" drawing up one side of his face and twisting his big red nose until he resembled a German clown.

"O, my mule's fair," I defended weakly.

"Nothing but an old dead mule," he spit out, grabbing old Jack's tail and giving him a yank that all but pulled him over. "Look at him, look at him," he rattled away like an auctioneer. "Go on, Mr. Colored Man, you can't work me that way." He continued stepping around old Jack, making pretentions to hit him on the head. Jack may have been slow in the field, but he was swift in dodging, and he didn't look where he dodged either. I was standing at his side holding the reins, when the fellow made one of his wild motions, and Jack nearly knocked my head off as he dodged. "Naw sir, if I considered a trade, that is if I considered a trade at all, I would have to have a lot of boot," he said with an important air.

"How much?" I asked nervously.

"Well, sir," he spoke with slow decision; "I would have to have twenty-five dollars."

"What!" I exclaimed, at which he seemed to weaken; but he didn't understand that my exclamation was of surprise that he only wanted twenty-five dollars, when I had expected to give him seventy-five dollars. I grasped the situation, however, and leaning forward, said hardly above a whisper, my heart was so near my throat: "I will give you twenty," as I pulled out my roll and held a twenty before his eyes, which he took as though afraid I would jerk it away; muttering something about it not being enough, and that he had ought to have had twenty-five. However, he got old Jack and the twenty, gathered his plugs and left town immediately. I felt rather proud of my new possession, but before I got through the field that afternoon I became suspicious. Although I looked my new mule over and over often during the afternoon while plowing, I could find nothing wrong. Still I had a chilly premonition, fostered, no doubt, by past experience, that something would show up soon, and in a few days it did show up. I learned afterward the trader had come thirty-five miles to trade me that mule.

The mule I had traded was only lazy, while the one I had received in the trade was not only lazy, but "ornery" and full of tricks that she took a fiendish delight in exercising on me. One of her favorites was to watch me out of her left eye, shirking the while, and crowding the furrow at the same time, which would pull the plow out of the ground. I tried to coax and cajole her into doing a decent mule's work, but it availed me nothing. I bore up under the aggravation with patience and fortitude, then determined to subdue the mule or become subdued myself. I would lunge forward with my whip, and away she would rush out from under it, brush the other horse and mule out of their places and throw things into general confusion. Then as soon as I was again straightened out, she would be back at her old tricks, and I am almost positive that she used to wink at me impudently from her vantage point. Added to this, the coloring matter with which the trader doped her head, faded, and she turned grey headed in two weeks, leaving me with a mule of uncertain and doubtful age, instead of one of seven going on eight as the trader represented her to be.

I soon had the enviable reputation of being a horse trader.

Whenever anybody with horses to trade came to town, they were advised to go over to the sod house north of town and see the colored man. He was fond of trading horses, yes, he fairly doted on it. Nevertheless with all my poor "horse-judgment" I continued to turn the sod over day after day and completed ten or twelve acres each week.

CHAPTER XII

THE HOMESTEADERS

OF NEIGHBORS, I had many. There was Miss Carter from old Missouri whose claim joined mine on the west, and another Missourian to the north of her; a loud talking German north of him, and an English preacher to the east of the German. A traveling man's family lived north of me; and a big, fat, lazy barber who seemed to be taking the "rest cure," joined me on the east. His name was Starks and he had drawn claim number 252. He had a nice, level claim with only a few buffalo wallows to detract from its value, and he held the distinction of being the most uncompromisingly lazy man on the Little Crow. This, coupled with the unpardonable fault of complaining about everything, made him nigh unbearable and he was known as the "Beefer." He came from a small town, usually the home of his ilk, in Iowa, where he had a small shop and owned three and a half acres of garden and orchard ground on the outskirts of the town. He would take a fiendish delight in relating and re-relating how the folks in his house back in Iowa were having strawberries, new peas, green beans, spring onions, and enjoying all the fruits of a tropical climate, while he was holding down an "infernal no-account claim" on the Little Crow, and eating out of a can.

A merchant was holding down a claim south of him, and a

banker lived south of the merchant. Thus it was a varied class of homesteaders around Calias and Megory, the first summer on the Little Crow. Only about one in every eight or ten was a farmer. They were of all vocations in life and all nationalities, excepting negroes, and I controlled the colored vote.

This was one place where being a colored man was an honorary distinction. I remember how I once requested the stage driver to bring me some meat from Megory, there being no meat shop in Calias, and it was to be left at the post office. Apparently I had failed to give the stage driver my name, for when I called for it, it was handed out to me, done up in a neat package, and addressed "Colored Man, Calias." My neighbors soon learned, however, that my given name was "Oscar," but it was some time before they could all spell or pronounce the odd surname.

During the month of June it rained twenty-three days, but I was so determined to break out one hundred and twenty acres, that after a few days of the rainy weather I went out and worked in the rain. Starks used to go up town about four o'clock for the mail, wearing a long, yellow slicker, and when he saw me going around the half-mile land he remarked to the bystanders: "Just look at that fool nigger a working in the rain."

Being the first year of settlement in a new country, there naturally was no hay to buy, so the settlers turned their stock out to graze, and many valuable horses strayed away and were lost. When it rained so much and the weather turned so warm, the mosquitoes filled the air and covered the earth and attacked everything in their path. When I turned my horses out after the day's work was done, they soon found their way to town, where they stood in the shelter of some buildings and fought mosquitoes. Their favorite place for this pastime was the post office, where Billinger had a shed awning over the board walk, the framework consisting of two-by-fours joined together and nailed lightly to the building, and on top of this he had laid a few rough boards. Under this crude shelter the homesteaders found relief from the broiling afternoon sun, and swapped news concerning the latest offer for their claims. The mosquitoes did not bother so much in even so slight an inclosure as this, so every night Jenny Mule would walk on to the board walk, prick up her ears and look in at the window. About this time the big horse would come along and begin to scratch his neck on one of the two-by-fours, and suddenly down would go Billinger's portable awning with a loud crash which was augmented by Jenny Mule getting out from under the falling boards. As the sound echoed through the slumbering village the big horse would rush away to the middle of the street, with a prolonged snort, and wonder what it was all about. This was the story Billinger told when I came around the next morning to drive them home from the storekeeper's oat bin where they had indulged in a midnight lunch. The performance was repeated nightly and got brother Billinger out of bed at all hours. He swore by all the Gods of Buddha and the people of South Dakota, that he would put the beasts up and charge me a dollar to get them.

Early one morning I came over and found that Billinger had remained true to his oath, and the horse and mule were tied to a wagon belonging to the storekeeper. Nearby on a pile of rock sat Billinger, nodding away, sound asleep. I quietly untied the rope from the wagon and peaceably led them home. Then Billinger was in a rage. He had a small, screechy tremulo voice and it fairly sputtered as he tiraded: "If it don't beat all; I never saw the like. I was up all last night chasing those darned horses, caught them and tied them up; and along comes Devereaux while I am asleep and takes horses, rope and all." The crowd roared and Billinger decided the joke was on him.

Miss Carter, my neighbor on the west, had her trouble too. One day she came by, distressed and almost on the verge of tears, and burst out: "Oh, Oh, Oh, I hardly know what to do."

I could never bear seeing any one in such distress and I became touched by her grief. Upon becoming more calm, she told me: "The banker says that the man who is breaking prairie on my claim is ruining the ground." She was simply heartbroken about it, and off she went into another spasm of distress. I saw the fellow wasn't laying the sod over smoothly because he had a sixteen-inch plow, and had it set to cut only about eight inches, which caused the sod to push away and pile up on edges, instead of turning and dropping into the furrow. I went with her and explained to the fellow where the fault lay. The next day he was doing a much better job.

Those who have always lived in the older settled parts of the country sometimes have exaggerated ideas of life on the homestead, and the following incident offers a partial explanation. Megory and Calias each had a newspaper, and when they weren't roasting each other and claiming their paper to be the only live and progressive organ in the country, they were "building" railroads or printing romantic tales about the brave homesteader girls. A little red-headed girl nicknamed "Jack" owned a claim near Calias. One day it was reported that she killed a rattlesnake in her house. The report of the great encounter reached eastern dailies, and was published as a Sunday feature story in one of the leading Omaha papers. It was accompanied by gorgeous pictures of the girl in a leather skirt, riding boots, and cowboy hat, entering a sod house, and before her, coiled and poised to strike, lay a monster rattlesnake. Turning on her heel and jerking the bridle from her horse's head, she made a terrific swing at Mr. Rattlesnake, and he, of course, "met his Waterloo." This, so the story read, was the eightieth rattlesnake she had killed. She was described as "rattlesnake Jack" and thereafter went by that name. She was also credited with having spent the previous winter alone on her claim and rather enjoyed the wintry nights and snow blockade. Now as a matter of fact, she had spent most of the previous winter enjoying the comforts of a front room at the Hotel Calias, going to the claim occasionally on nice days. She had no horse, and as to the eighty rattlesnakes, seventy-nine were myths, existing only in the mind of a prolific feature story writer for the Sunday edition of the great dailies. In fact she had killed one small young rattler with a button.

CHAPTER XIII

IMAGINATIONS RUN AMUCK

I DECIDED to utilize some of my spare time by doing a little freighting from Oristown to Calias. Accordingly, one fair morning I started for the former town. It began raining that evening, finally turning into a fine snow, and by morning a genuine South Dakota blizzard was raging. How the wind did screech across the prairie!

I was driving the big horse and Jenny Mule to a wagon loaded with two tons of coal. They were not shod, and the hillsides had become slick and treacherous with ice. At the foot of every hill Jenny Mule would lay her ears back, draw herself up like a toad, when teased, and look up with a groan, while the big horse trotted on up the next slope, pulling her share of the load.

When the wind finally went down the mercury fell to 25° below zero and my wrists, face, feet, and ears were frost bitten when I arrived at Calias. As is always the case during such severe weather, the hotel was filled, and laughing, story telling, and good cheer prevailed. The Nicholson boys asked "how I made it" and I answered disgustedly that I'd have made it all right if that Jennie Mule hadn't got faint hearted. The remark was received as a good joke and my suffering and annoyances of the trip slipped away into the past. That remark also had the further effect of giving Jennie Mule immortality. She became the topic of conversation and jest in hotel and post office lobbies, and even to this day the story of the "faint hearted mule" often affords splendid entertainment at festive boards and banquet halls of the Little Crow, when told by a Nicholson.

While working in the rain, the perspiration and the rain water had caused my body to become so badly galled, that I found considerable difficulty in getting around. To add to this discomfiture Jenny Mule was affected with a touch of "Maudism" at times, especially while engaged in eating grain. One night when I had wandered thoughtlessly into the barn, she gave me such a wallop on the right shin as to impair that member until I could hardly walk without something to hold to. As it had taken a fourteen-hundred-mile walk to follow the plow in breaking the one hundred and twenty acres, I was about "all in" physically when it was done.

As a means of recuperation I took a trip to Chicago. While there, the "call of the road" affected me; I got reinstated and ran a couple of months to the coast. Four months of free life on the plains, however, had changed me. After one trip I came in and found a letter from Jessie, saying she was sick, and although she never said "come and see me" I took it as an excuse and quit that P———n Company for good—and here it passes out of the story—went down state to M—boro, and spent the happiest week of my life.

After I had returned to Dakota, however, I contracted an imagination that worked me into a state of jealousy, concerning an individual who made his home in M—boro, and with whom I suspicioned the object of my heart to be unduly friendly. I say, this is what I suspicioned. There was no particular proof, and I have been inclined to think, in after years, that it was more a case of an over-energetic imagination run amuck. I contended in my mind and in my letters to her as well, that I should not have thought anything of it, if the "man in the case" had a little more promising future, but since his proficiency only earned him the munificent sum of three dollars per week, I continued to fret and fume, until I at last resolved to suspend all communication with her.

Now what I should have done when I reached this stage of imaginary insanity, was to have sent Miss Rooks a ticket, some money, and she would have come to Dakota and married me, and together we would have "lived happy ever after." As I see it now, I was affected with an "idealism." Of course I was not aware of it at the time—no young soul is—until they have learned by bitter experience the folly of "they should not do thus and so", and, of course, there is the old excuse, "good intentions." Somewhere I read that the road to—not St. Peter—is paved with good intentions. The result of my prolific imagination was that I carried out my resolutions, quit writing, and emotionally lived rather unhappily thereafter, for some time at least.

CHAPTER XIV

THE SURVEYORS

HE entire Little Crow reservation consisted of about two million acres of land, four-fifths of which was unopened and lay west of Megory County. Of the two million acres, perhaps one million, five hundred thousand ranged from fair to the richest of loam soil, underlaid with clay. The climatic condition is such that all kinds of crops grown in the central west, can be grown here. Two hundred miles north, corn will not mature; two hundred miles south, spring wheat is not grown; two hundred west, the altitude is too high to insure sufficient rainfall to produce a crop; but the reservation lands are in such a position that winter wheat, spring wheat, oats, rye, corn, flax, and barley do well. Ever since the drouth of '94, all crops had thrived, the rainfall being abundant, and continuing so during the first year of settlement. Oristown and other towns on the route of the railroad had waited twenty years for the extension, and now the citizens of Oristown estimated it would be at least ten years before it extended its line through the reservation; while the settlers, to the number of some eight thousand, hoped they would get the road in five years. However, no sleep was lost in anticipation. The nearest the reservation came to getting a railroad that summer was by the way of a newspaper in Megory, whose editor spent most of his time building roads into Megory from the north, south, and the east. In reality, the C. & R. W. was the only road likely to run to the reservation, and all the towns depended on its extension to overcome the long, burdensome freighting with teams.

With all the country's local advantages, its geographical location was such as to exclude roads from all directions except the one taken by the C. & R. W. To the south lay nine million acres of worthless sand hills, through which it would require an enormous sum of money to build a road. Even then there would be miles of track which would practically pay no interest on the investment. At that time there was no railroad extending the full length of the state from east to west, most lines stopping at or near the Missouri River. Since then two or three lines have been built into the western part of the state; but they experienced much difficulty in crossing the river, owing to the soft bottom, which in many places would not support a modern steel bridge. For from one to two months in the spring, floating ice gives a great deal of trouble and wreaks disaster to the pontoon.

A bird's eye view of the Little Crow shows it to look something like a bottle, the neck being the Missouri River, with the C. & R. W. tracks creeping along its west bank. This is the only feasible route to the Reservation and the directors of this road were fully aware of their advantageous position. The freight rates from Omaha to Oristown (a distance of two hundred and fifty miles) being as high as from Omaha to Chicago, a distance of five hundred miles.

But getting back to the settlers around and in the little towns on the Little Crow. The first thing to be considered in the extension was, that the route it took would naturally determine the future of the towns. Hedrick, Kirk, and Megory were government townsites, strung in a northwesterly direction across the country, ranging from eight to fifteen miles apart, the last being about five miles and a half east of the west line of the county. Now the county on the west was expected to be thrown open to settlement soon, would likely be opened under the lottery system, as was Megory county. After matters had settled this began to be discussed, particularly by the citizens of Megory, five and one-half miles from the Tipp County line. This placed Megory in the same position to handle the crowds coming into the next county, as Oristown had for Megory County, excepting Megory would have an advantage, for Tipp County was twice as large as Megory. When this was all considered, the people of Megory began to boost the town on the prospects of a future boom. The only uncertain feature of the matter then to be considered was which way the road would extend. That was where the rub came in, which way would the road go? This became a source of continual worry and speculation on the part of the towns, and the men who felt inclined to put money into the towns in the way of larger, better, and more commodious buildings; but when they were encouraged to do so, there was always the bogy "if." If the railroad should miss us, well, the man owning the big buildings was "stung," that was all, while the man with the shack could load it on two or four wagons, and with a few good horses, land his building in the town the railroad struck or started. This was, and is yet, one of the big reasons shacks are so numerous in a town in a new country, which expects a road but knows not which way it will come; and the officials of the C. & R. W. were no different from the directors of any other road. They were "mum" as dummies. They wouldn't tell whether the road would ever extend or not.

The Oristown citizens claimed it was at one time in the same uncertainty as the towns to the west, and for some fifteen or twenty years it had waited for the road. With the road stopping at Oristown, they argued, it would be fully ten years before it left, and during this time it could be seen, Oristown would grow into an important prairie city, as it should. Everything must be hauled into Oristown, as well as out. So it can be seen that Oristown would naturally boom. While nothing had been raised to the west to ship out, as yet, still there was a growing population on the reservation and thousands of carloads of freight and express were being hauled into and from Oristown monthly, for the settlers on the reservation; which filled the town with railroad men and freighters. Crops had been good, and every thing was going along smoothly for the citizens and property owners of Oristown. Not a cloud on her sky of prosperity, and as the trite saying goes: "Everything was lovely, and the goose hung high," during the first year of settlement on the Little Crow.

And now lest we forget Calias. Calias was located one and one half miles east, and three miles south of Megory, and five miles straight west of Kirk. If the C. & R. W. extending its line west, should strike all the government townsites, as was claimed by people in these towns, who knew nothing about it, and Calias, it would have run from Kirk to Megory in a very unusual direction. Indeed, it would have been following the section lines and it is common knowledge even to the most ignorant, that railroads do not follow section lines unless the section lines are directly in its path. If the railroad struck Kirk and Megory, it was a cinch it would miss Calias. If it struck Calias, perched on the banks of the Monca Creek, the route the Nicholsons, as promoters of the town, claimed it would take; the road would miss all the towns but Calias. This would have meant glory and a fortune for the promoters and lot holders of the town. It would also have meant that my farm, or at least a part of it, would in time be sold for town lots.

After I got so badly overreached in dealing in horses, for a time the opinion was general that the solitary negro from the plush cushions of a P————n would soon see that growing up with a new country was not to his liking, and would be glad to sell at any old figure and "beat it" back to more ease and comfort. This is largely the opinion of most of the white people, regarding the negro, and they are not entirely wrong in their opinion. I was quite well aware that such an opinion existed, but contrary to expectations, I rather appreciated it. When I broke out one hundred and twenty acres with such an outfit as I had, as against many other real farmers who had not broken over forty acres, with good horses and their knowledge of breaking prairie, acquired in states they had come from, I began to be regarded in a different light. At first I was regarded as an object of curiosity, which changed to appreciation, and later admiration. I was not called a free-go-easy coon, but a genuine booster for Calias and the Little Crow. I never spent a lonesome day after that.

The Nicholson Brothers, however, gave the settlers no rest, and created another sensation of railroad building by their new contention that the railroad would not be extended from Oristown, but that it would be built from a place on the Monca bottom two stations below Oristown, where the track climbed a four per cent grade to Fairview, then on to Oristown. They offered as proof of their contention that the C. & R. W. maintained considerable yardage there, and it does yet. Why it did, people did not know, and this kept everybody guessing. Some claimed it would go up the Monca Valley, as Nicholson claimed. This much can be said in favor of the Nicholsons, they were good boosters, or "big liars," as their rivals called them, and if one listened long and diligently enough they would have him imagine he could hear the exhaust of a big locomotive coming up the Monca Valley. While the people in the government town-sites persisted loudly that the C. & R. W. had contracted with the government before the towns were located, to strike these three towns, and that the government had helped to locate them; that furthermore, the railroad would never have left the Monca Valley, which it followed for some twenty miles after leaving the banks of the Missouri. All of which sounded reasonable enough, but the government and the railroad had entered into no agreement whatever, and the people in the government towns knew it, and were uneasy.

I had been on my claim just about a year, when one day Rattlesnake Jack's father came from his home on the Jim River and sold me her homestead for three thousand dollars. My dreams were at last realized, and I had become the owner of three hundred and twenty acres of land; but my money was now gone, when I had paid the one thousand, five hundred dollars down on the Rattle Snake Jack place, giving her back a mortgage for the remaining one thousand, five hundred at seven per cent interest, and it was a good thing I did, too. I bought the place early in April and in June the Interior Department rejected the proof she had offered the November before, on account of lack of sufficient residence and cultivation. The proof had been accepted by the local land office, and a final receipt for the remaining installments of the purchase price, amounting to four hundred and eighty dollars, was issued. A final receipt is considered to be equivalent to a patent or deed, but when Rattlesnake Jack's proof of residence got to the General Land Office in Washington, in quest of a patent, the commissioner looked it over, figured up the time she actually put in on the place, and rejected the proof, with the statement that it only showed about six month's actual residence. At that time eight month's residence was required, with six months within which to establish residence; but no proof could be accepted until after the claimant had shown eight month's actual and continuous residence.

From the time the settlers began to commute or prove up on the Little Crow, all proofs which did not show fully eight month's residence, were rejected. This was done mostly by the Register and Receiver of the Local Land Office, and many were sent back on their claims to stay longer. Many proofs were also taken by local U.S. Commissioners, County Judges, and Clerks of Courts, but these officers rarely rejected them, for by so doing they also rejected a four dollar and twenty-five cent fee. About one-third of the persons who offered proof at that time had them turned down at the Local Land Office. This gave the local Commissioners, County Judges, and Clerks of Courts, a chance to collect twice for the same work. It may be interesting to know that a greater percentage of proofs rejected were those offered by women. This was perhaps not due to the fact that the ladies did not stay on their claims, so much as it was conscientiousness. They could not make a forcible showing by saying that they had been there every night, like the men would claim, but would say instead that they had stayed all night with Miss So-and-So this time and with another that time, and by including a few weeks' visit at home or somewhere else, they would bungle their proofs, so they were compelled to try again.

A short time after this and evidently because so many proofs had been sent back, the Interior Department made it compulsory for the claimant to put in fourteen months' actual residence on the claim, before he could offer proof. With fourteen months, they were sure to stay a full eight months at least. This system has been very successful.

When Rattlesnake Jack was ordered back, after selling me the place, she wanted me to sign quit claim deed to her and accept notes for the money I had paid, which might have been satisfactory had it not been that she thought I had stopped to look back and failed to see the rush of progress the Little Crow was making; that the long anticipated news had been spread, and was now raging like a veritable prairie fire, and stirred the people of the Little Crow as much as an active stock market stirs the bulls on the stock exchange. The report spread and stirred the everyday routine of the settlers and the finality of humdrum and inactivity was abrupt. It came one day in early April. The rain had kept the farmers from the fields a week. It had been raining for nearly a month, and we only got a clear day once in a while. This day it was sloppy without, and many farmers were in from the country. We were all listening to a funny story Ernest Nicholson was telling, and "good fellows" were listening attentively. Dr. Salter, a physician, had just been laid on a couch in the back room of the saloon, "soused to the gills," when in the door John M. Keely, a sort of ne'er do well popular drummer, whose proof had been rejected some time before, and who had come back to stay "a while longer," stumbled into the door of the local groggery. He was greeted with sallies and calls of welcome, and like many of the others, he was "feeling good." He sort of leaned over, and hiccoughing during the intervals, started "I've," the words were spoken chokingly, "got news for you." He had by now got inside and was hanging and swinging at the same time, to the bar. Then before finishing what he started, called "Tom," to the bartender, "give me a whiskey before I", and here he leaned over and sang the words "tell the boys the news." "For the love of Jesus Keel" exclaimed the crowd in chorus "tell us what you know." He drained the glass at a gulp and finally spit it out. "The surveyors are in Oristown."

CHAPTER XV

"WHICH TOWN WILL THE R. R. STRIKE?"

THE drummer's information soon received corroboration from other sources, and although it seemed almost unbelievable, it was discussed incessantly and excitement ran high. These pioneers, who had braved the hardships of homestead life had felt that without the railroad they were indeed cut off from civilization. To them the advent of the surveyors in Oristown could mean only one thing—that their dreams of enjoying the many advantages of the railroad train, would soon materialize.

They fell to enumerating these advantages—the mail daily, instead of only once or twice a week; the ease with which they could make necessary trips to the neighboring towns; and most of all—the increase in the value of the land. With this last subject they became so wrought up with excitement and anxiety as to the truth of the report, that they could stay away from the scene of action no longer. Accordingly, buggies and vehicles of all descriptions began coming into Oristown from all directions. I hitched Doc and my new horse, Boliver, for which I had paid one hundred and forty dollars, to an old ramshackle buggy I had bought for ten dollars, and joined the procession.

Three miles west of Oristown we came upon a crowd of

circus-day proportion, and in their midst were the surveyors.

In their lead rode the chief engineer—a slender, wiry man with a black mustache and piercing eyes, that seemed to observe every feature of surrounding prairie. Behind came a wagon loaded with stakes, accompanied by several men, the leader of whom was setting these stakes according to the signal of the engineer from behind the transit. Others, on either side, were also driving stakes. They were not only running a straight survey, but were cross-sectioning as they went.

Even though the presence of these surveyors was now an established fact, these were days of grave uncertainties as to just what route the road would take. The suspense was almost equal to that of the criminal, as he awaits the verdict of the jury. The valleys and divides lay in such a manner that it was possible the survey would extend along the Monca, thus passing through Calias. On the other hand, it was probable that it would continue to the Northwest through Kirk and Megory, thus missing Calias altogether.

When the surveyors reached a point five miles west of Hedrick, they swerved to the northwest and advanced directly toward Kirk. This looked bad for Calias.

When Ernest Nicholson had learned that the surveyors were in Oristown, he had left immediately for parts unknown and had not returned. He was in reality the founder of Calias and many of the inhabitants looked to him as their leader, and depended upon him for advice. Although he had many enemies who heaped abuse and epithets upon him—calling him a liar, braggard and "wind jammer" when boasting of their own independence and self respect—now that a calamity was about to befall them, and their fond hopes for this priceless mistress of prairie were about to be wrecked upon the shoals of an imaginary railroad survey, they turned toward him for comfort, as moths turn to a flame. It was Ernest here and Ernest there. As the inevitable progress of the surveyors proceeded in a direct line for Hedrick, Kirk and Megory, the consternation of the Caliasites became more intense as time went on, and the anxiety for Ernest to return almost resolved itself into mutiny. It became so significant, that at one time it appeared that if Ernest had only appeared, the railroad company would have voluntarily run its survey directly to Calias, in order to avoid the humiliation of Ernest's seizing them by the nape of the neck and marching them, survey, cars and all, right into the little hamlet.

Now there was one thing everybody seemed to forget or to overlook, but which occurred to me at the time, and caused me to become skeptical as to the possibilities of the road striking Calias, and that was, if the railroad was to be built up the Monca Valley, then why had the surveyors come to Oristown, and why had they not gotten off at Anona, the last station in the Monca Valley, where the tracks climb the grade to Fairview.

Many of the Megory and Kirk boosters had taken advantage of Ernest's absence, and through enthusiasm attending the advent of the railroad survey, persuaded several of Calias' business men to go into fusion in their respective towns. The remaining handful consoled each other by prophecies of what Ernest would do when he returned, and plied each other for expressions of theories, and ways and means of injecting enthusiasm into the local situation. Thousands of theories were given expression, consideration, and rejection, and the old one that all railroads follow valleys and streams was finally adhered to. I was singled out to give corroborative proof of this last, by reason of my railroad experience.

I was suddenly seized with a short memory, much to my embarrassment, as I felt all eyes turned upon me. However, the crowd were looking for encouragement and spoke up in chorus:

"Don't the railroads always follow valleys?" It suddenly occurred to me, that with all the thousands of miles of travel to my credit and the many different states I had traveled through, with all their rough and smooth territory, I had not observed whether the tracks followed the valleys or otherwise. However, I intimated that I thought they did. "Of course they do," my remark was answered in chorus.

Since then I have noticed that a railway does invariably follow a valley, if it is a large one; and small rivers make excellent routes, but never crooked little streams like the Monca. When it comes to such creeks, and there is a table land above, as soon as the road can get out, it usually stays out. This was the situation of the C. & R. W. It came some twenty-five or thirty miles up the Monca, from where it empties into the Missouri. There are fourteen bridges across in that many miles, which were and still are, always going out during high water.

It came this route because there was no other way to come, but when it got to Anona, as has been said, it climbed a four per cent grade to get out and it stayed out.

CHAPTER XVI

MEGORY'S DAY

THE first day in May was a local holiday in Megory, held in honor of the first anniversary of the day when all settlers had to be on their claims; and it was raining. During the first years on the Little Crow we were deluged with rainfall, but this day the inclement weather was disregarded. It was Settler's Day and everybody for miles around had journeyed thither to celebrate—not only Settler's Day, but also the advent of the railroad. Only the day before, the surveyors had pitched their tents on the outskirts of the town, and on this day they could be seen calmly sighting their way across the south side of the embryo city. Megory was the scene of a continuous round of revelry. Five saloons were crowded to overflowing, and a score of bartenders served thousands of thirsty throats; while on the side opposite from the bar, and in the rear, gambling was in full blast. Professionals, "tin horns", and "pikers", in their shirt sleeves worked away feverishly drawing in and paying money to the crowd that surged around the Roulette, the Chuck-luck, and the Faro-bank. It seemed as though everybody drank and gambled. "This is Megory's Day," they called between drinks, and it would echo with "have another," "watch Megory grow."

Written in big letters and hung all along the streets were

huge signs which read "Megory, the gateway to a million acres of the richest land in the world." "Megory, the future metropolis of the Little Crow, Watch her grow! Watch her grow!" The board walk four feet wide could not hold the crowd. It was a day of frenzied celebration—a day when no one dared mention Nicholson's name unless they wanted to hear them called liars, wind jammers, and all a bluff.

Ernest was still in the East and no one seemed to know where he was, or what he was doing. The surveyors had passed through Megory and extended the survey to the county line, five miles west of the town. The right-of-way man was following and had just arrived from Hedrick and Kirk, where he had made the same offer he was now making Megory. "If" he said, addressing the "town dads" and he seemed to want it clearly understood, "the C. & R. W. builds to Megory, we want you to buy the right-of-way three miles east and four miles west of the town."

Then Governor Reulback, known as the "Squatter Governor," acting as spokesman for the citizens, arose from his seat on the rude platform, and before accepting the proposition—needless to say it was accepted—called on different individuals for short talks. Among others he called on Ernest Nicholson; but Frank, the Junior member of the firm, arose and answered that Ernest was away engaged in purchasing the C. & R. W. railroad and that he, answering for Ernest, had nothing to say. A hush fell on the crowd, but Governor Reulbach, who possessed a well defined sense of humor, responded with a joke, saying, "Mr. Nicholson's being away purchasing the C. & R. W. railroad reminds me of the Irishman who played poker all night, and the next morning, yawning and stretching himself, said, "Ol lost nine hundred dollars last night and seven and one-half of it was cash."

The backbone of the town was beginning to weaken, while there were many who continued to insist that there was hope. Others contracted rheumatism from vigils at the surveyor's camp, in vain hope of gaining some information as to the proposed direction of the right-of-way. The purchasing of the right-of-way and the unloading of carload after carload of contracting material at Oristown did little to encourage the belief that there was a ghost of a show for Calias.

In a few days corral tents were decorating the right-of-way at intervals of two miles, all the way from Oristown to Megory. In the early morning, as the sound of distant thunder, could be heard the dull thud of clods and dirt dropping into the wagon from the elevator of the excavator; also the familiar "jup" and the thud of the "skinner's" lines as they struck the mules, in Calias one and one-half miles away.

A very much discouraged and weary crowd met Ernest when he returned, but even in defeat this young man's personality was pleasing. He was frank in telling the people that he had done all that he could. He had gone to Omaha where his father in-law joined him, thence to Des Moines, where his father maintained his office as president of an insurance company, that made loans on Little Crow land. Together with two capitalists, friends of his father, they had gone into Chicago and held a conference with Marvin Hewitt, President of the C. & R. W. who had showed them the blue prints, and, as he put it, any reasonable man could see it would be utterly impossible to strike Calias in the route they desired to go. The railroad wanted to strike the Government town sites, but the president told them that if at any time he could do them a favor to call on him, and he would gladly do so.

In a few days a man named John Nodgen came to Calias. Towns which had failed to get a road looked upon him in the

way a sick man would an undertaker. He was a red-haired
Irishman with teeth wide apart and wildish blue eyes, who had
the reputation of moving more towns than any other one man.
He brought horses and wagons, block and tackle, and massive
steel trucks. He swore like a stranded sailor, and declared they
would hold up any two buildings in Calias.

The saloon was the first building deserted. The stock had
not been removed when the house movers arrived, and in some
way they got the door open and helped themselves to the
"booze," and when full enough to be good and noisy, began jack-
ing up the building that had been the pride of the hopeful
Caliasites. In a few weeks a large part of what had been Calias
was in Megory and a small part in Kirk.

It had stopped raining for a while, and several large buildings were still on the move to Megory when the rain set in
again. This was the latter part of July and how it did rain, every
day and night. One store building one hundred feet long had
been cut in two so as to facilitate moving, and the rains caught it
half way on the road to Megory. After many days of sticking
and floundering around in the mud, at a cost of over fourteen
hundred dollars for the moving alone, not counting the goods
spoiled, it arrived at its new home. The building in the beginning had cost only twenty-three hundred dollars, out of which
thirty cents per hundred had been paid for local freighting from
Oristown. The merchant paid one thousand dollars for his lot in
Megory, and received ten dollars for the one he left in Calias.

This was the reason why Rattlesnake Jack's father and I
could not get together when he came out and showed me
Rattlesnake Jack's papers. It was bad and I readily agreed with
him. I also agreed to sign a quit claim deed, thereby clearing the
place, so she could complete her proof. Everything went along
all right, until it came to signing up. Then I suggested that as I

had broken eighty acres of prairie, the railroad was in course of construction, and land had materially increased in valuation— having sold as high as five thousand dollars a quarter section— I should have a guarantee that he would sell the place back to me when the matter had been cleared up.

"I will see that you get the place back"—he pretended to reassure me—"when she proves up again."

"Then we will draw up an agreement to that effect and make it one thousand dollars over what I paid," I suggested.

"I will do nothing of the kind," he roared, brandishing his arms as though he wanted to fight, "and if you will not sign a quit claim without such an agreement, I will have Jack blow the whole thing, that is what I will do, do you hear?" He fairly yelled, leaning forward and pointing his finger at me in a threatening manner.

"Then we will call it off for today," I replied with decision, and we did. I confess however, I was rather frightened. In the beginning I had not worried, as he held a first mortgage of one thousand, five hundred dollars, I had felt safe and thought that they had to make good to me in order to protect their own interests. But now as I thought the matter over it began to look different. If he should have her relinquish, then where would I be, and the one thousand, five hundred dollars I had paid them?

I was very much disturbed and called on Ernest Nicholson and informed him how the matter stood. He listened carefully and when I was through he said:

"They gave you a warranty deed, did they not?"

"Yes, I replied, it is over at the bank of Calias."

"Then let it stay there. Tell him, or the old man rather, to have the girl complete sufficient residence, then secure you for all the place is worth at the time; then, and not before, sign a quit claim, and if they want to sell you the place, well and good;

if not, you will have enough to buy another." And I followed his advice.

It was fourteen months, however, before the Scotch-Irish blood in him would submit to it. But there was nothing he could do, for the girl had given me a deed to something she did not have title to herself, and had accepted one thousand, five hundred dollars in cash from me in return. As the matter stood, I was an innocent party.

About this time I became imbued with a feeling that I would like "most awfully well" to have a little help-mate to love and cheer me. How often I longed for company to break the awful and monotonous lonesomeness that occasionally enveloped me. At that time, as now, I thought a darling little colored girl, to share all my trouble and grief, would be interesting indeed. Often my thoughts had reverted to the little town in Illinois, and I had pictured Jessie caring for the little sod house and cheering me when I came from the fields. For a time, such blissful thoughts sufficed the longing in my heart, but were soon banished when I recalled her seeming preference for the three dollar a week menial, another attack of the blues would follow, and my day dreams became as mist before the sun.

About this time I began what developed into a flirtatious correspondence with a St. Louis octoroon. She was a trained nurse; very attractive, and wrote such charming and interesting letters, that for a time they afforded me quite as much entertainment, perhaps more, than actual company would have done. In fact I became so enamored with her that I nearly lost my emotional mind, and almost succumbed to her encouragement toward a marriage proposal. The death of three of my best horses that fall diverted my interest; she ceased the epistolary courtship, and I continued to batch.

Doc, my big horse, got stuck in the creek and was drowned.

The loss of Doc was hardest for me to bear, for he was a young horse, full of life, and I had grown fond of him. Jenny mule would stand for hours every night and whinny for him.

In November, Bolivar, his mate—the horse I had paid one hundred and forty dollars for not nine months before—got into the wheat, became foundered, and died.

While freighting from Oristown, in December, one of a team of dapple grays fell and killed himself. So in three months I lost three horses that had cost over four hundred dollars, and the last had not even been paid for. I had only three left, the other dapple gray, Jenny mule, and "Old Grayhead," the relic of my horse-trading days. I had put in a large crop of wheat the spring before and had threshed only a small part of it before the cold winter set in, and the snow made it quite impossible to complete threshing before spring.

That was one of the cold winters which usually follow a wet summer, and I nearly froze in my little old soddy, before the warm spring days set in. Sod houses are warm as long as the mice, rats, and gophers do not bore them full of holes, but as they had made a good job tunneling mine, I was left to welcome the breezy atmosphere, and I did not think the charming nurse would be very happy in such a mess "nohow." The thought that I was not mean enough to ask her to marry me and bring her into it, was consoling indeed.

Since I shall have much to relate farther along concerning the curious and many sided relations that existed between Calias, Megory, and other contending and jealous communities, let me drop this and return to the removal of Calias to Megory.

The Nicholson Brothers had already installed an office in the successful town, and offered to move their interests to that place and combine with Megory in making the town a metropolis. But the town dads, feeling they were entirely responsible for the road striking the town, with the flush of victory and the sensation of empire builders, disdained the offer.

In this Megory had made the most stupid mistake of her life, and which later became almost monumental in its proportions. It will be seen how in the flush of apparent victory she lost her head, and looked back to stare and reflect at the retreating and temporary triumph of her youth; and in that instant the banner of victory was snatched from her fingers by those who offered to make her apparent victory real, and who ran swiftly, skillfully, and successfully to a new and impregnable retreat of their own.

The Megory town dads were fairly bursting with rustic pride, and were being wined and dined like kings, by the citizens of the town—who had contributed the wherewith to pay for the seven miles of right-of-way. Besides, the dads were puffed young roosters just beginning to crow, and were boastful as well. So Nicholson Brothers got the horse laugh, which implied that Megory did not need them. "We have made Megory and now watch her grow. Haw! Haw! Haw! Watch her grow," came the cry, when the report spread that the town dads had turned Nicholson's offer down.

Megory was the big I am of the Little Crow. Then Ernest went away on another long trip. It was cold weather, with the ground frozen, when he returned.

CHAPTER XVII

ERNEST NICHOLSON'S RETURN—THE BUILDING
WEST OF TOWN—"WHAT'S IT ALL ABOUT"

T HE big hotel from Calias had not long since been unloaded and decorated a corner lot in Megory. All that remained in Calias were the buildings belonging to Nicholson Brothers, consisting of an old two-story frame hotel, a two-story bank, the saloon, drug store, their own office and a few smaller ones. It was a hard life for the Caliasites and the Megoryites were not inclined to soften it. On the other hand, she was growing like a mushroom. Everything tended to make it the prairie metropolis; land was booming, and buyers were plentiful. Capital was also finding its way to the town, and nothing to disturb the visible prosperity.

But a shrewd person, at that very time, had control of machinery that would cause a radical change in this community, and in a very short time too. This man was Ernest Nicholson, and referring to his return, I was at the depot in Oristown the day he arrived. There he boarded an auto and went west to Megory. On his arrival there, he ordered John Nogden to proceed to Calias, load the bank building, get all the horses obtainable, and proceed at once to haul the building to—no, not to Megory—this is what the Megoryites thought, when, with seventy-six head of horses hitched to it, they saw the bank of Calias coming toward Megory. But when it got to within half a mile of the south side, swerved off to the west. About six that evening, when the sun went down, the Bank of Calias was sitting on the side of a hill that sloped to the north, near the end of the survey.

Now what did it mean? That was the question that everybody began asking everybody else. What was up? Why was Ernest Nicholson moving the bank of Calias five miles west of Megory and setting it down on or near the end of the survey? There were so many questions being asked with no one to answer, that it amused me. Then someone suggested that it might be the same old game, and here would come a pause, then the question, "What old game?" "Why, another Calias?"—some bait to make money. Then, "Oh, I see," said the wise town dads, just a hoax. That answered the question, just a snare to catch the unwary. Tell them that the railroad would build to the Tipp County line. Sell them some lots, for that is what the "bluff" meant. Get their good money and then, Oh, Ha! Ha! Ha! it was too funny when one saw the joke, and Megoryites continued to laugh. Had not Nicholson Brothers said a whole lot about getting the railroad; and that it was sure coming up the Monca. It had come, had it not. Haw! Haw! Haw! Ho! Ho! Ho! just another Nicholson stall, Haw! Haw! Haw! and Nicholsons got the laugh again. The railroad is in Megory, and here it will stop for ten years. One hundred thousand people will come to Megory to register for Tipp County lands, and "Watch Megory grow" was all that could be heard.

Ernest would come to Megory, have a pleasant chat, treat the boys, tell a funny story, and be off. Nobody was mean enough or bold enough to tell him to his face any of the things they told to his back.

Ernest was never known to say anything about it. His scheme simply kept John Nogden moving buildings. He wrote checks in payment, that the bank of Calias cashed, for it was open for business the next day after it had been moved out on the prairie, five miles west of Megory.

The court record showed six quarter sections of land west of town had recently been transferred; the name of the receiver was unknown to anyone in Megory, but such prices, forty to fifty dollars per acre. The people who had sold, brought the money to the Megory banks, and deposited it. All they seemed to know was that someone drove up to their house and asked if they wanted to sell. Some did not, while others said they were only five miles from Megory, and if they sold they would have to have a big price, because Megory was the "Town of the Little Crow" and the gateway to acres of the finest land in the world, to be opened soon. "What is your price?" he would ask, and whether it was forty, forty-five or fifty per acre, he bought it.

This must have gone on for sixty days with everybody wondering "what it was all about", until it got on the nerves of the Megoryites; and even the town dads began to get a little fearful. When Ernest was approached he would wink wisely, hand out a cigar or buy a drink, but he never made anybody the wiser.

A lady came out from Des Moines, bought a lot, and let a contract for a hotel building 24x140, and work was begun on it immediately. This was getting ahead of Megory, where a hotel had just been completed 25x100 feet, said by the Megoryites to be the "best" west of a town of six thousand population, one hundred fifty miles down the road. Whenever anything like a real building goes up in a little town on the prairie, with their collection of shacks, it is always called "the best building" between there and somewhere else.

I shall not soon forget the anxiety with which the people

watched the building which continued to go up west of Megory, and still no one there seemed willing to admit that Nicholson Brothers were "live," but spent their argument in trying to convince someone that they were only wind jammers and manipulators of knavish plots, to immesh the credulous.

What actually happened was this, and Ernest told me about it afterwards in about the following words:

"Well, Oscar, after Megory turned our offer down, I knew there were just two things to do, and that was, to either make good or leave the country. Megory is full of a lot of fellows that have never known anything but Keya Paha county, and when the road missed Calias, and struck Megory, they took the credit for displaying a superior knowledge. I knew we were going to be the big laughing stock of the reservation, and since I did not intend to leave the country, I got to thinking. The more I pondered the matter, the more determined I became that something had to be done, and I finally made up my mind to do it." Ernest Nicholson was not the kind of a man to make idle declarations. "I went down to Omaha and saw some business friends of mine and suggested to them just what I intended to do, thence to Des Moines and got father, and again we went into Chicago and secured an appointment with Hewitt, who listened attentively to all that we had to say, and the import of this was that Megory, being over five miles east of the Tipp County line, it was difficult to drive range cattle that distance through a settled country. They are so unused to anything that resembles civilization, that ranchers hate to drive even five miles through a settled country, besides the annoyance it would habitually cause contrary farmers, when it comes to accommodating the ranchers. But that is not all. With sixty-six feet open between the wire fences, the range cattle at any time are liable to start a stampede, go right through, and a lot of damage follows. I showed him that most of the cattle men were still driving their stock north and shipping over the C. P. & St. L. Now knowing that the directors had ordered the extension of the line to get the cattle business, Hewitt looked serious, finally arose from his chair, and went over to a map that entirely covered the side of the wall and showed all the lines of the C. & R. W. He meditated a few minutes and then turned around and said: "Go back and buy the land that has been described." It all seemed simple enough when it was done.

By the time that the extension had been completed to Megory, the building that had been moved west of town had company in the way of many new ones, and by this time comprised quite a burg, and claimed the name of New Calias. The new was to distinguish between its old site and its present one. After Megory turned them down, Ernest had made a declaration or defiance that he would build a town on the Little Crow and its name would be Calias.

CHAPTER XVIII

COMES STANLEY, THE CHIEF ENGINEER

MEGORY was still on the boom, not quite as much as the summer before, but more than it was some time later, for as yet New Calias was still regarded as a joke, until one day Stanley, the same wiry-looking individual with the black mustache and the piercing eyes, got off the stage at Megory and began to do the same work he had started west of Oristown the year before.

Oh, it was a shame to thus wreck the selfish dreams of these Megoryites upon the rocks of their own shortsightedness. Stanley was followed a few days later by a grade contractor, who had been to Megory the summer before and who had became popular around town, and was known to be a good spender. They had bidden him good-bye along in December, and although nothing was said about it, the truth was, Megory did not wish to see any more railroad contractors, for a while, not for five or ten years anyway.

It is a peculiar thing that when a railroad stops at some little western burg, that it is always going to stay ten or twenty years. This has always been the case before, according to the towns at the end of the line, and at this time Megory was of the same opinion as regarded the extension to New Calias. So

Oristown had been in regard to the extension to Megory. But Trelway built the road to New Calias, and built it the quickest I ever saw a road built. The first train came to Megory on a Sunday in June—(Schedules always commence on Sunday) and September found the same train in Calias, the "New" having been dropped.

Megoryites admitted very grudgingly, a short time before, that the train would go on to Calias but would return to Megory to stay over night, where it left at six o'clock the following morning. Now at Megory the road had a "Y" that ran onto a pasture on a two years lease, while at Calias coal chutes, a "Y," a turning table, a round house, and a large freight depot were erected.

And then began one of the most bitter fights between towns that I ever saw or even read about.

Five miles apart, with Calias perched on another hill, and like the old site, could be seen from miles around. Now the terminus, it loomed conspicuously. It was a foregone conclusion that when the reservation to the west opened, Calias was in the right position to handle the crowds that came to the territory to the west, instead of Megory. Megory contended, however, that Calias, located on such a hill, could never hope for an abundance of good water and therefore could not compete with Megory, with her natural advantages, such as an abundance of good soft water, which was obtainable anywhere in town.

There are certain things concrete in the future growth of a prairie town; the first is, has it a railroad; the next is, is the agricultural territory sufficient to support a good live town (a fair sized town in either one of the Dakotas has from one thousand to three thousand inhabitants); and last, are the business men of the town modern, progressive, and up to date. In this respect Calias had the advantage over Megory, as will be seen later.

Megory became my post office address after Calias had moved to its new location, and about that time the first rural mail route was established on the reservation. Megory boasted of this. The other things it boasted of, was its great farming territory. For miles in every direction tributary to the town, the land was ideal for farming purposes, and at the beginning of the bitter rivalry between the two towns, Megory had the big end of the farm trade. They could see nothing else but Megory, which helped the town's business considerably.

CHAPTER XIX

IN THE VALLEY OF THE KEYA PAHA. THE RIVALS. THE VIGILANTS

NOTHING is more essential to the up-building of the small western town, than a good agricultural territory, and this was where Calias found its first handicap. When it had moved to its new location, scores of investors had flocked to the town, paying the highest prices that had ever been paid for lots in a new country town, of its kind, in the central west.

Twenty-five miles south of the two towns, where a sand stream known as the Keya Paha wends its way, is a fertile valley. It had been settled thirty years before by eastern people, who hauled their hogs and drove their cattle and sheep fifty miles in a southerly direction, to a railroad. Although the valley could not be surpassed in the production of corn, wheat, oats, and alfalfa, the highlands on either side are great mountains of sand, which produce nothing but a long reddish grass, that stock will not eat after it reaches maturity, and which stands in bunches, with the sand blown from around its roots, to such an extent that riding or driving over it is very difficult.

These hills rise to heights until they resemble the Sierras, and near the top, on the northwest slope of each, are cave-like holes where the strong winds have blown a squeegee.

The wagon road to the railway on the south was sandy and made traveling over it slow and hazardous by the many pits and dunes. Therefore, it is to be seen, when the C. & R. W. pushed its line through Megory County, everything that had been going to the road on the south began immediately to come to the road on the north—where good hard roads made the traveling much easier, and furthermore, it was only half the distance.

Keya Paha County was about as lonely a place as I had ever seen. After the sun went down, the coyotes from the adjacent sand hills, in a series of mournful howls, filled the air with a noise which echoed and re-echoed throughout the valley, like the music of so many far-away steam calliopes and filled me with a cold, creepy feeling. For thirty years these people had heard no other sound save the same monotonous howls and saw only each other. The men went to Omaha occasionally with cattle, but the women and children knew little else but Keya Paha County.

During a trip into this valley the first winter I spent on the homestead, in quest of seed wheat, I met and talked with families who had children, in some instances twenty years of age, who had never seen a colored man. Sometimes the little tads would run from me, screaming as though they had met a lion or some other wild beast of the forest. At one place where I stopped over night, a little girl about nine years of age, looked at me with so much curiosity that I became amused, finally coaxing her onto my knee. She continued to look hard at me, then meekly reached up and touched my chin, looked into my eyes, and said: "Why don't you wash your face?" When supper was ready went to the sink and washed my face and hands; she watched me closely in the meanwhile, and when I was through, appeared to be vexed and with an expression as if to say: "He has cleaned it thoroughly, but it is dirty still."

About twenty years previous to this time, or about ten years after settlement in this valley, the pioneers were continually robbed of much of their young stock. Thieving outlaws kept up a continuous raid on the young cattle and colts, driving them onto the reservation, where they disappeared. This continued for years, and it was said many of the county officials encouraged it, in a way, by delaying a trial, and inasmuch as the law and its procedure was very inadequate, on account of the county's remote location, the criminals were rarely punished.

After submitting to such until all reasonable patience had been exhausted, the settlers formed "a vigilant committee," and meted out punishment to the evil doers, who had become over-bold and were well known. After hanging a few, as well as whipping many, the vigilantes ridded the county of rustlers, and lived in peace thereafter.

At the time the railroad was built to Megory there was little activity other than the common routine attending their existence. But with Megory twenty-five miles to the north, and many of her former active and prosperous citizens living there; and while board walks and "shack" buildings still represented the Main Street, Megory was considered by the people of the valley very much of a city, and a great place to pay a visit. Many had never seen or ridden on a railroad train, so Megory sounded in Keya Paha County as Chicago does to the down state people of Illionis.

The people of Keya Paha County had grown prosperous, however, and the stock shipments comprised many train loads, during an active market. Practically all this was coming to Megory when Calias began to loom prominent as a model little city.

I could see two distinct classes, or personages, in the leaders of the two towns. Beginning with Ernest Nicholson, the head of the firm of Nicholson Brothers and called by Megoryites "chief" "high mogul," the "big it" and "I am," in absolute control of Calias affairs; and the former Keya Paha County sand rats—as they are sometimes called—running Megory. The two contesting parties presented a contrast which interested me.

The Nicholson Brothers were all college-bred boys, with a higher conception of things in general; were modern, free and up-to-date. While Megory's leaders were as modern as could be expected, but were simply outclassed in the style and perfection that the Calias bunch presented. Besides, the merchants and business men—in the "stock yards west of Megory," as Calias was cartooned by a Megory editor, were much of the same ilk. And referring to the cartoon, it pictured the editor of the Calias News as a braying jackass in a stock pen, which brought a great laugh from Megoryites, but who got it back, however, the next week by being pictured as a stagnant pond, with two Megory editors as a couple of big bull-frogs. This had the effect of causing the town to begin grading the streets, putting in cement walks and gutters, for Megory had located in the beginning in an extremely bad place. The town was located in a low place, full of alkali spots, buffalo wallows underlaid with hardpan, which caused the surface to hold water to such an extent, that, when rain continued to fall any length of time, the cellars and streets stood in water.

But Megory had the start, with the largest and best territory, which had by this time been developed into improved farms; the real farmer was fast replacing the homesteader. It had the biggest and best banks. Regardless of all the efficiency of Calias, it appeared weak in its banking. Now a farmer could go to Nicholson Brothers, and get the largest farm loan because the boys' father was president of an insurance company that made the loan, but the banks there were short in the supply of time loans on stock security, but Calias' greatest disadvantage was, that directly west in Tipp County the Indians had taken their allotments within seven or eight miles of the town, and there was hardly a quarter section to be homesteaded.

Now there was no doubt but that in the course of time the Indian allotments would be bought, whenever the government felt disposed to grant the Indian a patent; which under the laws is not supposed to be issued until the expiration of twenty-five years. People, however, would probably lease the land, break it up and farm it; but that would not occur until some future date, and Calias needed it at the present time.

A western town, in most instances, gets its boom in the beginning, for later a dry rot seems an inevitable condition, and is likely to overtake it after the first excitement wears away. Resurrection is rare. These were the conditions that faced the town on the Little Crow, at the beginning of the third year of settlement.

CHAPTER XX

THE OUTLAW'S LAST STAND

A FTER the vigilantes had frightened the outlaws into abandoning their operations in the valley, the thieves skulked across the reservation to a strip of country some twenty-five miles northeast of where Megory now stands. Here, on the east, the murky waters of the Missouri seek their level; to the north the White River runs like a cow-path through the foot hills—twisting and turning into innumerable bends, with its lime-like waters lapping the sides, bringing tons of shale from the gorgeous, dark banks, into its current; while on the south runs the Whetstone, inclosed by many rough, ragged brown hills, and to the west are the breaks of Landing Creek. In an angle between these creeks and rivers, lies a perfect table land known as Yully Flats, which is the most perfectly laying land and has the richest soil of any spot on the Little Crow. It took its name from a famous outlaw and squaw-man, by the name of Jack Yully. With him the thieves from the Keya Paha Valley found co-operation, and together had, a few years previously operated as the most notorious band of cattle rustlers the state had known. For a hundred miles in every direction this band plundered, stole, and ran the cattle and horses onto the flats, where they were protected by the breaks of the creeks and rivers, referred to. Mixed with half, quarter, eighth and six-teenth breeds, they knew every nook and crook of the country. These operations had lasted until the year of the Little Crow opening, and it was there that Jack Yully made his last stand.

He had for many years defied the laws of the county and state, and had built a magnificent residence near a spring that pours its sparkling waters into a small lake, where now stands a sanitarium. Yully had been chief overseer, dictator, and arbitrator of the combined forces of Little Crow and Keya Paha County outlaws and mixed bloods. The end came when, on a bright day in June, a posse led by the United States Marshal sneaked across the Whetstone and secreted themselves in a cache between Yully's corral and the house. Yully was seen to enter the corral and having laid a trap, a part of the men, came in from another direction and made as if to advance when Yully made a run for his house, which took him alongside the men hidden. Before he could change his course he was halted and asked to surrender. He answered by dropping to the opposite side of the horse and began firing. In the skirmish that followed the horse was shot and fell on Yully, but in the shot's exchange two of the posse and Yully were killed.

CHAPTER XXI

THE BOOM

THIS valuable tract of land comprising about fifty thousand acres had been entered after the opening, by settlers, and lay about as near to Kirk as it did to Megory, hence its trade was sought by both towns, but with Kirk getting the larger part until Megory established a mill, which paid two cents more for wheat, and the farmers took advantage by hauling most of their produce to the former town. This included another strip of rich territory to the north of Megory and west of Landing Creek, where the soil is a rich gumbo, and the township thickly settled so it is readily seen that Megory was advantageously situated to draw from all directions. This soon brought such a volume of business into the town as to make the most fastidious envy it, and the Megoryites were well aware of their enviable position. The town continued to grow in a sound, substantial way.

Nicholson Brothers began leading booster trade excursions to the north, south, and east, with Ernest at the head in a big "Packard" making clever speeches and inviting all the farmers to come to Calias, where a meal at the best hotel was given free. A good, live, and effective commercial club was organized, which guaranteed to pay all a hog, cow, or calf would bring on the Omaha market, minus the freight and expenses.

Ernest would explain with deep which sincerity which impressed the farmers of the valley, as well as the settlers on the Little Crow, that Calias wanted a share of their business, and was willing to sacrifice profit for two years in order to have the farmers come to the town and get acquainted, to see what the merchants, bankers and real estate dealers had to offer. In making this offer the people of Calias had the advantage over Megory, in that it derived profits from other sources, chiefly from great numbers of transients who were beginning to fill the hotels, restaurants, saloons, and boarding houses of the town. Being the end of the road and the place where practically every settler coming to Tipp County must stay at least one night, it stood to reason they could make such an inducement and stick to it.

However, this was countered immediately by Megoryites who promptly organized a commercial club and began the same kind of bid for trade. Thus the small ranchmen of the valley found themselves an object of much importance and began to awaken a little.

Now the land of the reservation had taken on a boom such as had never been realized, or dreamed of. Land in the states of Iowa, Minnesota, Illinois, and Nebraska had doubled in valuation in the previous ten years, and was still on the increase in value. Crops had been good and money was plentiful; with a number of years of unbroken prosperity, the farmers had paid off mortgages and had a good surplus in the bank. Their sons and daughters were looking for newer fields. Retired farmers with their land to rent now, instead of the customary one-third delivered, demanded and received from two-fifths to one-half, or cash, from three to five and six dollars per acre. And with the prices in these states ranging from ninety to one hundred and fifty dollars per acre, which meant from fifteen to twenty-five thousand dollars to buy a quarter section, which the renters felt was too high to ever be paid for by farming it. Therefore, western lands held an attraction, where with a few thousand dollars, some stock, and machinery a man could establish a good home. As this land in southern South Dakota is in the Corn Belt, the erstwhile investor and home-seeker found a haven.

There is always more or less gossip as regards insufficient moisture in a new country. The only thing to kill this bogy is to have plenty of rain, and plenty of rain had fallen on the Little Crow, too much at times. Large crops of everything had been harvested, but if the first three years had been wet, this fourth was one of almost continual rainfall.

In the eastern states the corn crop had been badly drowned out on the low lands, and rust had cut the yield of small grain considerably, while on the rolling land of the Little Crow the season was just right and everything grew so rank, thick and green that it gave the country, a raw prairie until less than four years before, the appearance of an old settled country. It looked good to the buyers and they bought. Farms were sold as soon as they were listed. The price at the beginning of the year had been from twenty-five to forty dollars per acre, some places more, but after the first six months of the year it began to climb to forty-five and then to fifty dollars per acre. Those who owned Little Crow farms became objects of much importance. If they desired to sell they had only to let it be known, and a buyer was soon on hand.

The atmosphere seemed charged with drunken enthusiasm. Everybody had it. There was nothing to fear. Little Crow land was the best property to be had, better, they would declare, than government bonds, for its value was increasing in leaps and bounds. Choice farms close to town, if bought at fifty dollars per acre, could be sold at a good profit in a short time.

This was done, and good old eastern capital continued to be paid for the land.

The spirit of unrest that seem to pervade the atmosphere of the community was not altogether the desire to have and to hold, but more, to buy and to sell. Homesteads were sold in Megory county and the proceeds were immediately reinvested in Tipp, where considerable dead Indian land could be purchased at half the price.

At about that time the auto fever began to infect the restless and over-prosperous settlers, and business men alike. That was the day of the many two-cylinder cars. They made a dreadful noise but they moved and moved faster than horses. They sailed over the country, the exhaust of the engine making a cracking noise. The motion, added to the speed, seemed to thrill and enthuse the investor until he bought whether he cared to or not.

In previous years, when capital was not so plentiful, and when land was much cheaper and slower to sell, the agent drove the buyer over the land from corner to corner, cross-wise and angling, and the buyer would get out here and there and with a spade dig into the ground, and be convinced as to the quality of the soil. He then pondered the matter over for days, weeks, and sometimes months. Then maybe he would go back and bring "the woman." The land dealers seriously object to buyers bringing "the woman" along, especially if the farm he has to sell has any serious drawbacks, such, for instance, as a lack of water. There were numerous farms on the high lands of the Little Crow where water could not be found, but they were invariably perfect in every other respect. The perfection in the laying of the land and quality of the soil was severely offset by the inability to get water. While on the rougher and less desirable farms water can be easily obtained in the draws and the hills. But the high lands were the more attractive and were sold at higher prices and much quicker, regardless of the obvious defects.

Now if "the woman" was brought to look it over one of the first inquires she made would be, "Now is there plenty of water?" Furthermore she was liable to steal a march on the dealer by having her husband hire a livery team, and with the eastern farmer and his wife drive out to the place and look the farm over without the agent to steer them clear of the bad places. They not only looked it over, but made inquiries of the neighbors as to its merits. Now country people have the unpardonable habit of gossip, and have complicated many deals of the real-estate men by this weakness, even caused many to fall through, until, the land sharks are usually careful to prevent a buyer from having a conversation with "Si."

In my case, however, this was quite different. I was known as "a booster", and since my land was located between the Monca and Megory—this was considered the cream of the county as to location soil, and other advantages—instead of being nervous over meeting me, the dealers would drive into the yard or into the fields, and as I liked to talk, introduce the prospective buyers to me and we would engage in a long conversation at times. I might add that exaggerated tales were current, which related how I had run as P————n porter, saved my money, come to the Little Crow, bought a half section, and was getting rich. The most of the buyers from Illinois, Iowa, Minnesota and Nebraska were unused to seeing colored farmers, and my presence all alone on the former reserve added to their interest. In my favor was the fact that my service in the employ of the P————n Company had taken me through nearly every county in the central states and therefore, always given to observation, I could talk with them concerning the counties they had come from.

Land prices continued to soar. Higher and higher they went

and to boost them still higher, as well as to substantiate the values, the bogy concerning insufficient moisture was drowned in the excessive rainfall. From April until August it poured, and the effect on the growing crops in the east became greater still in the way of drowned out corn-fields and over-rank stems of small grain that grew to abnormal heights and with the least winds lodged and then fell to the ground. The crops on the reservation could not have been better and prices were high.

CHAPTER XXII

THE PRESIDENT'S PROCLAMATION

COINCIDENT with the expectation came the president's proclamation throwing four thousand claims in Tipp county open to settlement under the lottery system at six dollars per acre. Among the towns designated in the proclamation where the people could make application for a claim, Megory and Calias were nearest to the land. These were the places where the largest crowds were expected. Therefore, the citizens of these two vigorous municipalities began extensive preparations to "entertain the crowds." Megory, being more on the country order, made more homelike preparations. Among the many "conveniences" prepared were a ladies' rest room and information bureau, which were located in a large barn previously used for storing hay.

Calias, under the criticism that as soon as the road extended farther west it would be as dead as Oristown—now all but forgotten—prepared to "get theirs" while the crowds were in town. And they did, but that is ahead of the story.

The time for the opening approached. People seemingly from every part of the universe, and from every vocation in life, drifted into the towns. Among these were included the investors, who stated that in the event of a failure to draw they

127

would buy deeded land. Next in order were the gamblers, from the "tin horn" and "piker" class to the "fat" professionals. Although every precaution was taken to keep out the characters of the city's underworld, who had characterized former openings, both towns were fully represented with a large share of pick-pockets, con-men, lewd women and their consorts.

The many vacant lots on Main street of both the towns were decorated with the typical scene at land openings. There were little tents with notaries assisted by many beautiful girls to "prepare your application." There were many hotels with three and four beds to a room, as well as "rooms to let" over all the places of business containing two stories or more. There were tents with five hundred cots, and "lest we forget," there were the numerous "drinking fountains," with bars the length of the building, behind which were scores of bartenders to serve the "how dry I am," on one side. On the other, in tents, back rooms and overhead could be heard the b-r-r-r of the little ivory marble as it spun a circuit over the roulette wheel, and the luck cages, where the idle sports turned them over for their own amusement, to pass away the time. The faro-bank and numerous wheels of fortune also had a place. From the rear came the strains of ragtime music. These were some of the many attractions that met the trains carrying the first arrivals on the night of October fifth.

CHAPTER XXIII

WHERE THE NEGRO FAILS

ONG before I came west and during the years I had spent on the homestead, my closest companion was the magazines. From the time Thomas W. Lawson's "Frenzied Finance" had run as a serial article in a leading periodical, to Ida M. Tarbell's "The History of the Standard Oil Company," I fairly devoured special articles on subjects of timely interest. I enjoyed reading anything that would give me a more complete knowledge of what made up this great country in which we live and which all Americans are given to boasting of as the "greatest country in the world."

And this brings to my mind certain conditions which exist concerning the ten odd millions of the black race in America; and more, this, in itself had a tendency to open wider the gap between a certain class of the race and myself.

There are two very distinct types or classes, among the American negroes. I am inclined to feel that this is more prominent than most people are aware. I have met and known those who are quick to think, practical, conservative as well as progressive, while there are those who are narrow in their sympathies and short-sighted in their views. Now as a matter of argument, my experience has taught me there are more of this class than most colored people have any idea.

The worst feature of this situation, however, is that a large number of the latter class have commingled with the former in such a way as to easily assume all the worthy proportions. They are a sort of dog in the manger, and are not in accord with any principle that is practical and essential to the elimination of friction and strife between the races.

Among the many faults of this class is, that they do not realize what it takes to succeed, nor do they care, but spend their efforts loudly claiming credit for the success of those who are honest in their convictions and try to prove themselves indispensable citizens. Nothing is more obvious and proves this more conclusively than to take notice, as I have, of their own selection of reading matter.

Now, for instance, a few years ago a series of articles under the title of "Following the Color Line" appeared in a certain periodical, the work of a very well known writer whose specialty is writing on social conditions, strikes, etc.

In justice to all concerned, the writer described the conditions which his articles covered, just as he found them and in this, in my opinion, he differed largely from many of the southern authors whose articles are still inclined to treat the Ethiopians as a whole, as the old "time worn" aunt and uncle. Not intending to digress, I want to put down here, that negroes as a whole are changing to some extent, the same as the whites and no liberty-loving colored man appreciates being regarded as "aunt" or "uncle" even though some of these people were as honorable as could be. This is a modern age.

Now getting back to the discussion that I seem to have for the moment forgotten and as regards the article, while worthy in every respect, it was no different in its way from any number of other articles published at that time, as well as now, that deal on great and complex questions of the day. Yet, this article caused thousands of colored people, who never before bought a magazine or book, to subscribe for that magazine. It was later published in book form and is conspicuous in the libraries of many thousands of colored families.

What I have intended to put down in this lengthy discourse regarding my race is, if they see or hear of an article concerning the race, they will buy that magazine, to read the article spoken of and nothing more.

Since living in the state, as a recreation I was in the habit of taking trips to Chicago once or twice a year, and as might be expected I would talk of South Dakota. In the course of a conversation I have related a story of someone's success there and would be listened to with unusual attention. As I had found in them many who were poor listeners, at these times when I found myself the object of so much undivided attention I would warm up to the subject until it had evolved into a sort of lecture, and remarks of, "my," "you don't say so," and "just think of it" would interrupt me—"and a colored man." No, I would correct, the least bit hesitant, a white man. Then, just like the sun disappearing behind a cloud, all interest would vanish; furthermore, I have on occasions of this kind had attention of a few minutes before turned to remarks of criticism for taking up the time relating the success of a white man. The idea is prevalent among this class that all white people should be rich, and regardless of how ideal the success has been, I learned that no white person could be accepted as an example for this class to follow.

By reading nothing but discussions concerning the race, by all but refusing to accept the success of the white race as an example and by welcoming any racial disturbance as a conclusion that the entire white race is bent in one great effort to hold him—the negro, down, he can not very well feel the thrill of modern progress and is ignorant as to public opinion. Therefore he is unable to cope with the trend of conditions and has become so condensed in the idea that he has no opportunity, that he is disinteresting to the public. One of the greatest tasks of my life has been to convince a certain class of my racial acquaintances that a colored man can be anything.

Now on the entire Little Crow reservation, less than eight hundred miles from Chicago, I was the only colored man engaged in agriculture, and moreover, from Megory to Omaha, a distance of three hundred miles. There was only one other negro family engaged in the same industry.

Having lived in the cities, I therefore, was not a greenhorn, as some of them would try to have me feel, when they referred to their clubs and social affairs.

Among the many facts that confronted me as I meditated the situation, one dated back to the time I had run on the road. The trains I ran on carried thousands monthly into the interior of the northwest. Among these were a great number of emigrants fresh from the old countries, but there was seldom a colored person among them, and those few that I had seen, with few exceptions, went on through to the Pacific coast cities and engaged in the same occupation they had followed in the east.

During these trips I learned the greatest of all the failings were not only among the ignorant class, but among the educated as well. Although more agreeable to talk to, they lacked that great and mighty principle which characterizes Americans, called "the initiative." Colored people are possible in every way that is akin to becoming good citizens, which has been thoroughly proven and is an existing fact. Yet they seem to lack the "guts" to get into the northwest and "do things." In seven or eight of the great agricultural states there were not enough colored farmers to fill a township of thirty-six sections.

Another predominating inconsistency is that there is that "love of luxury." They want street cars, cement walks, and electric lights to greet them when they arrive. I well remember it was something near two years before I saw a colored man on the reservation, until the road had been extended. They had never come west of Oristown, but as the time for the opening arrived, the kitchens and hotel dining-rooms of Megory and Calias were filled with waiters and cooks.

During the preparation for the opening the commercial club of Megory had lengthy circulars printed, with photographs of the surrounding country, farms, homes, and the like, to accompany. These circulars described briefly the progress the country had made in the four years it had been opened to settlement, and the opportunities waiting. By giving the name and address the club would send these to any address or person, with the statement, "by the request" of whoever gave the name.

I gave the name of not less than one hundred persons, and sent them personally to many as well. I wrote articles and sent them to different newspapers edited by colored people, in the east and other places. I was successful in getting one colored person to come and register—my oldest brother.

CHAPTER XXIV

"AND THE CROWDS DID COME."
THE PRAIRIE FIRE

THE registration opened at twelve o'clock Monday morning. Seven trains during the night before had brought something like seven thousand people. Of this number about two thousand got off at Megory, and the remainder went on through to Calias. The big opening was on, and the bid for patronage made the relations between the towns more bitter than ever.

After the first few days, however, the crowds, with the exception of a few hundred, daily went on through to Calias and did not heed the cat calls and uncomplimentary remarks from the railway platform at Megory. Among these remarks flung at the crowded trains were: "Go on to Calias and buy a drink of water," "Go on to Calias and pay a dime for the water to wash your face"—water was one of Calias's scarcities, as will be seen later. However, this failed to detract the crowd.

The C. & R. W. put on fifteen regular trains daily, and the little single track, unballasted and squirmy, was very unsafe to ride over and the crowded trains had to run very slowly on this account. Because of the fact that it was difficult to find adequate side tracking, it took two full days to make the trip from Omaha to Calias and return.

All the day and night the "toot, toot" of the locomotives could be heard and the sound seemed to make the country seem very old indeed. Megory's brass band—organized for the purpose—undaunted, continued to play frantically at the depot to try to induce the crowded trains to unload a greater share, but to no avail, although the cars were stuffed like sandwiches.

Those times in Calias were long to be remembered. As the trains disgorged the thousands daily it seemed impossible that the little city could care for such crowds. The sidewalks were crowded from morn till night. The registration booths and the saloons never closed and more automobiles than I had ever seen in a country town up to that time, roared, and with their clattering noise, took the people hurriedly across the reservation to the west.

Along toward the close of the opening a prairie fire driven by a strong west wind raced across Tipp county in a straight line for Calias. Although fire guards sixty feet wide had been burned along the west side of the town, it soon became apparent that the fire would leap them and enter the town, unless some unusual effort on the part of the citizens was made to stop it.

It was late in the afternoon and as seems always the case, a fire will cause the wind to rise, and it rose until the blaze shut out the western horizon. It seemed the entire world to the west was afire.

Ten thousand people, lost in sight-seeing, gambling and revelry, all of a sudden became aware of the approaching danger, and began a rush for safety. To the north, south, and east of the town the lands were under cultivation, therefore, a safe place from the fire that now threatened the town. All business was suspended, registration ceased, and the huge cans containing more than one hundred thousand applications for lands, were loaded on drays and taken into the country and deposited in the center of a large plowed field, for safety. The gamblers put their gains into sacks and joined the surging masses, and with grips got from the numerous check rooms, all the people fled like stampeding cattle to a position to the north of town which was protected by a corn field on the west.

Ernest Nicholson, leading the business men and property owners, bravely fought the oncoming disaster. The chemical engine and water hose were rushed forward but were as pins under the drivers of a locomotive. The water from the hose ran weakly for a few minutes and then with a blowing as of an empty faucet, petered out from lack of water. The strong wind blew the chemical into the air and it proved as useless. The fire entered the city. One house, a magnificent residence, was soon enveloped in flames, which spread to another, and still to another.

The thousands of people huddled on a bare spot, but safe, watched the minature city of one year and the gate-way to the homesteads of the next county, disappear in flames.

Megoryites, seeing the danger threatening her hated rival five miles away, called for volunteers who readily responded and formed bucket brigades, loaded barrels into wagons, filled them with water and burned the roads in the hurry-up call to the apparently doomed city.

I could see the fire from where I was harvesting flax ten miles away, and the cloud of smoke, with the little city lying silent before, it reminded me of a picture of Pompeii before Vesuvius. It looked as if Calias were lost. Then, like a miracle, the wind quieted down, changed, and in less than twenty minutes was blowing a gale from the east, starting the fire back over the ground over which it had burned. There it sputtered, flickered, and with a few sparks went out, just as L. A. Bell pulled onto the scene with lathered and bloody eyed mules drawing a tank of Megory's water, and was told by the Nicholson

Brothers—who were said to resemble Mississippi steamboat roustabouts on a hot day—that Calias didn't need their water.

Following the day of the high wind which brought the prairie fire that so badly frightened the people of the town, the change of the wind to the east brought rain, and about two hundred automobiles that had been carrying people over Tipp county into the town. I remember the crowds but have no idea now many people there were, but that it looked more like the crowds on Broadway or State street on a busy day than Main Street in a burg of the prairie. This was the afternoon of the drawing and a woman drew number one, while here and there in the crowd that filled the street before the registration, exclamations of surprise and delight went up from different fortunates hearing their names called, drawing a lucky number. I felt rather bewildered by so much excitement and metropolitanism where hardly two years before I had hauled one of the first loads of lumber on the ground to start the town. I could not help but feel that the world moved swiftly, and that I was living, not in a wilderness—as stated in some of the letters I had received from colored friends in reply to my letter that informed them of the opening—but in the midst of advancement and action.

When the drawing was over and the crowds had gone, it was found that the greatest crowds had registered not at Calias—but at a town just south, in Nebraska, which received forty-five thousand while Calias came second with forty-three thousand and Megory only received seven thousand, something like one hundred fifteen thousand in all having applied.

The hotels in Calias had charged one dollar the person and some of the large ones had made small fortunes, while the saloons were said to have averaged over one thousand dollars a day.

After the opening, land sold like hot hamburger sandwiches had a few weeks before.

CHAPTER XXV

THE SCOTCH GIRL

IT HAD been just four years since I bought the relinquishment and seven since leaving southern Illinois. I had been very successful in farming although I had made some very poor deals in the beginning, and when my crops were sold that season I found I had made three thousand, five hundred dollars. Furthermore, I had in the beginning sought to secure the best land in the best location and had succeeded. I had put two hundred eighty acres under cultivation, with eight head of horses—I had done a little better in my later horse deals—and had machinery, seed and feed sufficient to farm it. My efforts in the seven years had resulted in the ownership of land and stock to the value of twenty thousand dollars and was only two thousand dollars in debt and still under twenty-five years of age.

During the years I had spent on the Little Crow I had "kept batch" all the while until that summer. A Scotch family had moved from Indiana that spring consisting of the father, a widower, two sons and two daughters. One of the boys worked for me and as it was much handier, I boarded with them.

The older of the two girls was a beautiful blonde maiden of twenty summers, who attended to the household duties, and considering the small opportunities she had to secure an education, was an unusually intelligent girl. She had composed some verses and songs but not knowing where to send them, had never submitted them to a publisher. I secured the name of a company that accepted some of her writings and paid her fifty dollars for them. She was so anxious to improve her mind that I took an interest in her and as I received much literature in the way of newspapers and magazines and read lots of copy-right books, I gave them to her. She seemed delighted and appreciated the gifts.

Before long, however, and without any intention of being other than kind, I found myself being drawn to her in a way that threatened to become serious. While custom frowns on even the discussion of the amalgamation of races, it is only human to be kind, and it was only my intention to encourage the desire to improve, which I could see in her, but I found myself on the verge of falling in love with her. To make matters more awkward, that love was being returned by the object of my kindness. She, however, like myself, had no thought of being other than kind and grateful. It placed me as well as her in an awkward position—for before we realized it, we had learned to understand each other to such an extent, that it became visible in every look and action.

It reached a stage of embarrassment one day when we were reading a volume of Shakespeare. She was sitting at the table and I was standing over her. The volume was "Othello" and when we came to the climax where Othello has murdered his wife, driven to it by the evil machinations of Iago, as if by instinct she looked up and caught my eyes and when I came to myself I had kissed her twice on the lips she held up.

After that, being near her caused me to feel awkwardly uncomfortable. We could not even look into each other's eyes, without showing the feeling that existed in the heart.

Now during the time I had lived among the white people, I

had kept my place as regards custom, and had been treated with every courtesy and respect; had been referred to in the local papers in the most complimentary terms, and was regarded as one of the Little Crow's best citizens.

But when the reality of the situation dawned upon me, I became in a way frightened, for I did not by any means want to fall in love with a white girl. I had always disapproved of inter-marriage, considering it as being above all things, the very thing that a colored man could not even think of. That we would become desperately in love, however, seemed inevitable.

Lived a man—the history of the American Negro shows—who had been the foremost member of his race. He had acquitted himself of many honorable deeds for more than a score of years, in the interest of his race. He had filled a federal office but at the zenith of his career had brought disappointment to his race and criticism from the white people who had honored him, by marrying a white woman, a stenographer in his office.

They were no doubt in love with each other, which in all likelihood overcame the fear of social ostracism, they must have known would follow the marriage. I speak of love and presume that she loved him for in my opinion a white woman, intelligent and respectable and knowing what it means, who would marry a colored man, must love him and love him dearly. To make that love stronger is the feeling that haunts the mind; the knowledge that custom, tradition, and the dignity of both races are against it. Like anything forbidden, however, it arouses the spirit of opposition, causing the mind to battle with what is felt to be oppression. The sole claim is the right to love.

These thoughts fell upon me like a clap of thunder and frightened me the more. It was then too, that I realized how pleasant the summer just passed had been, and that I had not been in the least lonesome, but perfectly contented, aye, happy. And that was the reason.

During the summer when I had read a good story or had on mind to discuss my hopes, she had listened attentively and I had found companionship. If I was melancholy, I had been cheered in the same demure manner. Yet, on the whole, I had been unaware of the affection growing silently; drawing two lonesome hearts together. With the reality of it upon us, we were unable to extricate ourselves from our own weak predicament. We tried avoiding each other; tried everything to crush the weakness. God has thus endowed. We found it hard.

I have felt, if a person could only order his mind as he does his limbs and have it respond or submit to the will, how much easier life would be. For it is that relentless thinking all the time until one's mind becomes a slave to its own imaginations, that brings eternal misery, where happiness might be had.

To love is life—love lives to seek reply—but I would contend with myself as to whether or not it was right to fall in love with this poor little white girl. I contended with myself that there were good girls in my race and coincident with this I quit boarding with them and went to batching again, to try to successfully combat my emotions. I continued to send her papers and books to read—I could hardly restrain the inclinations to be kind. Then one day I went to the house to settle with her father for the boy's work and found her alone. I could see she had been crying, and her very expression was one of unhappiness. Well, what is a fellow going to do. What I did was to take her into my arms and in spite of all the custom, loyalty, or the dignity of either Ethiopian or the Caucasian race, loved her like a lover.

It was during a street carnival at Megory sometime before the Tipp county opening, when one afternoon in company with

three or four white men, I saw a nice looking colored man coming along the street. It was very seldom any colored people
came to those parts and when they did, it was with a show
troupe or a concert of some kind. Whenever any colored people
were in town, I had usually made myself acquainted and welcomed them—if it was acceptable, and it usually was—so when
I saw this young man approaching I called the attention of my
companions, saying, "There is a nice-looking colored man." He
was about five feet, eleven, of a light brown complexion, and
chestnut-like hair, neatly trimmed. He wore glasses and was
dressed in a well-fitting suit that matched his complexion. He
had the appearance of being intelligent and amiable.

I was in the act of starting to speak, when one of the fellows
nudged me and whispered in my ear, that it was one of the
Woodrings from a town a short distance away in Nebraska, who
was known to be of mixed blood but never admitted it.

According to what I had been told, the father of the three
boys was about half negro but had married a white woman, and
this one was the youngest son. Needless to say I did not speak
but kept clear of him.

There is a difference in races that can be distinguished in
the features, in the eyes, and even if carefully noted, in the sound
of the voice.

It seemed the family claimed to be part Mexican, which
would account for the darkness of their complexion. But I had
seen too many different races, however, to mistake a streak of
Ethiopian. Having been in Mexico, I knew them to be almost
entirely straight-haired (being a cross between an Indian and a
Spaniard). When I observed this young man, I readily distinguished the negro features; the brown eyes, the curly hair, and
the set of the nose.

The father had come into the sand hills of Nebraska some

thirty-five years before, taken a homestead, but from where he came from no one seemed to know. It was there he married his white wife, and to the union was born the three sons, Frank, the eldest, Will, and Len, the youngest.

The father sold the homestead some twenty years before and moved to another county, and had run a hotel since in the town of Pencer, where they now live.

Unlike his younger brother, Frank, the eldest son, could easily have passed for a white, that is, so long as no one looked for the streak. But when the fellow whose timely information had kept me from embarrassing myself, and perhaps from insulting the young man, a few minutes later called out, "Hello, Frank!" to a tall man, one look disclosed to my scrutiny the negro in his features. I was not mistaken. It was Frank Woodring.

In view of the fact, that in some chapters of this story I dwell on the negro, and on account of the insistence of many of them who declare they are deprived of opportunities on account of their color, I take the privilege of putting down here a sketch of this Frank Woodring's life. And although these people deny a relation to the negro race, it was well known by the public in that part of the country, that they were mixed, for it had been told to me by every one who knew them, therefore the instance cannot be regarded altogether as an exception.

Shortly after coming to Pencer, he went to work for an Iowa man on a ranch near by, and later a prosperous squaw-man, who owned a bank, took him in, where in time he became book-keeper and all round handy man, later assistant cashier. The ranchman whom Woodring had worked for previous to entering the bank, bought the squaw-man out, made Woodring cashier, and sold to him a block of stock and took his note for the amount. In time Woodring proved a good banker and his efficient management of the institution, which had been a State bank with a capital stock of twenty-five thousand dollars, had been incorporated into a National bank and the capital increased to fifty thousand dollars, and later on to one hundred thousand dollars. He dealt in buying and selling land as well as feeding cattle, on the side, and had prospered until he was soon well-to-do. Coincident with this prosperity he had been made president of not only that bank—whose footing was near a half-million dollars—but of some other three or four local banks in Nebraska, also a Megory county bank at Fairview—which is the county depository—and a large bank and trust company at the town of Megory, with a capital stock of sixty thousand dollars. Today Frank Woodring is one of the wealthiest men in northwest Nebraska.

The local ball team of their town was playing Megory that day, and a few hours later out at the ball park, I was shouting for the home team with all my breath, the batter struck a foul, and when I turned to look where the ball went, there, standing on the bench above me, between two white girls, and looking down at me with a look that betrayed his mind, was Len Woodring. Our eyes met for only the fraction of a minute but I read his thoughts. He looked away quickly, but I shall not soon forget that moment of racial recognition.

And now when I found my affections in jeopardy regarding the love of the Scotch girl, I thought long and seriously over the matter, and pictured myself in the place of the Woodring family, successful, respected, and efficient business men, but still members of the down-trodden race. I pondered as to whether I could make the sacrifice. Maybe they were happy, the boys had never known or associated with the race they denied, and maybe were not so conscientious as myself, although the look of Len's had betrayed what was on his mind.

I had learned that throughout these Dakotas and Nebraska,

that other lone colored men who had drifted from the haunts and homes of the race, as I had—maybe discontented, as I had been—and had with time and natural development, through the increase in the valuation of their homesteads or other lands they had acquired, grown prosperous and had finally, with hardly an exception, married into the white race. Even the daughter of the only colored farmer between the Little Crow and Omaha was only prevented from marrying a white man, at the altar, when it was found the law of the state forbids it.

I could diagnose their condition by my own. Life in a new country is always rough in the beginning. In the past it had taken ten and fifteen years for a newly opened country to develop into a state of cultivation and prosperity, that the Little Crow had in the four years.

At the time it had been opened to settlement, the reaction from the effects of the dry years and hard times of 93–4 and 5 had set in and at that time, with plenty of available capital, the early extension of the railroad, and other advantages too numerous to mention, life had been quite different for the settlers. Such advantages had not been the lot of the homesteader twenty and thirty years before.

These people had no doubt been honorable and had intended to remain loyal to their race, but long, hard years, lean crops, and the long, lonesome days had changed them. It is easier to control the thoughts than the emotions. The craving for love and understanding pervades the very core of a human, and makes the mind reckless to even such a grave matter as race loyalty. In most cases it had been years before these people had the means and time to get away for a visit to their old homes, while around them were the neighbors and friends of pioneer days, and maybe, too, some girl had come into their lives—like this one had into mine—who understood them and was kind and

146

sympathetic. What worried me most, however, even frightened me, was, that after marriage and when their children had grown to manhood and womanhood, they, like the Woodring family, had a terror of their race; disowning and denying the blood that coursed through their veins; claiming to be of some foreign descent; in fact, anything to hide or conceal the mixture of Ethopian. They looked on me with fear, sometimes contempt. Even the mixed-blood Indians and negroes seemed to crave a marriage with the whites.

The question uppermost in my mind became, "'Would not I become like that, would I too, deny my race?" The thought was a desperate one. I did not feel that I could become that way, but what about those to come after me, would they have to submit to the indignities I had seen some of these referred to, do, in order that they may marry whites and try to banish from memory the relation of a race that is hated, in many instances, for no other reason than the coloring matter in their pigment. Would my life, and the thought involved and occupied my mind daily, innocent as my life now appeared, lead into such straits if I married the Scotch girl. It became harder for me, for at that time, I had not even a correspondence with a girl of my race. As I look back upon it the condition was a complicated affair. I confess at the time, however, that I was on the verge of making the sacrifice. This was due to the sights that had met my gaze when I would go on trips to Chicago, and such times I would return home feeling disgusted.

CHAPTER XXVI

THE BATTLE

SOME time after the opening it was announced from Washington that the Land Office, which was located in one of the larger towns of the state, about one hundred and fifty miles from the Little Crow, would be moved to one of the towns in the new territory. The Land Office is something like a County Seat in bringing business to a town, and immediately every town in Megory County began a contest for the office. However, it was soon seen that it was the intention of the Interior Department to locate it in either Megory or Calias. So the two familiar rivals engaged in another battle. But in this Megory held the high card.

That was about the time the insurgents and stalwarts were in a struggle to get control of the State's political machinery. It had waxed bitter in the June primaries of that year and the insurgents had won. Calias had supported the losing candidate, who had been overwhelmingly defeated, and both senator and one representative in Congress from the state were red-hot insurgents. The Nicholson Brothers, bowing to tradition, were stand pats. Their father had been a stalwart before them in Iowa, where Cummins had created so much commotion with his insurgency.

Ernest, with his wife, had left for the Orient to spend the winter. After leaving, the announcement came that the land office would be moved. Even had he been in Calias the result would likely have been the same, but I had a creepy feeling that had he been on the ground Megory would have had to work considerably harder at least.

After sending many men from each town down to the National Capital, the towns fought it out. With, as I have stated, and which was to be expected, with both Senators recommending Megory as having advantages over Calias in the way of an abundant supply of water and a National Bank with a capital stock of fifty thousand dollars, the Interior Department decided in favor of Megory, and Calias lost.

Ernest, on hearing of the fight, hurriedly returned, went in to Washington, secured an appointment with the Secretary and is said to have made a worthy plea for Calias; but to no avail and the Megoryites returned home the heroes of the day.

I was away at the time, but was told a good share of the men of Megory were drunk the greater part of the week.

Some evidence of the rejoicing was visible on my return, in the loss of an eye, by a little gambler who became too enthusiastic and run up against a "snag." What amused me most, however, was an article written especially for one of the Megory papers by a keeper of a racket store and a known shouter for the town. The article represented the contest as being a big prize fight on the Little Crow and read something like this:

BIG PRIZE FIGHT ON THE LITTLE CROW

PRINCIPALS

MEGORY, THE METROPOLIS OF THE

LITTLE CROW

REPUTATION, THE SQUARE DEAL

CALIAS BOASTER

REPUTATION GRAFTING

SCENE.—LITTLE CROW RESERVATION.

TIME.—A.D. 190—REFEREE—WASHINGTON, D.C.

SECONDS FOR MEGORY.—FLACKLER,

OF THE MEGORY NATIONAL.

FRED CROFTON, POSTMASTER.

FOR CALIAS, MAYOR ROSIE AND A HAS-BEEN,

FORMERLY OF WASHINGTON.

Round one. September. Principals enter the ring and refuse to shake hands, referee Washington, D. C. announces fight to be straight Marquis of Queensbury. No hitting in the clinches, and a clean break; a fight to the finish. They are off. Calias leads with a left to the face, Megory countering with a right to the ribs, they clinch. Referee breaks them, then they spar and as the gong sounded appeared evenly matched.

Round two. October. They rush to the center of the ring and clinch, referee tells them to break. Just as this is done Calias lands a terrific left to Megory's jaw following with a right to the body, and Megory goes down for the count of nine, getting up with much confusion, only to be floored again with a right to the temple. Megory rises very groggy, when Calias lands a vicious left to the mouth, a right to the ear just as the gong sounded, saving her from a knock-out. They go to their corners with betting three to one on Calias and no takers. During the one minute's rest the crowd whooped it up for Calias, thousands coming her way. Megory looked serious, sitting in the corner thinking how she had fallen down on some well-laid plans.

Round three. November. They rush to a clinch and spar. Referee cautions Calias for butting. They do some more sparring, and both seem cautious, with honors even at the end of the third round.

Round four. December. They rush to the center of the ring and begin to spar, then like a flash, Megory lands a terrific swing on Calias' jaw, following it up with a right to the heart. Calias cries foul, but referee orders her to proceed, while Megory, with eyes flashing and distended nostrils, feints and then like the kick of a mule, lands a hard left to the mouth, following in quick succession with jolts, swings, jabs and upper cuts. Mayor Rosie wants to throw up the sponge, but the referee says fight. Megory, with a left to the face and right to the stomach, then rushing both hands in a blow to the solar plexus, Calias falls and is counted out with Megory winning the prize—Great Land Office.

CHAPTER XXVII

THE SACRIFICE—RACE LOYALTY

ETTING back to the affair of the Scotch girl, I hated to give up her kindness and friendship. I would have given half my life to have had her possess just a least bit of negro blood in her veins, but since she did not and could not help it any more than I could help being a negro, I tried to forget it, straightened out my business and took a trip east, bent on finding a wife among my own.

As the early morning train carried me down the road from Megory, I hoped with all the hope of early manhood, I would find a sensible girl and not like many I knew in Chicago, who talked nothing but clothes, jewelry, and a good time. I had no doubt there were many good colored girls in the east, who, if they understood my life, ambition and morality, would make a good wife and assist me in building a little empire on the Dakota plains, not only as a profit to ourselves, but a credit to the negro race as well. I wanted to succeed, but hold the respect and good will of the community, and there are few communities that will sanction a marriage with a white girl, hence, the sacrifice.

I spent about six weeks visiting in Chicago and New York, finally returning west to southern Illinois to visit a family in C—dale, near M—boro, who were the most prosperous colored people in the town. They owned a farm near town, nine houses and lots in the city, and were practical people who understood business and what it took to succeed.

They had a daughter whom I had known as a child back in the home town M—plis, where she had cousins that she used to visit. She had by this time grown into a woman of five and twenty. Her name was Daisy Hinshaw. Now Miss Hinshaw was not very good-looking but had spent years in school and in many ways was unlike the average colored girl. She was attentive and did not have her mind full of cheap, showy ideals. I had written to her at times from South Dakota and she had answered with many inviting letters. Therefore, when I wrote her from New York that I intended paying her a visit, she answered in a very inviting letter, but boldly told me not to forget to bring her a nice present, that she would like a large purse. I did not like such boldness. I should have preferred a little more modesty, but I found the purse, however, a large seal one in a Fifth Avenue shop, for six dollars, which Miss Hinshaw displayed with much show when I came to town.

The town had a colored population of about one thousand and the many girls who led in the local society looked enviously upon Miss Hinshaw's catch—and the large seal purse—and I became the "Man of the Hour" in C—dale.

The only marriageable man in the town who did not gamble, get drunk and carouse in a way that made him ineligible to decent society, was the professor of the colored school. He was a college graduate and received sixty dollars a month. He had been spoiled by too much attention, however, and was not an agreeable person.

Miss Hinshaw was dignified and desired to marry, and to marry somebody that amounted to something, but she was so bold and selfish. She took a delight in the reports, that were going the rounds, that we were engaged, and I was going to have her come to South Dakota and file on a Tipp County homestead relinquishment that I would buy, and we would then get married.

The only objector to this plan was myself. I had not fallen in love with Miss Hinshaw and did not feel that I could. Daisy was a nice girl, however, a little odd in appearance, having a light brown complexion, without color or blood visible in the cheeks; was small and bony; padded with so many clothes that no idea of form could be drawn. I guessed her weight at about ninety pounds. She had very good hair but grey eyes, that gave her a cattish appearance.

She had me walking with her alone and permitted no one to interfere. She would not introduce me to other girls while out, keeping me right by her side and taking me home and into her parlor, with her and her alone, as company.

One day I went up town and while there took a notion to go to the little mining town, to see the relatives who had got me the job there seven years before. But it was ten miles, with no train before the following morning. Just then the colored caller called out a train to M—boro and St. Louis, and all of a sudden it occurred to me that I had almost forgotten Miss Rooks. Why not go to M—boro? I had not expected to pay her a visit but suddenly decided that I would just run over quietly and come back on the train to C—dale at five o'clock that afternoon. I jumped aboard and as M—boro was only eight miles, I was soon in the town, and inquiring where she lived.

I found their house presently—they were always moving— and just a trifle nervously rang the bell. The door was opened in a few minutes and before me stood Jessie. She had changed quite a bit in the three years and now with long skirts and the eyes looked so tired and dream-like. She was quite fascinating, this I took in at a glance. She stammered out, "Oh! Oscar Devereaux," extending her hand timidly and looking into my eyes as though afraid. She looked so lonely, and I had thought a great deal of her a few years ago—and perhaps it was not all dead—and the next moment she was in my arms and I was kissing her.

I did not go back to C—dale on the five nor on the eight o'clock—and I did not want to on the last train that night. I was having the most carefree time of my life. They were hours of sweetest bliss. With Jessie snugly held in the angle of my left arm, we poured out the pent-up feelings of the past years. I had a proposition to make, and had reasons to feel it would be accepted.

The family had a hard time making ends meet. Her father had lost the mail carrier's job and had run a restaurant later and then a saloon. Failing in both he had gone to another town, starting another restaurant and had there been assaulted by a former admirer of Jessie's, who had struck him with a heavy stick, fracturing the skull and injuring him so that for weeks he had not been able to remember anything. Although he was then convalescing, he was unable to earn anything. Her mother had always been helpless, and the support fell on her and a younger brother, who acted as special delivery letter carrier and received twenty dollars a month, while Jessie taught a country school a mile from town, receiving twenty-five dollars per month. This she turned over to the support of the household, and made what she earned sewing after school hours, supply her own needs. It was a long and pitiful tale she related as we walked together along a dark street, with her clinging to my arm and speaking at times in a half sob. My heart went out to her, and I wanted to help and said: "Why did you not write to me, didn't you know that I would have done something?"

"Well," she answered slowly, "I started to several times, but was so afraid that you would not understand." She seemed so weak and forlorn in her distress. She had never been that way when I knew her before, and I felt sure she had suffered, and I was a brute, not to have realized it. Twelve o'clock found me as reluctant to go as five o'clock had, but as we kissed lingeringly at the door, I promised when I left C—dale two evenings later I would stop off at M—boro and we would discuss the matter pro and con. This was Saturday night.

The next morning I called to see Daisy. I was unusually cheerful, and taking her face in my hands, blew a kiss. She looked up at me with her grey eyes alert and with an air of suspicion, said: "You've been kissing somebody else since you left here." Then leading me into the parlor in her commanding way, ordered me to sit down and to wait there until she returned. She had just completed cleaning and dusting the parlor and it was in perfect order. She seemed to me to be more forward than ever that morning, and I felt a suspicion that I was going to get a curtain lecture. However, I escaped the lecture but got stunned instead.

Daisy returned in about an hour, dressed in a rustling black silk dress, with powdered face and her hair done up elegantly and without ceremony or hesitation planted herself on the settee and requested, or rather ordered me to take a seat beside her. She opened the conversation by inquiring of South Dakota, and took my hand and pretended to pare my finger nails. I answered in nonchalant tones but after a little she turned her head a little slantingly, looked down, began just the least hesitant, but firmly: "Now what arrangements do you wish me to make in regard to my coming to South Dakota next fall?"

For the love of Jesus, I said to myself, if she hasn't proposed. Now one advantage of a dark skin is that one does not show his inner feeling as noticeably as those of the lighter shade, and I do not know whether Miss Hinshaw noticed the look of embarrassment that overspread my countenance. I finally found words to break the deadly suspense following her bold action.

"Oh!" I stammered more than spoke, "I would really rather not make any arrangements, Daisy."

"Well," she said, not in the least taken back, "a person likes to know just how they stand."

"Yes," of course, I added hastily. "You see," I was just starting in on a lengthy discourse trying to avoid the issue, when the door bell rang and a relative of mine by the name of Menloe Robinson, who had attended the university the same time Miss Hinshaw had, but had been expelled for gambling and other bad habits, came in. He was a bore most of the time with so much of his college talk, but I could have hugged him then, I felt so relieved, but Miss Hinshaw put in before he got started to talking, wickedly, that of course if I did not want her she could not force it.

The next day at noon I left for St. Louis but did not mention that I was scheduled to stop off at M—boro. Miss Hinshaw had grown sad in appearance and looked so lonely I felt sorry for her and kissed her good-bye at the station, which seemed to cheer her a little. She was married to a classmate about a year later and I have not seen her since.

Jessie was glad to see me when I called that evening in M—boro, and we went walking again and had another long talk. When we got back, I sang the old story to which she answered with, "Do you really want me?"

"Sure, Jessie, why not." I looked into her eyes that seemed just about to shed tears but she closed them and snuggled up closely, and whispered, "I just wanted to hear you say you wanted me."

CHAPTER XXVIII

THE BREEDS

ERE the story may have ended, that is, had I taken her to the minister, but as everybody had gone land crazy in Dakota and I had determined to own more land myself, I told her how I could buy a relinquishment and she could file on it and then we would marry at once. Now when a young man and a girl are in love and feel each other to be the world and all that's in it, it is quite easy to plan, and Miss Rooks and I were no exception. Had we been in South Dakota instead of Southern Illinois, and had it been the month of October instead of January, nine months before, we would have carried out our plans, but since it was January we mutually agreed to wait until the nine months had elapsed, but something happened during that time which will be told in due time.

I enjoyed feeling that I was at last engaged. It was positively delightful, and when I left the next morning to visit my parents in Kansas, I was a very happy person. While visiting there, shooting jack-rabbits by day and boosting Dakota to the Jayhawkers half the night, I'd write to Miss Rooks sometime during each twenty-four hours, and for a time received a letter as often. Two sisters were to be graduated from the high school the following June, and wanted to come to Dakota in the fall and take up claims, but had no money to purchase relinquishments. I agreed to mortgage my land and loan the money, but when all was arranged it was found one of them would not be old enough in time, so my grandmother, who had always possessed a roving spirit, wanted to come and so it was settled.

When I got back to Dakota and jumped into my spring work it was with unusual vigor and contemplation, and all went well for a while. Soon, however, I failed to hear from Jessie and began to feel a bit uneasy. When three weeks had passed and still no letter, I wrote again asking why she did not answer my letters. In due time I heard from her stating that she had been afraid I didn't love her and that she had been told I was engaged to Daisy, and as Daisy would be the heir to the money and property of her parents she felt sure my marriage to Miss Hinshaw would be more agreeable to me than would a marriage with her, who had only a kind heart and willing mind to offer, so she had on the first day of April married one whom she felt was better suited to her impoverished condition.

Now, what she had done was, in her effort to break off the prolonged courtship of the little fellow referred to in the early part of this story (and who was still working for three dollars a week), she had commenced going with another—a cook forty-two years of age, and had thought herself desperately in love with him at the time. I had not even written to Miss Hinshaw and knew nothing whatever of any engagement. I was much downcast for a time, and like some others who have been jilted, I grew the least bit wicked in my thoughts, and felt she would not find life all sunshine and roses with her forty-two-year-old groom. Lots of excitement was on around Megory and Calias, and as I liked excitement, I soon forgot the matter.

With the location of the land office in Megory and its subsequent removal from east of the Missouri, it was found there was only one building in the town, outside of the banks, that contained a vault, and a vault being necessary, it became expedient for the commercial club to provide an office that contained one. Two prosperous real-estate dealers, whose office contained a vault, readily turned over their building to the register and receiver until the land office building, then under construction, should be completed. A building twenty-five by sixty feet was built in the street just in front of the office, to be used as a temporary map room, and to be moved away as soon as the filing was over.

The holders of lucky numbers had been requested to appear at a given hour on a certain day to offer filings on Tipp county claims. By the time the filing had commenced, the hotels of both towns were filled, and tents covered all the vacant lots, while one hundred and fifty or more autos, to be hired at twenty-five dollars per day, did a rushing business. The settlers seemed to be possessed of abundant capital, and deposits in the local banks increased out of all proportion to those of previous times.

Besides the holders of numbers, hundreds of other settlers, who had purchased land in Megory county, were moving in at the same time, bringing stock, machinery, household goods and plenty of money. Those were bountiful days for the locators and land sharks.

When Megory county opened for settlement a few years previous, it was found that the Indians had taken practically all their allotments along the streams, where wood and water were to be had. The most of these allotments were on the Monca, bottom below Old Calias. In fact, they had taken the entire valley that far up. The timber along the creek was very small, being stunted from many fires, and consisted mostly of cottonwood, elm, box-elder, oak and ash. All but the oak and ash being easily susceptible to dry rot, were unfit for posts or anything except for shade and firewood. This made the valley lands cheaper than the uplands.

The Indians were always selling and are yet, what is furnished them by the government, for all they can get. When given the money spends it as quickly as he possibly can, buying fine horses, buggies, whiskey, and what-not. Their only idea being that it is to spend. The Sioux Indians, in my opinion, are the wealthiest tribe. They owned at one time the larger part of southern South Dakota and northern Nebraska, and own a lot of it yet. Be it said, however, it is simply because the government will not allow them to sell.

The breeds near Old Calias were easily flattered, and when the white people invited them to anything they always came dressed in great regalia, but after the settlers came there was not much inter-marrying, such as there had been before. A family of mixed-bloods by the name of Cutschall, owned all the land just south of Old Calias, in fact the site where Calias had stood, was formerly the allotment of a deceased son. The father, known as old Tom Cutschall, was for years a landmark on the creek.

Now and then Nicholson Brothers had invited the Cutschalls to some of their social doings, which made the Cutschalls feel exalted, and higher still, when Ernest suggested he could get them a patent for their land and then would buy it. This suited Cutschalls dandy. Ernest offered seven thousand dollars for the section, and they accepted. At that time, by recommending the Indian to be a competent citizen and able to care for himself, a patent would be granted on proper recommendation, and Nicholson Brothers attended to that and got Mrs. Cutschall the patent. Tom, her husband, being a white man, could not be allotted, and she had been given the section as the head of the family. It is said they spent the seven thousand dollars in one year. The company of which the father of the

Nicholson Brothers was president made a loan of eight thousand dollars on the land, and shortly afterward they sold it for twenty-three thousand dollars. The lots had brought more than one hundred thousand dollars in Calias and were still selling, so this placed the "Windy Nicholsons," as they had been called by jealous Megoryites, in a position of much importance, and they were by this time recognized as men of no small ability.

Years before Megory county was opened to settlement, many white men had drifted onto the reservation and had engaged in ranching, and had in the meantime married squaws. This appears to have been done more by the French than any other nationality, judging by the many French names among the mixed-bloods. Among these were a family by the name of Amoureaux, consisting of four boys and several girls. The girls had all married white men, and the little while Old Calias was in existence, two of the boys, William and George, used to go there often and were entertained by the Nicholson Brothers with as much splendor as Calias could afford. The Amoureaux were high moguls in Little Crow society during the first two years and everybody took off their hats to them. They were called the "rich mixed-bloods," and were engaged in ranching and owned great herds in Tipp county. When they shipped it was by the trainloads. The Amoureaux and the Colones, another family of wealthy breeds, were married to white women, and the husbands, as heads of families, held a section of land and the children each held one hundred and sixty acres.

Before the Nicholson Brothers had left Old Calias and before they had reached the position they now occupied, as I stated, they had shown the Amoureaux a "good time." They did not have much Indian blood in their veins, being what are called quarter-breeds, having a French father and a half-blood Indian mother, and were all fine looking. George had seven children and the family altogether had eleven quarter sections of land and two thousand head of cattle, so there was no reason why he should not have been the "big chief," but so much society and paid-for notoriety had brought about a change to him and his brother. William, who had always been a money-maker and a still bigger spender, with the fine looks thrown in, had shown like a skyrocket before bursting.

A rich Indian is something worth associating with, but a poor one is of small note. The Amoureaux spent so freely that in a few years they were all in, down and out—had nothing but their allotments left, and these the government would not give patents to, the Colones had done likewise, and together they had all moved into Tipp county.

Now there was another Amoureaux, the oldest one of the boys, who like the others had "blowed his roll," but happened to have an allotment in the very picturesque valley of the Dog Ear, in Tipp county, near the center of the county, and when a bunch of promoters decided to lay out a town they made a deal with Oliver, taking him into the company, he furnishing the land and they the brains. They laid out the site and began the town, naming it "Amoureaux" in honor of the breed, which made Oliver feel very big, indeed.

CHAPTER XXIX

IN THE VALLEY OF THE DOG EAR

T HE boom in Megory and Calias took such proportions that it made every investor prosperous, a goodly number of whom sold out, settled in Amoureaux, and the beautiful townsite soon became one of the most popular trade centers in the new county. It was the only townsite where trees stood, and the investors thought it a great thing that they would not have to wait a score of years to grow them.

Among the money investors in the town was old Dad Durpee, the former Oristown and Megory stage driver. When talking with him one day he told me he had saved three thousand dollars while running the stage line and had several good horses besides. "Dad," as he was familiarly called, had invested a part of his bank account in a corner lot and put up a two-story building, and soon became an Amoureaux booster. Old "Dad" opened up a stage line between Calias and the new town, but this line did not pay as well as the old one, for no one rode with him except when the weather was bad, as the people were all riding now in automobiles. In a short time every line of business was represented in Amoureaux and when the settlers began to arrive, Amoureaux did a flourishing business.

In coming from Calias, the trail led over a monstrous hill,

and from the top "Amro," the name having been shortened, nestling in the valley below, reminding me of Mexico City as it appeared from the highlands near Cuernavaca. A party from Hedrick, by the name of Van Neter, built a hotel fifty by one hundred feet, with forty rooms, and during the opening and filing made a small fortune. The house was always full and high prices were charged, and thus Amro prospered.

During the month of April the promoters succeeded in having the governor call an election to organize the county, the election to be held in June following. The filing had been made in April and May, and as conditions were, no one could vote except cowboys, Indians and mixed-bloods. In the election Amro won the county seat, and settlers moving into the county were exceedingly mortified over the fact, having to be governed eighteen months by an outlaw set who had deprived them of a voice in the organization of the county. As Amro had won, it soon became the central city and grew, as Calias had grown, and in a short time had a half-dozen general stores, two garages, four hotels, four banks, and every other line of business that goes to make up a western town. Its four livery barns did all the business their capacity would permit, while the saloons and gamblers feasted on the easy eastern cash that fell into their pockets. In July the lot sales of the government towns were held, but only one amounted to much, that town being farthest west and miles from the eastern line of the county. This was Ritten, and under a ruling of the Interior Department, a deposit of twenty-five dollars was accepted on an option of sixty days, after which a payment of one-half the price of the lot was required. Here it must be said that almost every dollar invested on the Little Crow had been doubled in a short time, and in many instances a hundred dollars soon grew to a thousand or more.

Practically all the lowest number holders had filed around Ritten, including numbers one and two. Ever since the opening of Oklahoma in 1901, when number one took a claim adjoining the city of Lawton, and the owner is said to have received thirty thousand dollars for it, the holder of number one in every opening of western land since has been a vary conspicuous figure, and this was not lost on the holder of number one in Tipp county—who was a divorced woman. She took her claim adjoining the town of Ritten, which fact brought the town considerable attention. The lots in the town brought the highest price of any which had been sold in any town on the Little Crow, up to that time, several having sold for from one thousand, two hundred to one thousand, four hundred dollars and one as high as two thousand and fifty dollars.

The town of Amro, being surrounded by Indian allotments, had few settlers in its immediate vicinity. The Indians, profiting by their experience in Megory county, where they learned that good location meant increase in the value of their lands, had, in selecting allotments, taken nearly all the land just west of Amro, as they had taken practically all of the good land just west of Calias in the eastern part of Tipp county. The good land all over the county had been picked over and the Indians had selected much of the best, but Tipp county is a large one, and several hundred thousand acres of good land were available for homesteading, though much scattered as to location.

When July arrived and still no surveyors for the railroad company had put in their appearance, it was feared that no extension work would be commenced that year, but shortly after the lot sale at Ritten, the surveyors arrived in the county and ran a survey west from Calias eleven miles to a town named after the Colones, referred to, striking the town, then proceeding northwest, missing Amro and crossing the Dog Ear about two miles north of the town, then following a divide almost due west to the county line on the west, running just south of a conspicuous range of hills known as the "Red Hills," missing every town in the county except Colone. This caused a temporary check in the excitement around Amro, but as it had the county seat it felt secure, as a county seat means much to a western village, and felt the railroad would eventually go there. In fact the citizens of the town boasted that the road could not afford to miss it, pointing with pride to the many teams to be seen in her streets daily and the bee-like activity of the town in general. I visited the town many times, but from the first time I saw the place I felt sure the railroad would never go there as two miles to the north was the natural divide, that the survey had followed all the way from Colone to the Dog Ear and on to the west side of the county, which is a natural right-of-way. When I argued with the people in the town, that Amro would not get the railroad, I brought out a storm of protest.

CHAPTER XXX

ERNEST NICHOLSON TAKES A HAND

AFTER completing the first survey, however, the surveyors returned, and made another that struck Amro. This survey swerved off from the first survey to the southwest between Colone and Amro and struck the valley of a little stream known as Mud Creek, which empties into the Dog Ear at Amro. But being a most illogical route, I felt confident the C. & R. W. had no intention of following it, perhaps only making the survey out of courtesy to the people in Amro, or possibly to show to the state railroad commissioners, if they became insistent, why they could not strike the town.

About this time Ernest Nicholson appeared on the scene, and purchased a forty acre tract of land north of the town, for which he paid fifty-five dollars an acre, later paying ten thousand dollars for a quarter, joining the forty. Still later he purchased the entire section of heirship land, belonging to a man named Jim Riggins, an Oristown city justice, and a former squaw-man, whose deceased wife had owned the land. For this section of land the Nicholsons paid thirty-five thousand dollars. The price staggered the people of Amro, who declared Nicholson had certainly gone crazy. They set up a terrible "howl." "What were the d— Nicholsons sticking their noses into Tipp county towns for? Were they not satisfied with Calias, where they had grafted everybody out of their money?" No, the trouble, they all agreed, was that Ernest wanted to run the county and wanted to be the "big stick." But they consoled themselves for awhile with the fact that Amro had the county seat and was growing. The settlers were trading in Amro, for Amro had what they needed. An indignation meeting was held, where with much feeling they denounced the actions of Ernest Nicholson in buying land north of the town and announcing that he would build a town such as the Little Crow had never dreamed of, and that Amro should at once begin to move over to the new townsite and save money; but they were hot. Old Dad Durpee, in his shirt sleeves, corduroy and boots, his shaggy beard flowing, declared that the low-down, stinking, lying cuss would not dare to ask him to move to the town he had as yet not even named; but Ernest, at the wheel of a big new sixty-horse power Packard, continued to buy land along the railroad survey all the way to the west line of the county. In fact he bought every piece of land that was purchasable.

I watched this fight from the beginning, with interest, for I had become well enough acquainted with Ernest to feel that he knew what he was about. When the surveyors had arrived in Calias, Ernest had gone to Chicago. In declaring the road could not miss Amro the people were much like inhabitants of Megory had been a few years before. While they prattled and allowed their ego to rule, they should have been busy, and when it was seen that the town might not get the railroad, they should have gone to Chicago and seen Marvin Hewitt, putting the proposition squarely before him, and requested that if he could not give them the road, to give them a depot, if they moved to the line of the survey. By that time it was a town with two solid blocks of business houses and many good merchants and bankers. I often wondered how such men could be so pin-headed, sitting back, declaring the great C. & R. W. railway could not afford to miss a little burg like Amro, but from previous observations and experience I felt sure they would wait until the last dog was dead, before trying to see what they could do. And they did.

In the meantime the promoters, who were nearly all from Megory or somewhere in Megory county, had learned that Ernest Nicholson was nobody's fool. They hooted the Nicholsons, along with the rest of the town, declaring Ernest to be anything but what he really was, until they had roused enough excitement to make Amro seem like a "good thing." Then they quietly sold their interest to the Amoureaux Brothers, who raked up about all that was left of the fortune of a few years previous, and paid six thousand, six hundred dollars for the interest of the promoters which made the Amoureaux the sole owners of the townsite and placed them in obvious control of the town's affairs, and again in the white society they liked so well.

All the Calias lumber yards owned branch yards at Amro and everybody continued to do a flourishing business. The Amroites paid little attention to the platting of the townsite to the north, nor made a single effort to ascertain which survey the railroad would follow, but continued to boast that Amro would get the road. About this time Ernest Nicholson called a meeting in Amro, inviting all the business men to be present and hear a proposition that he had to make, stating he hoped the citizens of the town and himself could get together without friction or ill-feeling. The meeting was held in Durpee's hall and everybody attended; some out of curiosity, some out of fear, and but few with any expectation or intention of agreeing to move to the north townsite. Ernest addressed the meeting, first thanking them for their presence, then plunged headlong into the purpose of the meeting. He explained that it was quite impossible for the road to go to Amro, this he had feared before a survey was made, but that he had ascertained while in Chicago that the road would not strike Amro. He then read a letter from Marvin Hewitt, the "man of destiny," so far as the location of the railroad was concerned, which stated that the road would be extended and the depot would be located on section twenty, which was the section Ernest had purchased. Then he brought up the matter of the distribution of lots which was, that to every person who moved or began to move to the new townsite within thirty days, one-half of the purchase price of the lot would be refunded. The price of the business lots ranged from eight hundred to two thousand dollars, while residence lots were from fifty to three hundred. "Think it over," he said, in closing, and was gone.

Needless to say they paid little attention to the proposition. The Amro Journal "roasted" and cartooned the Nicholson Brothers in the same way Megory papers had done, on account of the town of Calias.

After thirty days had elapsed, the Nicholsons warned the people of Amro that it was the last opportunity they would have to accept his proposition, and when they paid no attention to his warning, he named the new town. I shall not soon forget how the people outside of the town of Amro laughed over the name applied to the new town, as its application to the situation was so accurate and descriptive of later events, that I regret I must substitute a name for the purposes of this story, but which is the best I am able to find, "Victor."

Instead of moving to Victor, taking advantage of choice of location and the purchase of a lot at half price, the Amroites began making improvements in their town, putting down cement walks ten feet wide the length of the two business blocks and walks on side streets as well. A school election was called and as a result an eleven-thousand-dollar school house was erected, a modern two-story building, with basement and gymnasium. The building was large enough to hold all the population of Amro if all the men, women and children were of school age, and still have room for many more. This act brought a storm of criticism from the settlers, and even many of the people of the town thought it quite a needless extravagance; but Van Neter, who was strong for education and for Amro, had put it through and figured he had won a point. He was the county superintendent. Most of the people claimed the town would soon grow large enough to require the building, and let it go at that.

People began drifting into Victor, buying lots and putting up good buildings. Nicholsons announced a lot sale and preparations began for much active boosting for the new town. In the election to be held a year later, they hoped to wrest the county seat from Amro.

When Ernest Nicholson saw the improvements being made in Amro and no sign of moving the town, he began to scheme, and I could see that if Amro wasn't going to move peacefully he would help it along in some other way. However, nothing was done before the lot sale, which was advertised to take place in the lobby of the Nicholson Brothers' new office building in Calias.

On the date advertised for the lot sale, crowds gathered and many who had no intentions of investing, attended the sale out of curiosity. I took a crowd to Calias from Megory, among whom was Joy Flackler, cashier of the Megory National Bank, who stated that Frank Woodring had loaned the Nicholsons fifty thousand dollars to buy the townsite. Megoryites still held a grudge against the Nicholsons, and Flackler seemed to wish they had asked the loan of him so he might have had the pleasure of turning them down.

The second day of the lot sale, a bunch of bartenders, gamblers and Amro's rougher class appeared on the scene and distributed handbills which announced that Amro had contracted for a half section on the survey north of the town and would move in a body if moving was necessary. The crowd styled themselves "Amro knockers," whose purpose it was to show prospective lot buyers that in purchasing Victor lots they were buying "a pig in a poke." The knocking was done mostly in saloons, where the knockers got drunk and were promptly arrested before the sale started. The sale went along unhindered. The auctioneer, standing above the crowds, waxed eloquent in pointing out the advantages, describing Sioux City on the east and Deadwood and Lead on the west, and explaining that eventually a city must spring up in that section of the country, that would grow into a prairie metropolis of probably ten thousand people, and whether the crowd before him took his eloquence seriously or not, they at least had the chance at the choice of the lots and locations, and eighty-four thousand dollars worth of lots were sold.

CHAPTER XXXI

THE McCRALINES

AS BEFORE mentioned, I was given largely to observation and to reading and was fairly well posted on current events. I was always a lover of success and nothing interested me more after a day's work in the field than spending my evening hours in reading. What I liked best was some good story with a moral. I enjoyed reading stories by Maude Radford Warren, largely because her stories were so very practical and true to life. Having traveled and seen much of the country, while running as a porter for the P———n Company, I could follow much of her writings, having been over the ground covered by the scenes of many of her stories. Another feature of her writings which pleased me was the fact that many of the characters, unlike the central figures in many stories, who all become fabulously wealthy, were often only fairly successful and gained only a measure of wealth and happiness, that did not reach prohibitive proportions.

Perhaps I should not have become so set against stories whose heroes invariably became multi-millionaires, had it not been for the fact that many of the younger members of my race, with whom I had made acquaintance in my trips to Chicago and other parts of the country, always appeared to intimate in their conversation, that a person should have riches thrust upon them if they sacrificed all their "good times," as they termed it, to go out west. Of course the easterner, in most stories, conquers and becomes rich, that is, after so much sacrifice. The truth is, in real life only about one in ten of the eastern people make good at ranching or homesteading, and that one is usually well supplied with capital in the beginning, though of course there are exceptions. Colored people are much unlike the people of other races. For instance, all around me in my home in Dakota were foreigners of practically all nations, except Italians and Jews, among them being Swedes, Norwegians, Danes, Assyrians from Jerusalem, many Austrians, some Hungarians, and lots of Germans and Irish, these last being mostly American born, and also many Russians. The greater part of these people are good farmers and were growing prosperous on the Little Crow, and seeing this, I worked the harder to keep abreast of them, if not a little ahead. This was my fifth year and still there had not been a colored person on my land. Many more settlers had some and Tipp county was filling up, but still no colored people. My white neighbors had many visitors from their old homes and but few had visitors at some time to see them and see what they were doing.

During my visit to Kansas the spring previous, I had found many prosperous colored families, most of whom had settled in Kansas in the seventies and eighties and were mostly ex-slaves, but were not like the people of southern Illinois, contented and happy to eke a living from the farm they pretended to cultivate, but made their farms pay by careful methods. The farms they owned had from a hundred and sixty acres to six hundred and forty acres, and one colored man there at that time owned eleven hundred acres with twelve thousand dollars in the bank.

Wherever I had been, however, I had always found a certain

class in large and small towns alike whose object in life was obviously nothing, but who dressed up and aped the white people.

After Miss Rooks had married I was again in the condition of the previous year, but during the summer I had written to a young lady who had been teaching in M—boro and whom I had met while visiting Miss Rooks. Her name was Orlean McCraline, and her father was a minister and had been the pastor of our church in M—pls when I was a baby, but for the past seventeen years had been acting as presiding elder over the southern Illinois district. Miss McCraline had answered my letters and during the summer we had been very agreeable correspondents, and when in September I contracted for three relinquishments of homestead filings, I decided to ask her to marry me but to come and file on a Tipp county claim first.

To get the money for the purchase of the relinquishments, I had mortgaged my three hundred and twenty acres for seven thousand, six hundred dollars, the relinquishments costing in the neighborhood of six thousand, four hundred dollars. October was the time when the land would be open to homestead filing, and Miss McCraline had written that she would like to homestead. After sending my sister and grandmother the money to come to Dakota, I went to Chicago, where I arrived one Saturday morning. I had, since being in the west, stopped at the home of a maiden lady about thirty-five years of age, and in talking with her I had occasion to speak of the family. Evidently she did not know I had come to see Orlean, or that I was even acquainted with the family. I spoke of the Rev. McCraline and asked her if she knew him.

"Who, old N. J. McCraline?" she asked. "Humph," she went on with a contemptuous snort. "Yes, I know him and know him to be the biggest old rascal in the Methodist church. He's lower than a dog," she continued, "and if it wasn't for his family they would have thrown him out of the conference long ago, but he has a good family and for that reason they let him stay on, but he has no principle and is mean to his wife, never goes out with her nor does anything for her, but courts every woman on his circuit who will notice him and has been doing it for years. When he is in Chicago he spends his time visiting a woman on the west side. Her name is Mrs. Ewis."

This recalled to my mind that during the spring I had come to Chicago I had become acquainted with Mrs. Ewis' son and had been entertained at their home on Vernon Avenue where at that time the two families, McCraline and Ewis, rented a flat together, and although I had seen the girls I had not become acquainted with any of the McCraline family then. Orlean was the older of the two girls. What Miss Ankin had said about her father did not sound very good for a minister, still I had known in southern Illinois that the colored ministers didn't always bear the best reputations, and some of the colored papers I received in Dakota were continually making war on the immoral ministers, but since I had come to see the girl it didn't discourage me when I learned her father had a bad name although I would have preferred an opposite condition.

I went to the phone a few minutes after the conversation with Miss Ankin and called up Miss McCraline, and when she learned I was in the city she expressed her delight with many exclamations, saying she did not know I would arrive in the city until the next day and inquired as to when I would call.

"As nothing is so important as seeing you," I answered. "I will call at two o'clock, if that is agreeable to you."

She assured me that it was and at the appointed hour I called at the McCraline home and was pleasantly received. Miss McCraline called in her mother, whom I thought a very pleasant lady. We passed a very agreeable evening together, going over on State street to supper and then out to Jackson Park. I found Miss McCraline a kind, simple, and sympathetic person; in fact, agreeable in every way.

I had grown to feel that if I ever married I would simply have to propose to some girl and if accepted, marry her and have it over with. I was tired of living alone on the claim and wanted a wife and love, even if she was a city girl. I felt that I hadn't the time to visit all over the country to find a farmer's daughter. I had lived in the city and thought if I married a city girl I would understand her, anyway. I could not claim to be in love with this girl, nor with anyone else, but had always had a feeling that if a man and woman met and found each other pleasant and entertaining, there was no need of a long courtship, and when we came in from a walk I stated the object of my trip.

Miss McCraline was acquainted with a part of the story for, as stated, she had been teaching in M—boro at the time I went there to see Miss Rooks, and had seen her take up with the cook and marry foolishly. She had stated in her letters that she had been glad that I wrote to her and that she thought Miss Rooks had acted foolishly, and when I explained my circumstances and stated the proposition she seemed favorable to it. I told her to think it over and I would return the next day and explain it to her mother.

When I called the next morning and talked with her and her mother, they both thought it all right that Orlean should go to Dakota and file on the homestead, then we would marry and live together on the claim, but her mother added somewhat nervously and apparently ill at ease, that I had better talk with her husband. As the Reverend was then some three hundred and seventy-five miles south of Chicago attending conference, I couldn't see how we could get together, but we put in the

Sunday attending church and Sunday School, and that evening went to a downtown theatre where we saw Lew Dokstader's ministrels with Neil O'Brien as captain of the fire department, which was very funny and I laughed until my head ached.

The next day was spent in trying to communicate with the Reverend over the long distance but we did not succeed. Fortunately, at about five o'clock Mrs. Ewis came over from the west side. I had known Mrs. Ewis to be a smart woman with a deeper conviction than had Mrs. McCraline, whom she did not like, but as Mrs. McCraline was in trouble and did not know which way to turn, Mrs. Ewis was approached with the subject. Orlean was an obedient girl and although she wanted to go with me, it was evident that I must get the consent of her parents. She was nearly twenty-seven years old and girls of that age usually wish to get married. Her younger sister had just been married, which added to her feeling of loneliness. The result of the consultation with Mrs. Ewis, as she afterward explained to me, was that it was decided that it would not be proper for Orlean to go alone with me but if I cared to pay her way she would accompany us as chaperon. I was getting somewhat uneasy as I had paid twelve hundred dollars into the bank at Megory for the relinquishment, which I would lose if someone didn't file on the claim by the second of October. It was then about September twenty-fifth and I readily consented to incur the expense of her trip to Megory, where we soon landed. While I had been absent my sister and grandmother had arrived. On October first, all three were ready to file on their claims, and Dakota's colored population would be increased by three, and four hundred and eighty acres of land would be added to the wealth of the colored race in the state. Hundreds of others had purchased relinquishments and were waiting to file also. A ruling of the department had made it impossible to file before October first, and when it was seen that only a small number would be able to file on that day, the register and receiver inaugurated a plan whereby all desiring to file on Tipp county claims should form a line in front of the land office door, and when the office opened, the line should file through the office in the order in which they stood, and numbers would be issued to them which would permit them to return to the land office and make their filings in turn, thereby avoiding a rush and the necessity of remaining in line until admitted to the land office.

CHAPTER XXXII

A LONG NIGHT

EOPLE began forming into line immediately after luncheon, on the afternoon of the last day of September and continued throughout the afternoon. When I saw such a crowd gathering, I got my folks into the line. When it is taken into consideration that the land office would not open until nine o'clock the next morning, this seemed like a foolish proceeding. It was then four o'clock and the crowd would have to remain in line all night to hold their places (to be exact, just seventeen hours). Remaining in line all night was not pleasantly anticipated, and nights in October in South Dakota are apt to get pretty chilly, but the line continued to increase and by ten o'clock the street in front of the land office was a surging mass of humanity, mostly purchasers of relinquishments, waiting for the opening of the land office the next morning and to be in readiness to protect the claim they had contracted for. Hot coffee and sandwiches were sold and kept appetites supplied, and drunks mixed here and there in the line kept the crowd wakeful, many singing and telling stories to enliven the occasion. I held the place for my fiancee through the night, and although I had become used to all kinds of roughness, sitting up in the street all the long night was far from pleasant.

About two o'clock in the morning, squatters, who had spent the early part of the night on the prairie in order to be on their claims after midnight, began to arrive and took their places at the foot of the line. All land not filed on by the original number holders was to be open for filing as soon as the land office opened, and squatters had from midnight until the opening of the land office in which to beat the man who waited to file, before locating on the land, a squatters right holding first in such cases. Many had hired autos to bring them in from the reservation immediately after midnight, or as soon after midnight as they had made some crude improvements on the land. Many auto loads arrived with a shout and claimants leaped from the tonneaus, falling into line almost before the vehicles had stopped. The line wound back and forth along the street like a snake and formed into a compact mass. Until after sunrise the noisy autos kept a steady rush, dumping their weary passengers into the street.

By the time the land office opened in the morning, the line filled the street for half a block, and fully seventeen hundred persons were waiting for a chance to enter the land office. An army of tired, swollen-eyed and dusty creatures they appeared, some of whom commenced dealing their positions in the line to late comers, having gotten into line for speculation purposes only, and offered their places for from ten to twenty-five dollars, and in a few instances places near the door sold for as high as fifty dollars.

Under a ruling of the land officials, no filings were to be accepted except from holders of original numbers until October first, and this ruling made it expedient for holders of relinquishments of early numbers to get into line early, as the six months allowed for establishing residence expired for the first hundred original numbers on that day, and in cases where residence had not been properly established, the land would be open to contest

as soon as this period had expired. Many hundreds had purchased relinquishments, hence the value placed on the positions
nearest the land-office door. It was three o'clock by the time the
line had passed through the land office and received their numbers. The land office closed at four o'clock for the day, which left
but one hour for the protection of those who must offer their filings that day or face the chances of a contest.

Some had protected their claims by going into the land
office before the ruling was made and filing contests on the
claims for which they held relinquishments, but most of the
buyers had not thought of such a thing, and land grafters had
complicated matters by filing contests on various claims for
which they knew relinquishments would be offered and then
withdrawing the contest, for a consideration. This practice met
with strong disapproval as most of the people had invested for
the purpose of making homes, and the laws made it impossible
to change the circumstances. These transactions had to be completed before the line formed, however, as after the line formed
no one could enter the land office to offer either filing, relinquishment or contest, without a number issued by the officials.
The line was full of such grafters, and as not more than one
hundred filings could be taken in a day, it can readily be seen
that some of the relinquishment holders were in danger of losing out through a contest offered before they had an opportunity to file.

The crowds that flock to land openings, like other games of
chance, are made up in a measure of speculators, people who
journey to one of the registration points and make application
for land, figuring that if they should draw an early number (that
is, in the first five hundred) they would file, no thought of making a home, but simply to sell the relinquishment for the largest
possible price.

When the filings were made, about sixty had dropped out of the first five hundred and even more out of the second five hundred, evidently thinking they were not likely to get enough for the relinquishment to pay them for their trouble and original investment, since it cost them a first payment of two hundred and six dollars on the purchase price of six dollars per acre and a locating fee of twenty-five dollars, and in some cases the first expense reached three hundred dollars. If the relinquishment was not sold before the six months allowed for establishing residence expired, it was necessary to establish residence making sufficient improvement for that purpose, or lose the money invested.

Out of the first four thousand numbers some two thousand had filed, and practically half of this number had contracted to sell their relinquishments. The buyers had deposited the amount to be paid in some bank to the credit of the claimant, to be turned over when the purchaser had secured filing on the land, the bank acting as agent between the parties to the transaction.

I shall long remember October 1, 190— in Megory—called the "Magic City," and claiming a population of three thousand, but probably not exceeding one thousand, five hundred actual inhabitants, though filled with transients from the beginning of the rush a year before, and had at no time during this period less than two thousand, five hundred persons in the town.

My bride-to-be and my grandmother had received numbers 138 and 139 which would likely be called to file the second day, while my sister received 170. On the afternoon of the second, Orlean, and my grandmother, who had raised a family in the days of slavery, and was then about seventy-seven years of age, were called, and came out of the land office a few minutes later with their blue papers, receipts for the two hundred six dollars, first payment and fees, which I had given the agent before they entered the land office. Their agent went into the land office with them to see that they got a straight filing, which they received. My sister, however, was not called that day and the next day being Sunday, she would not be called until the following Monday.

The place my grandmother had filed on had been bought by a Megory school teacher, who had paid one thousand, four hundred dollars to a real estate dealer for the relinquishment of the same place. The claimant had issued two relinquishments, which was easy enough to do, though the relinquishment accompanied by his land office receipt was the only bona fide one and we had the receipt. The teacher had stood in line the long night through, behind my sister and then lost the place. The dealer who sold her the relinquishment was very angry, as he was to get six hundred dollars in the deal, giving the claimant only eight hundred. When I learned this and that the teacher had lost out I was very sorry for her, but it was a case of "first come first served," and many other mix-ups between buyers and dealers had occurred. I went to the teacher and apologized as best I could. She looked very pitiful as she told me how she had taught so many years to save the money and her dreams had been of nothing but securing a claim. Her eyes filled with tears and she bent her head and began crying, and thus I left her.

The next morning I sent Miss McCraline and Mrs. Ewis back to Chicago and proceeded to the claims of my sister and grandmother, which I found to be good ones. I had whirled around them in an auto before I bought them, and though being satisfied that they laid well I had not examined the soil or walked across them.

In a week I had two frame houses, ten by ten, built on them and within another week they had commenced living on them. Shortly after they moved onto the claims came one of the biggest snowstorms I had ever seen. It snowed for days and then came warm weather, thawing the snow, then more snow. The corn in the fields had not been gathered nor was it all gathered before the following April.

Most of the settlers in the new county were from twenty to fifty miles from Calias and winter caught many of them without fuel, and the suffering from cold was intense. The snow continued to fall until it was about four feet deep on the level. Fortunately I had hauled enough coal to last my folks through the winter, and they had only to get to Ritten, a distance of eight miles, to get food. I had just gathered two loads out of a ninety-acre field. Being snowbound, with nothing to do, I watched the fight between Amro and Victor, with interest.

XXXIII

THE SURVIVAL OF THE FITTEST

AFTER the lot sale Amro still refused to move. It was then Ernest Nicholson said the town had to be overcome somehow and he had to do it. The business men of the town continued to hold meetings and pass resolutions to stick together. They argued that all they had to do to save the town was to stick together. This was the slogan of each meeting. The county seat no doubt held them more than the meetings, but it was not long before signs of weakening began to appear here and there along the ranks.

Victor to the north, in the opinion of the people abroad, would get the road; lots were being bought up and business people from elsewhere were continuing to locate and erect substantial buildings in the new town, and then it was reported that Geo. Roane, who had recently sold his livery barn in Amro where he had made a bunch of money, had bought five lots in Victor, paying fancy prices for them but getting a refund of fifty per cent if he moved or started his residence hotel by January first. This report could not be confirmed as Roane could not be found, but soon conflicting reports filled the air and old Dad Durpee, who loved his corner lot in Amro like a hog loves corn, made daily trips up and down Main street, railing the boys. The more he talked the more excited he became. "My good men!" he would shout, with his arms stretched above his head like Billy Sunday after preaching awhile. "Stick together! Stick together! We've got the best town in the best county, in the best state in the best country in the world. What more do you want?" He would fairly rave, with his old eyes stretched widely open, and his shaggy beard flowing in the breeze. He continued this until he bored the people and weakened the already weakening forces.

There were many good business men in Amro, among them young men of sterling qualities, college-bred, ambitious and with dreams of great success and of establishing themselves securely. Many of them had sweethearts in the east, and desired to make a showing and profit as well, and how were they to do this in a town in which even outsiders, though they might not admire the Nicholsons, were predicting failure for those who remained, and declaring they were foolish to stay. This young blood was getting hard to control, and to hold them something more had to be done than declaring Ernest Nicholson to be trying to wreck the town and break up their homes. Poor fools—I would think, as I listened to them, talking as though Ernest Nicholson had anything to do with the railroad missing the town. It was simply the mistaken location.

It had been an easy matter for the promoters, whose capital was mostly in the air, to locate Amro on the allotment of Oliver Amoureaux, because they could do so without paying anything, and did not have to pay fifty-five dollars an acre for deeded land as Nicholson had done. Being centrally located and with enough buildings to encourage the building of more, they induced the governor to organize the county when few but illiterate Indians and thieving mixed-bloods could vote, fairly stealing the county seat before the bona-fide settlers had any chance to express themselves on the matter. They had doggedly invested more money in cement walks and other improvements, when disinterested persons had criticized their actions, loading the township with eleven thousand dollars, seven per cent interest bearing bonds, that sold at a big discount, to build a school house large enough for a town three times the size of Amro. This angered the settlers and being dissatisfied because they were disfranchised by the rascals who engineered the plan, Amro began rapidly to lose outside sympathy.

Ernest Nicholson had a pleasing personality and forceful as well. He was a king at reasoning and whenever a weak Amorite was in Calias he was invited into the townsite company's office which was luxuriously furnished, the walls profusely decorated with the pictures of prominent capitalists and financiers of the middle west, some of whom were financing the schemes of the fine looking young men who were trying to show these struggling waifs of the prairie the inevitable result.

All that was needed was to break into the town in some way or other, for it was essential that Amro be absorbed by Victor before the election, ten months away. The town should be entirely broken up. If it still existed, with or without the road, it had a good chance of holding the county seat. A county seat is a very hard thing to move. In fact, according to the records of western states, few county seats have ever been moved.

Megory's county seat was located forty miles from Megory, in the extreme east end of the county, where the county ran to a point and the river on the north and the south boundary of the county formed an acute angle; yet the county seat remains at Fairview and the voters keep it there, where no one but a handful of farmers and the few hundred inhabitants of the town reside. When trying to remove the county seat every town in the county jumps into the race, persisting in the contention that their town is the proper place for the county seat and when election comes, the farmers who represent from sixty-five to ninety per cent of the vote in states like Dakota, vote for the town nearest their farm, thinking only of their own selfish interests and forgetting the county's welfare, as the victor must have a majority of all votes cast. Another example of this condition is near where this story is written, on the east bank of the Missouri. It is a place called Keeler, the most God-forsaken place in the world, with only three or four ramshackle buildings and a post office, with little or no country trade, yet this is a county seat, the capital of one of the leading counties of the state; while half a dozen good towns along the line of the C. M. & St. L. road, cart their records and hold court in Keeler, twenty miles from the railroad. Every four years for thirty years the county seat has been elected to stay at Keeler, as no town can get a majority of all votes cast against Keeler, which doesn't even enter the race.

All of these facts had their bearing on Ernest Nicholson in his office at Calias, and had helped to hold Amro together, until Van Neter was called into Calias and into the private office of "King Ernest" as Amro had named him. What passed in that office at this interview is a matter of conjecture, but when Van Neter came out of the office he carried a check for seven thousand, five hundred dollars and Ernest Nicholson became the owner of the two-story, fifty by one hundred foot hotel and lot, Amro's most popular corner. When this news reached Amro pandemonium reigned, business men passed from one place of business to another talking in low tones, and shaking their heads significantly, while old Dad Durpee, nearer maniac than ever before, went the rounds of the town shouting in a high staccato tone: "What do you think of it? What do you think of the ornery, low-down rascal's selling out. Selling out to that band of dirty thieves and town wreckers. By the living gods!"

With his arms folded like a tragedian, eyes rolled to the skies and his form reared back until his knees stuck forward, then raising his hand he solemnly swore: "I'll stay in Amro! I'll stay in Amro! I'll stay in Amro," until his voice rose to a hoarse scream. "I'll stay in Amro until the town is deserted to the last d—n building and the last dog is dead." And he did, though I cannot say as to the last dog.

Nicholson had the hotel closed and although the snow was more than knee-deep on the level, a force of carpenters at once began cutting the building in two, preparatory to moving it to the new town. Old Machalacy Finn, a one-armed, hatchet-faced Irishman, with a long sandy mustache and pop-eyes, who had moved brick buildings in the windy city, was sent to Amro and declared in Joe Cook's saloon that he'd put that damned cracker-box in Victor in fifteen days, and armed with a force of carpenters and laborers, the plaster was soon knocked off the walls of the largest and best building in Amro and thrown into the streets; while the new cement walks, only fifty feet in front and one hundred by eight at the side, were broken into slabs and piled roughly aside, then huge timbers twenty-four by thirty-two inches and sixty feet long, from the redwood forests of Washington, followed the jackscrews and blocks under the building. Two sixty-horse power mounted tractors, with double boilers and horse power locomotive construction, low wheels and high cabs, where the engineer perched like a bird, steamed into the town and prepared to pull the structure from its foundations.

The crowd gathered to watch as the powerful engines began to cough and roar, with an occasional short puff, like fast passenger engines on the New York Central, the power being sufficient to tear the building to splinters. Creaking in every joint, the hotel building began slowly moving out into the street.

The telephone wires, which belonged to the Nicholsons, had been cut and thrown aside and the town was temporarily without telephonic communication. The powerful engines easily pulled the hotel between banks of snow, which had been shoveled aside to make room for the passing of the building across the grades and ditches and on toward Victor. A block and tackle was used whenever the building became stuck fast and in a few days the hotel was serving the public on a corner lot in Victor, where it added materially to the appearance of the town.

Following in the footsteps of old Calias, the town, now being broken by the removal of the hotel, the dark cellar over which it stood gaping like an open grave, to be gazed into at every turn, became of small consequence, and in Victor the price of corner lots had advanced from one thousand, five hundred to two thousand and three thousand dollars, while inside lots were being offered at from one thousand, two hundred to one thousand, eight hundred dollars which had formerly priced from eight hundred to one thousand, two hundred dollars. This did not discourage those who wanted to move to the new town. All that was desired by former rock-ribbed Amroites was to get to Victor. They talked nothing but Victor. The name of Amro was almost forgotten.

Before the hotel building had fairly left the town, other traction engines were brought to the town. The snow was a great hindrance and to get coal hauled from Calias cost seventy-five cents a hundred. Labor and board was high, and in fact all prices for everything were very high. It was in the middle of one of the cold winters of the plains, but money had been made in Amro and was offered freely in payment for moving to the new town. It was bitter cold and the snow was light and drifting, the ground frozen under the snow two feet deep, but the frozen ground would hold up the buildings better than it would when the warm weather came and started a thaw. The soil being underlaid with sand it would be impossible to move buildings over it, if rain should come, as it would be likely to do in the spring, and with the melted snow to hinder, it would then be very difficult to move the buildings. It was small wonder that they were anxious to get away from the disrupted town at this time, and the road between Amro and Victor became a much used thoroughfare.

The traction engines pounding from early morning until late at night filled the air with a noise as of railroad yards, while the happy faces of the owners of the buildings arriving in Victor, and the anxious ones waiting to be moved, gave material for interesting study of human nature.

George Roane had built a new barn in Victor and was much pleased over having sold the old one in Amro before the town went to pieces, thereby saving the expense of removal and getting a refund of fifty per cent of the purchase price of the lots he purchased in Victor. Many buildings continued to arrive from Amro, and new ones being erected did credit to the name of the new town by growing faster than any of the towns on the reservation, including Calias or Megory.

CHAPTER XXXIV

EAST OF STATE STREET

I HAD in due time heard from Orlean saying she and Mrs. Ewis had arrived safely home. She wrote: "When I came into the house mama grabbed me and held me for a long time as though she was afraid I was not real. She had been so worried while I was away and was so glad I had returned before father came." They had received a telegram from her father saying that he had again been appointed presiding elder of the Cairo district and would be home within a few days.

I judged from what Mrs. Ewis had told me that the Reverend was not much of a business man and a hard one to make understand a business proposition or to reason with. He had only two children, and Orlean, as Mrs. Ewis informed me, was his favorite. She had always been an obedient girl, was graduated from the Chicago high school and spent two years at a colored boarding school in Ohio that was kept up by the African M. E. Church, had taught two years, but had not secured a school that year.

She had saved a hundred dollars out of the money she had earned teaching school. The young man who married her sister worked for a trading-stamp corporation and received thirteen dollars a week, while the Reverend was supposed to receive about a thousand dollars a year as presiding elder. There were some twelve or fifteen churches on his circuit, where quarterly conference was held every three months, and each church was expected to contribute a certain amount at that time. Each member was supposed to give twenty-five cents, which they did not always do.

In a town like M——boro, for instance, where the church had one hundred members, not over twenty-five are considered live members; that is, only twenty-five could be depended upon to pay their quarterly dues regularly, the others being spasmodic, contributing freely at times or nothing at all for a long time.

Orlean often laughed as she told me some of the many ways her father had of making the "dead ones" contribute, but with all the tricks and turns the position was not a lucrative one, there being no certainty as to the amount of the compensation. Mrs. Ewis told me the family had always been poor and got along only by saving in every direction. I could see this as Orlean seemed to have few clothes and had worn her sister's hat to Dakota.

Her sister was said to be very mean and disagreeable, and if anyone in the family had to do without anything it was never the sister. She was quarrelsome and much disliked while Orlean was the opposite and would cheerfully deprive herself of anything necessary. Her mother, Mrs. Ewis went on to tell me, was a "devil, spiteful and mean and as helpless as a baby." I believed a part of this but not all. I had listened to Mrs. McCraline, and while I felt she was somewhat on the helpless order, I did not believe she was mean, nor a "devil." Meanness and deviltry are usually discernible in the eyes and I had seen none of it in the eyes of either Mrs. McCraline or Orlean, but I did not like Ethel, and from what little Miss Ankin told me about the Reverend I was inclined to believe that he was likely to be the "devil," and Mrs. Ewis' information regarding Mrs. McCraline was probably inspired by jealousy.

I remembered that back in M—pls the preachers' wives were timid creatures, submissive to any order or condition their "elder" husbands put upon them, submitting too much in order to keep peace, never raising a row over the gossip that came to their ears from malicious "sisters" and church workers. As long as I could remember the colored ministers were accused of many ugly things concerning them and the "sisters," mostly women who worked in the church, but I had forgotten it until I now began hearing the gossip concerning Rev. McCraline.

Orlean, her father and her brother-in-law had begun buying a home on Vernon avenue for which they were to pay four thousand, five hundred dollars. Of this amount three hundred dollars had been paid, one hundred by each of them. It was a nice little place, with eight rooms and with a stone front. Ethel had not paid anything, using her money in preparation for her wedding, which had taken place in September. Claves and her father had spent two hundred on it, which seemed very foolish, and were pinched to the last cent when it was done.

Claves had borrowed five dollars from his brother when they went on the wedding trip, to pay for a taxi to the depot. The wedding tour and honeymoon lasted two weeks and was spent in Racine, Wisconsin, sixty miles north of Chicago. They had just returned when I went to Chicago. When I first called, Mrs. Claves did not come down but when we returned to the house she condescended to come down and shake hands. She put on enough airs to have been a king's daughter.

With the three hundred dollars already paid on the home, they figured they should be able to pay for it in seven years in monthly installments of thirty-five dollars, paying the interest upon the principal at the same time, excepting two thousand which was in a first mortgage and drew five per cent and payable semi-annually. The house was in a quiet neighborhood much unlike the south end of Dearborn street and Armour avenue where none but colored people live.

The better class of Chicago's colored population was making a strenuous effort to get away from the rougher set, as well as to get out of the black belt which is centered around Armour, Dearborn, State and Thirty-first. Here the saloons, barbershops, restaurants and vaudeville shows are run by colored people, also the clubs and dance houses. East from State street to the lake, which is referred to by the colored people of the city as "east of State," there is another and altogether different class. Here for a long while colored people could hardly rent or buy a place, then as the white population drifted farther south, to Greenwood avenue, Hyde Park, Kenwood and other parts now fashionable districts, some of the avenues including Wabash, Rhodes, Calumet, Vernon and Indiana began renting to colored people and a few began buying.

Chicago is the Mecca for southern negroes. The better class continued to desert Dearborn and Armour and paid exorbitant rent for flats east of State street. Some lost what they had made on Armour avenue where rent was sometimes less than one-half what was charged five blocks east, and had to move back to Armour. As more colored people moved toward the lake more white people moved farther south, rent began falling and real estate dealers began offering former homes of rich families first for rent then for sale, and many others began buying as Rev. McCraline had done, making a small cash payment, and in this way otherwise unsalable property was disposed of at from five to ten per cent more than it would have brought at a cash sale.

The place they were buying could have been purchased for three thousand, eight hundred dollars or four thousand dollars in cash. After moving east of State street, these people formed into little sets which represented the more elite, and later developed into a sort of local aristocracy, which was not distinguished so much by wealth as by the airs and conventionality of its members, who did not go to public dances on State street and drink "can" beer. Here for a time they were secure from the vulgar intrusion of the noisy "loud-mouths," as they called them, of State street. The last time I was in Chicago, State street, the "dead line," had been crossed and a part of Wabash avenue is almost as noisy and vulgar as Dearborn. Beer cans, rough clubs and dudes were becoming as familiar sights as on Armour, and a large part of that part of the east side is so filled up with colored people that it is only a question of time until it will be a part of the black belt.

Orlean's brother-in-law had come to Chicago several years previous from a stumpy farm in the backwoods of Tennessee. He was the son of a jack-legged preacher and was very ignorant, but had been going with the girl he married some six years and she had trained him out of much of it and when he finally figured in the two hundred dollar wedding referred to, he felt himself admitted into society and highly exalted. He thought the Reverend a great man, Mrs. Ewis had told me, referring to him as a Simian-headed negro who tried to walk and act like the Reverend. The McCralines, especially Ethel, referred to themselves as the "best people." I thought they were. They were not wicked, and I also guessed that Ethel felt very "aristocratic," and I wondered whether I would like the Reverend. He seemed to be regarded as a sort of monarch judging from the way he was spoken of by the family, but I had a "hunch" that he and I were not going to fall in love with each other. Still I hoped not to be the one to start any unpleasantness and would at least wait until I met him before forming an opinion. I received a letter from him when he returned from the conference. He did not write a very brilliant letter but was very reasonable, and tried to appear a little serious when he referred to my having his daughter come to South Dakota and file on land. He concluded by saying he thought it a good thing for colored people to go west and take land.

I received another letter from Orlean about the same time telling me how her father had scolded her about going to the theatre with me the Sunday night I had taken her, and pretended, as he had to me, to be very serious about the claim matter, but she wrote like this: "I know papa, and I could see he was just pleased over it all that he just strutted around like a rooster." She wanted to know when I was going to send the ring, but as I had not thought about it I do not recall what answer I made her, but do remember that my trip to get her and Mrs. Ewis and send them home again, including my own expenses, amounted to one hundred sixty dollars, besides the cost of the land, and having had to pay my sister's and grandmother's way also and get them started on their homesteads had taken all of the seven thousand, six hundred dollars I had borrowed on my land; that I was snow-bound with my corn in the field and my wheat still unthreshed. I began to write long letters trying to reason this out with her. She was willing to listen to reason but seemed so unhappy without the ring, and I imagined as I read her letters that I could see tears. She said when a girl is engaged she feels lost without a ring, "and, too," here she seemed to emphasize her words, "everybody expects it." I was sure she was telling the truth, for with girls "east of State street," and west as well, the most important thing in an engagement is the ring, sometimes being more important than the man himself.

When I lived in Chicago and since I had been living in Dakota and going to Chicago once a year, I knew that Loftis

Brothers had more mortgages on the moral future and jobs of the young society men, for the diamonds worn by their sweethearts or wives, than would appear comforting to the credit man. It made no difference what kind of a job a man might have, as all the way from a boot-black or a janitor to head waiters and post office clerks were included, and their women folks wore some size of a diamond. I asked myself what I was to do. I could not hope to begin changing customs, so I bought a forty dollar diamond set in a small eighteen-karat ring which "just fit," as she wrote later in the sweetest kind of a letter.

I had written I was sorry that I could not be there to put it on (such a story!). I had never thought of diamond rings or going after my wife after spending so much on preliminaries. What I had pictured was what I had seen, while running to the Pacific coast, girls going west to marry their pioneer sweethearts, who sent them the money or a ticket. They had gone, lots of them, to marry their brawny beaux and lived happily "ever after," but the beaux weren't negroes nor the girls colored. Still there are lots of colored men who would be out west building an empire, and plenty of nice colored girls who would journey thither and wed, if they really understood the opportunities offered; but very few understand the situation or realize the opportunities open to them in this western country.

I had expected to get married Christmas but the snow had put a stop to that plan. Besides, I was so far behind in my work and had no place to bring my wife. I had abandoned my little "soddy" and was living in a house on the old townsite, where I intended staying until spring. Then I would build and move onto my wife's homestead in Tipp county. When Christmas came grandma and sister came down from Ritten and stayed while I went to Chicago. I could scarcely afford it but it had become a custom for me to spend Christmas in Chicago and I wanted to know Orlean better and I wanted to meet her father. I had written her that I wasn't coming and when I arrived in the city and called at the house her mother was surprised, but pleasantly. I thought she was such a kind little soul. She promised not to tell Orlean I was in the city (Orlean had secured a position in a downtown store—ladies' furnishings—and received five-fifty per week) but couldn't keep it and when I was gone she called up Orlean and told her I was in the city. When I called in the evening, instead of surprising Orlean, I was surprised myself. The Reverend hadn't arrived from southern Illinois but was expected soon.

Orlean had worked long enough to buy herself a new waist and coat, and Mrs. Ewis, who was a milliner, had given her a hat, and she was dressed somewhat better than formerly. The family had wanted to give her a nice wedding, like Ethel's, but found themselves unable to do so. The semi-annual interest on their two-thousand-dollar loan would be due in January and a payment also, about one hundred and fifty dollars in all. The high cost of living in Chicago did not leave much out of eighteen dollars and fifty cents per week, and colored people in southern Illinois are not very prompt in paying their church dues, especially in mid-winter; in fact, many of them have a hard time keeping away from the poorhouse or off the county, and when the Reverend came home he was very short of money.

I remember how he appeared the evening I called. He had arrived in town that morning. He was a large man standing well over six feet and weighed about two hundred pounds, small-boned and fleshy, which gave him a round, plump appearance, and although he was then near sixty not a wrinkle was visible in his face. He was very dark, with a medium forehead and high-bridged nose, making it possible for him to wear nose-glasses, the nose being very unlike the flat-nosed negro. The large square upper-lip was partly hidden by a mustache sprinkled with gray, and his nearly white hair, worn in a massive pompadour, contrasted sharply with the dark skin and rounded features. His great height gave him an unusually attractive appearance of which he, I later learned, was well aware and made the most. In fact, his personal appearance was his pride, but his eye was not the eye of an intelligent or deep thinking man. They reminded me more of the eyes of a pig, full but expressionless, and he could put on airs, such a drawing-up and spreading-out, seeming to give the impression of being hard to approach.

When introduced to him I had another "hunch" we were not going to like each other. I was always frank, forward and unafraid, and his ceremonious manner did not affect me in the least. I went straight to him, taking his hand in response to the introduction and saying a few common-place things. They were very home-like for city people, inviting me to supper and treating me with much respect. The head of the table was occupied by the Reverend when he was at home and by Claves when the Reverend was away. I could readily see where Ethel got her airs. It took him about thirty minutes to get over his ceremonious manner, after which we talked freely, or rather, I talked. He was a poor listener and, although he never cut off my discourse in any way, he didn't listen as I had been used to having people listen, apparently with encouragement in their eyes, which makes talking a pleasure, so I soon ceased to talk. This, however, seemed still more awkward and I grew to feel a trifle displeased in his company.

On the following Sunday we went to morning service on Wabash avenue at a big stone structure. It appeared to be a rule of the household that the girls should go out together. This displeased me very much, as I had grown to dislike Ethel and Claves did not interest me. Both talked of society and "swell people" they wanted me to meet, putting it in such a way as to have me feel I was meeting my betters, while the truth of the matter was that I did not desire to meet any of their friends nor to have them with us anywhere we went. When church services were over we went to spend the time before Sunday School opened, with some friends of theirs named Latimer, who lived on Wabash avenue near the church, and who were so nearly white that they could easily have passed for white people.

The family consisted of Mr. and Mrs. Latimer and Mr. Latimer's sister, and were the most interesting people I had ever met on any of my trips to Chicago. They inquired all about Dakota and whether there were many colored settlers in the state, listening to every word with careful attention and approving or disapproving with nods and smiles. While they were so deeply interested, Claves, who had a reputation for "butting in" and talking too much, interrupted the conversation, blurting out his opinion, stopping me and embarrassing them, by stating that colored people had been held in slavery for two hundred years and since they were free they did not want to go out into the wilderness and sit on a farm, but wanted to be where they could have freedom and convenience, and this was sanctioned by a friend of Claves's who was still more ignorant than he. This angered Orlean and when we were outside even Ethel expressed her disgust at Claves' ignorance.

They told me that the Latimers were very well-to-do, owning considerable property besides the three-story building where they lived. To me this accounted for their careful attention, for it is my opinion that when you find a colored man or woman who has succeeded in actually doing something, and not merely pretending to, you will find an interesting and reasonable person to converse with, and one who will listen to a description of conditions and opportunities with marked intelligence.

Orlean and I attended a few shows at the downtown the-atres during the week, the first being a pathetic drama which our friends advised us to see entitled "Madam X". I did not like it at all. The leading character is the wife of a business man who has left her husband and remains away from him two years, pre-sumably discouraged over his lack of affection; is very young and wants to be loved, as the "old story" goes, and the husband is too busy to know that she is unhappy. She returns after two years and asks forgiveness and love, but is turned away by the husband. Twenty years later, in the closing act, a court scene decorates the stage; a woman is on trial for killing the man she has lived with unlawfully. She had been a woman of the street and lived with many others before living with the one mur-dered. The young lawyer who has her case, is her son, although he is not aware of this fact. He has just been admitted to the bar and this is his first case, having been appointed to the defense by the court. He takes the stand and delivers an eloquent address on behalf of the woman, who appears to be so saturated with liquor and cocaine as to be quite oblivious of her surroundings. She expires from the effect of her dissipations, but just before death she looks up and recognizes her son, she having been the young wife who left her home twenty-two years before. The unhappy father, who had suffered as only a deserted husband can and who had prayed for many years for the return of the wife, is present in the court room and together with the son, are at her side in death. As the climax of the play is reached, sup-pressed sobs became audible in the balcony, where we had seats. The scene was pathetic, indeed, and I had hard work keeping back the tears while my betrothed was using her handkerchief freely.

What I did not like about the play was the fact of her going away and taking up an immoral life instead of remaining pure and returning later to her husband. The husband, as the play goes, had not been a bad man and was unhappy throughout the play, and I argued this with Orlean all the way home. Why did she not remain good and when she returned he could have gathered her into his arms and "lived happy ever after." Not only my fiancee but most other women I have talked with about the play contend that he could have taken her back when she returned and been good to her. The man who wrote the play may have been a tragedian but the management that put it on the road knew a money-maker and kept it there as long as the people patronized the box office.

The next play we attended suited me better as, to my mind, it possessed all that "Madam X" lacked and, instead of weakness and an unhappy ending, this was one of strength of character and a happy finale. It was "The Fourth Estate," by Joseph Medill Patterson, who served his apprenticeship in writing on the Chicago Tribune. It was a newspaper play and its interest centered around one Wheeler Brand, who, through the purchase of a big city daily by a western man, with the bigness to hand out the truth regardless of the threats of the big advertisers, becomes managing editor. He relentlessly goes after one Judge Barteling whose "rotten" decisions had but sufficed to help "big business" and without regard to their effect upon the poor. The one really square decision was recalled before it took effect. To complicate matters the young editor loves the judge's daughter and while Brand holds a high place in Miss Barteling's regard, he is made to feel that to retain it he must stop the fight on her father. Brand pleads with her to see the moral of it but is unable to change her views. One evening Brand secures a flashlight photo and telephone witnesses of an interview with the judge, the photo showing the judge in the act of handing him a ten-thousand-dollar bribe. Late that night Brand has the article exposing this transaction in type and ready for the press when the proprietor, who has heretofore been so pleased with Brand's performance, but whose wife has gained an entrance into society through the influence of Judge Barteling, enters the office with the order to "kill the story."

This was a hard blow to the coming newspaper man. The judge calls and jokes him about being a smart boy but crazed with ideals, but is shocked when he turns to find his daughter has entered the office and has heard the conversation. He tells her to come along home with papa, but she decides to remain with Brand. She has thought her father in the right all along, but now that she has heard her father condone dishonesty she can no longer think so. Wheeler disobeys orders and sends the paper to press without "killing the story," and "all's well that ends well."

In a week or so I was back in Dakota where the thermometer registered twenty-five below with plenty of snow for company. I received a letter from the Reverend shortly after returning home saying they hoped to see me in Chicago again soon. I did not know what that meant unless it was that I was expected to return to be married, but as I had been to Chicago twice in less than four months and had suggested to Orlean that she come to Megory and be married there, I supposed that it was all settled, but this was where I began to learn that the McCraline family were very inconsiderate.

I had not claimed to be wealthy or to have unlimited amounts of money to spend in going to and from Chicago, as though it were a matter of eighty miles instead of eight hundred. I had explained to the Reverend that it was a burden rather than a luxury to be possessed of a lot of raw land, until it could be cultivated and made to yield a profit. I recalled that while talking with the Reverend in regard to this he had nodded his head in assent but with no facial expression to indicate that he understood or cared. The more I knew him the more I disliked him, and was very sorry that Orlean regarded his as a great man, although his immediate family were the only ones who regarded him in that light. I had learned to expect his ceremonious manner but was considerably tried by his apparent dullness and lack of interest or encouragement of practical ideas.

I put volumes into my letters to Orlean, trying to make clear why she should condescend to come to Megory and be quietly married instead of obliging me to return to Chicago. I had no more money, as it was expensive to keep my grandmother and sister on their claims. They had no money and I had no outside support, not even the moral support of my people nor of Orlean's, who all seemed to take it for granted that I had plenty of ready money. I had not taken a cent out of the crop I had raised, the corn still standing in the field, with a heavy snow on the ground and my small grain still unthreshed.

However, my letters were in vain. Miss McCraline could see no other way than that if I cared for her I'd come and marry her at home, which she contended was no more than right and would look much better. I sighed wearily over it all and began to suspect I was "in the right church, but in the wrong pew."

CHAPTER XXXV

AN UNCROWNED KING

TOWARD spring the snow melted and with gum boots I plunged into the cold, wet corn field and began gathering the corn. It was nasty, cold work. The damp earth sent cold chills up through my limbs and as a result I was ill, and could do nothing for a week or more. In desperation I wrote the Reverend and being a man, I hoped he'd understand. I told him of my sickness and the circumstances, of Orlean's claim and of my crops to be put in. It was then April and soon the oats, wheat and barley should be seeded. It was a business letter altogether, but I never heard from him, and later learned that he had read only a part of the letter.

While in Chicago, one evening I had called at the house and found the household in a ferment of excitement, with everyone saying nothing and apparently trying to look as small and scarced as possible, while in their midst, standing like a jungle king and in a plaided bathrobe, the Reverend was pouring a storm of abuse upon his wife and shouting orders while the wife was trotting to and fro like a frightened lamb, protesting weakly. The way he was storming at her made me feel ashamed but after listening to his tirade for some fifteen minutes I was angry enough to knock him down then and there. He reminded

211

me more of a brute than a pious minister. When he had finally exhausted himself he turned without speaking to me and strode up the stairs, head reared back and carrying himself like a brave soldier returning from war. I wondered then how long it would be before I would be commanded as she had been. Shortly afterward I could hardly control the impulse to take her in my arms and comfort her. She was crying quietly and looked so pitiful. I was told she had been treated in a like manner off and on for thirty years.

As stated, I did not hear from the Reverend and when I wrote to Orlean I implied that I did not think her father much of a business man. Perhaps this was wrong, at least when I received another letter from her it contained the receipt for the payment on the claim, and the single sheet of paper comprising the letter conveyed the intelligence that since she thought it best not to marry me she was forwarding the receipt with thanks for my kindness and hopes for future success. I received the letter on Friday. Saturday night I went into Megory and took the early Sunday morning train bound for Chicago and to marry her, and while I did not think she had treated me just right I would not allow a matter of a trip to Chicago to stand in the way of our marriage. I had an idea her father was indirectly responsible. He and I were much unlike and disagreed in our discussions concerning the so-called negro problem, and in almost every other discussion in which we had engaged.

Arriving in Omaha I sent a telegram to Orlean asking her not to go to work that day, as I would be in Chicago in the morning. At the depot I called up the house and Claves answered the phone and was very impertinent, but before he said much Orlean took the receiver and without much welcome started to tell me about the criticisms of her father in my letters.

"You are not taking it in the right way," I hurriedly told her.

"I'll come to the house and we'll talk it over. You will see me, won't you?"

"Yes," she answered hesitatingly, appearing to be a little frightened. Then added, "I'll do you that honor."

The Reverend had returned to Southern Illinois, and when I entered the house the rest of the family appeared to have been holding a consultation in the kitchen, which they had, as Orlean informed me later, with Orlean standing poutingly to one side. She commenced telling me what she was not going to do, but I went directly to her, and gathered her in my arms, with her making a slight resistance but soon succumbing. I looked down at her still pouting face and remonstrated teasingly.

Ethel broke in, her voice resembling a scream, protesting against such boldness on my part, saying: "Orlean doesn't want you and she isn't going to go onto your old farm." Here Orlean silenced her saying that she would attend to that herself, and took me to the front part of the house, with her mother tagging after us in a sort of half-stupor and apparently not knowing what to do. We sat down on the davenport where she began giving me a lecture and declaring what she was not going to do. Her mother interposed something that angered me, though I do not now recall what it was, and a look of dissatisfaction came into my face which Orlean observed.

"Don't you scold mama," she finished. "Now, do you hear?"

"Yes, dear," I answered, meekly, with my arm around her waist and my face hidden behind her shoulder. "Anything more?"

"Well, well." She appeared at a loss to know what further to say or how to proceed.

Ethel remarked afterward to her mother that Orlean had not been near me a half hour until she was listening to everything I said.

She finally succeeded in getting off to work after commanding me to free her as she wanted to get away to think. Her mother bristled up with an, "I'll talk to you." This was entirely to my liking. I loved her mother as well as my own and had no fear that we would not soon agree, and we did. She couldn't be serious with me very long. She persisted in saying, however:

"I want my husband to know you are here and to know all about this. You must not expect to run in and get his daughter just like something wild, nor you just must not!"

"All right, mother," I assented. "But I must hurry back to Dakota, you know, for I can't lose so much time this time of year."

"You're the worst man I ever saw for always being in a hurry. I—I'll—well, I do declare!" And she bustled off to the kitchen with me following and talking.

"Oh, can't I get away from you? This is just awful, Mr. Devereaux."

"Don't you like the name?" I put in winningly and cutting off her discourse, and in spite of her attempt at seriousness she smiled.

"It is a beautiful name," she admitted, looking at me slyly out of her small black eyes. She was part Indian, just a trifle, but sufficient to give her black eyes instead of brown, as most colored people have, and she had long black hair.

Before Orlean returned from the store her mother and I were like mother and son and Orlean seemed pleased, while Ethel looked at Claves and admitted that I would get Orlean, anyhow. The only thing necessary now was to reach the elder, and the next morning we spent a couple of hours trying to locate him by telephone. We finally succeeded, as I thought, but he denied later he was the party, though I would have sworn to the voice being his as I could hear him distinctly. In answer to my statement that we were ready to marry he shouted in a frantic voice:

"I don't approve of it! I don't approve of it! I don't approve of it!" and kept shouting it over and over until the operator called the time was up.

A letter had been sent him by special delivery the day I arrived and the following morning a reply was received stating that if Orlean married me, without my convincing him that I was marrying her for love, and not to hold down a Dakota claim, she would be doing so without his consent. In discussing the matter later Ethel, who had become resigned to the inevitable, said:

"If you want to get along with papa you must flatter him. Just make him think he is a king."

"Ah," I thought. "Here is where I made my mistake."

I had started wrong. "Just make him think he is a king, His Majesty Newton Jasper." The idea kept revolving in my mind as I realized the reason I had not made good with him. I was too plain and sincere. I must flatter him, make him think he was what he was not, and my failure to do that was the reason for his listening to me in such an expressionless manner.

Somewhere I had read that to be a king was to look wise and say nothing. This is what he had done. Evidently he liked to feel great. I recalled the name he was known by, "the Reverend N. J.," and I had heard him spoken of jokingly as the "Great N. J." The N. J. was for Newton Jasper. Ha! Ha! The more I thought of his greatness the more amused I became. I might have settled the matter easily if I had no objection to flattering him. He arrived home the next morning and was sitting in the parlor when I called, trying to look serious, and surveying me as I entered, just as a king might have done a disobedient subject. I had been so free and without fear for so long that it was beyond my ability to shrivel up and drop as he continued to look me over. I proceeded to tell him all that I had written in my letter to him, the one he had not read, but did not intimate that I knew he had not read it.

In the dining room where we gathered a few minutes later, with the family assembled in mute attention, he asked Orlean whether she wanted to marry me and live in Dakota and she admitted that she did. Then turning to me he began a lengthy discourse with many ifs and if nots and kept it up until I cut in with:

"My dear people, when I first came to see Orlean I didn't profess love. Circumstances had not granted us the opportunity, but we entered a mutual agreement that we would wait and see whether we could learn to love each other or not." Hesitating a moment, I looked at Orlean and gaining confidence as I met her soft glance, I went on: "I cannot guarantee anything as to the future. We may be happy, and we may not, but I hope for the best."

That seemed to satisfy him and he was very nice about it afterward. Orlean and I had been to the court house the day previous and got the license, and when her father told us we should go and get the license we looked at each other rather sheepishly, and stammered out something, but went down town and bought a pair of shoes instead. When we arrived home preparations were being made for the wedding. The elder called up the homes of two bishops who lived in the city, and when he found one sick and the other out of town he was somewhat disappointed, as it had always been his desire to have his daughters married by a bishop. He had failed in the first instance and was compelled to accept the services of the pastor of one of the three large African M. E. Churches of the city at the wedding of Ethel, and had to call upon this pastor again but found he also was out of the city. He finally secured the services of another pastor, by whom we were married in the presence of some twenty or more near friends of the family, Orlean wearing her sister's wedding dress and veil. The dress was becoming and I thought her very beautiful. I wore a Prince Albert coat and trousers to match which belonged to Claves and were too small and tight, making me uncomfortable. I was not long in getting out of them after undergoing the ordeal of being kissed by all the ladies present. Mrs. Ewis invited us to spend the evening at her home and the next day we left for South Dakota.

CHAPTER XXXVI

A SNAKE IN THE GRASS

USUALLY in the story of a man's life, or in fiction, when he gets the girl's consent to marry, first admitting the love, the story ends; but with mine it was much to the contrary. The story did not end there, nor when we had married that afternoon at two o'clock. Instead, my marriage brought the change in my life which was the indirect cause of my writing this story. From that time adventures were numerous. We arrived in Megory several hours late and remained over night at a hotel, going to the farm the next morning and then to the house I had rented temporarily.

I breathed a sigh of relief when I looked over the fields, and saw that the boy I hired had done nicely with the work during my absence. The next night about sixty of the white neighbors gave us a charivari and my wife was much pleased to know there was no color prejudice among them. We purchased about a hundred dollars worth of furniture in the town and at once began house-keeping. My bride didn't know much about cooking, but otherwise was a good housekeeper, and willing to learn all she could. She was not a forceful person and could not be hurried, but was kind and good as could be, and I soon became very fond of her and found marriage much of an improvement over living alone.

In May we went up to her claim and put up a sod house and stayed there awhile, later returning to Megory county to look after the crops. Our first trouble occurred in about a month. I was still rather angry over the Reverend's obliging me to spend the money to go to Chicago. This had cost me a hundred dollars which I needed badly to pay the interest on my loan. Letters began coming from the company holding the mortgages, besides I had other obligations pending. I had only fifty dollars in the bank when I started to Chicago and while there drew checks on it for fifty more, making an overdraft of fifty dollars which it took me a month to get paid after returning home. The furniture required for housekeeping and improvements in connection with the homesteads took more money, and my sister went home to attend the graduation of another sister and I was required to pay the bills. My corn was gathered and I now shelled it. As the price in Megory was only forty cents at the elevators I hauled it to Victor, where I received seventy and sometimes seventy-five cents for it, but as it was thirty-five miles, that took time and the long drive was hard on the horses. Orlean's folks kept writing letters telling her she must send money to buy something they thought nice for her to have, and while no doubt not intending to cause any trouble, they made it very hard for me. Money matters are usually a source of trouble to the lives of newly-weds and business is so cold-blooded that it contrasts severely with love's young dream.

My position was a trying one for the reason that all the relatives on both sides seemed to take it for granted that I should have plenty of money, and nothing I could say or do seemed to change matters. From his circuit the Reverend wrote glowing letters to his "daughter and son," of what all the people were saying. Everybody thought she had married so well; Mr. Deveraux, or Oscar, as they put it, was of good family, a successful young man, and was rich. I hadn't written to him and called him "dear father."

Perhaps this is what I should have done. In a way it would have been easy enough to write, and since my marriage I had no letters to spend hours in writing. Perhaps I should have written to him, but when a man is in the position I faced, debts on one side and relatives on the other, I thought it would not do to write as I felt, and I could not write otherwise and play the hypocrite, as I had not liked him from the beginning, and now disliked him still more because I could find no way of letting him know how I felt. This was no doubt foolish, but it was the way I felt about it at the time. My father-in-law evidently thought me ungrateful, and wrote Orlean that I should write him or the folks at home occasionally, but I remained obdurate. I felt sure he expected me to feel flattered over the opinions of which he had written in regard to my being considered rich, but I did not want to be considered rich, for I was not. I had never been vain, and hating flattery, I wanted to tell her people the truth. I wanted them to understand, if they did not, what it took to make good in this western country, and that I had a load and wanted their encouragement and invited criticism, not empty praise and flattery.

Before I had any colored people to discourage me with their ignorance of business or what is required for success, I was stimulated to effort by the example of my white neighbors and friends who were doing what I admired, building an empire; and to me that was the big idea. Their parents before them knew something of business and this knowledge was a goodly heritage. If they could not help their children with money they at least gave their moral support and visited them and encouraged them with kind words of hope and cheer. The people in a new country live mostly on hopes for the first five or ten years. My parents and grandparents had been slaves, honest, but ignorant. My father could neither read nor write, had not succeeded in a large way, and had nothing to give me as a start, not even practical knowledge. My wife's parents were a little different, but it would have been better for me had her father been other than "the big preacher" as he was referred to, who in order to be at peace with, it was necessary to praise.

What I wanted in the circumstances I now faced was to be allowed to mould my wife into a practical woman who would be a help in the work we had before us, and some day, I assured her, we would be well to do, and then we could have the better things of life.

"How long?" She would ask, weeping. She was always crying and so many tears got on my nerves, especially when my creditors were pestering me with duns, and it is Hades to be dunned, especially when you have not been used to it.

"Oh!" I'd say. "Five or ten years."

And then she'd have another cry, and I would have to do a lot of petting and persuading to keep her from telling her mother. This all had a tendency to make me cross and I began to neglect kissing her as much as I had been doing, but she was good and had been a nice girl when I married her. She could only be made to stop crying when I would spend an hour or two petting and assuring her I still loved her, and this when I should have been in the fields. She would ask me a dozen times a day whether I still loved her, or was I growing tired of her so soon. She was a veritable clinging vine. This continued until we were both decidedly unhappy and then began ugly little quarrels, but when she would be away with my sister to her claim in Tipp county I would be so lonesome without her, simple as I thought she was, and days seemed like weeks.

One day she was late in bringing my dinner to the field where I was plowing, and we had a quarrel which made us both so miserable and unhappy that we were ashamed of ourselves. By some power for which we were neither responsible, our disagreements came to an end and we never quarreled again.

The first two weeks in June were hot and dry, and considerable damage was done to the crops in Tipp county and in Megory county also. The winds blew from the south and became so hot the young green plants began to fire, but a big rain on the twenty-fourth saved the crops in Megory county. About that time the Reverend wrote that he would come to see us after conference, which was then three months away.

One day we were going to town after our little quarrels were over, and I talked kindly with Orlean about her father and tried to overcome my dislike of him, for her sake. I had learned by that time just how she had been raised, and that was to praise her father. She would say:

"You know, papa is such a big man," or "He is so great."

She had begun to call me her great and big husband, and I think that had been the cause of part of our quarrels for I had discouraged it. I had a horror of praise when I thought how silly her father was over it, and she had about ceased and now talked more sensibly, weighing matters and helping me a little mentally.

We talked of her father and his expected visit. She appeared so pleased over the prospect and said:

"Won't he make a hit up here? Won't these white people be foolish over his fine looks and that beautiful white hair?" And she raised her hands and drew them back as I had seen her do in stroking her father's hair.

I agreed with her that he would attract some attention and changed the subject. When we returned home she gave me the letter to read that she had written to him. She was obedient and did try so hard to please me, and when I read in the letter she had written that we had been to town and had talked about him all the way and were anxious for him to visit us; that we had agreed that he would make a great impression with the people out here, I wanted very much to tell her not to send that letter as it placed me in a false light, and would cause him to think the people were going to be crazy about him and his distinguished appearance; but she was watching me so closely that I could not be mean enough to speak my mind and did not offer my usual criticism.

A short time before her father arrived, a contest was filed against Orlean's claim on the ground that she had never established a residence. We had established residence, but by staying much of the time in Megory county had laid the claim liable to contest. The man who filed the contest was a banker in Amro, this bank being one of the few buildings left there. I knew we were in for a big expense and lots of trouble, which I had feared, and had been working early and late to get through my work in Megory county and get onto her claim permanently.

We did not receive the Reverend's letter stating when he would arrive so I was not at the train to meet him, but happened to be in town on horse back. In answer to my inquiries, a man who had come in on the train gave me a description of a colored man who had arrived on the same train, and I knew that my father-in-law was in town. I went to the hotel and found he had left his baggage but had gone to the restaurant, where I found him. He seemed pleased to be in Megory and after I explained that I had not received his letter, I went to look up a German neighbor who was in town in a buggy, thinking I would have the Reverend ride out with him. When we got ready to go the German was so drunk and noisy that the Reverend was frightened and remarked cautiously that he did not know whether he wanted to ride out with a drunken man or not. The German heard him and roared in a still louder tone:

"You don't have to ride with me. Naw! Naw! Naw!"

The elder became more frightened at this and hurriedly ducked into the hotel, where he stayed. I hitched a team of young mules to the wagon the next morning and sent Orlean to town after him.

The Reverend seemed to be carried away with our lives on the Little Crow, and we got along fine until he and I got to arguing the race question, which brought about friction. It was as I had feared but it seemed impossible to avoid it. He had the most ancient and backward ideas concerning race advancement I had ever heard. He was filled to overflowing with condemnation of the white race and eulogy of the negro. In his idea the negro had no fault, nor could he do any wrong or make any mistake. Everything had been against him and according to the Reverend's idea, was still. This he would declare very loudly. From the race question we drifted to the discussion of mixed schools.

The Reverend had educated his girls with the intention of making teachers of them and would speak of this fact with much pride, speaking slowly and distinctly like one who has had years of oratory. He would insist that the public schools of Chicago have not given them a chance. "I am opposed to mixed schools," he would exclaim. "They are like everything else the white people control. They are managed in a way to keep the colored people down."

Here Orlean dissented, this being about the only time she did openly disagree with him. She was firm in declaring there was no law or management preventing the colored girls' teaching in Chicago if they were competent.

"In the first place," she carefully continued, "the school we attended in Ohio does not admit to teach in the city."

In order to teach in the city schools it is either necessary to be a graduate of the normal, or have had a certain number of years' experience elsewhere. I do not remember all the whys, but she was emphatic and continued to insist that it was to some extent the fault of the girls, who were not all as attentive to books as they should be; spending too much time in society or with something else that kept them from their studies, which impaired their chances when they attempted to enter the city schools.

She held up instances where colored girls were teaching in Chicago schools and had been for years, which knocked the foundation from his argument.

There are very few colored people in a city or state which has mixed schools, who desire to have them separated. The mixed schools give the colored children a more equal opportunity and all the advantage of efficient management. Separate schools lack this. Even in the large cities, where separate schools are in force, the advantage is invariably with the white schools.

Another advantage of mixed schools is, it helps to eliminate so much prejudice. Many ignorant colored people, as well as many ignorant white people, fill their children's minds with undue prejudice against each race. If they are kept in separate schools this line becomes more distinct, with one colored child filling the mind of other colored children with bad ideas, and the white child doing likewise, which is never helpful to the community. By nature, in the past at least, the colored children were more ferocious and aggressive; too much so, which is because they have not been out of heathenism many years. The mixed school helps to eliminate this tendency.

With the Reverend it was a self-evident fact, that the only thing he cared about was that it would be easier for the colored girls to teach, if the schools were separate. I was becoming more and more convinced that he belonged to the class of the negro race that desires ease, privilege, freedom, position, and luxury without any great material effort on their part to acquire it, and still held to the time-worn cry of "no opportunity."

Following this disagreement came another. I had always approved of Booker T. Washington, his life and his work in the uplift of the negro. Before his name was mentioned I had decided just about how he would take it, and I was not mistaken. He was bitterly opposed to the educator.

CHAPTER XXXVII

THE PROGRESSIVES AND THE
REACTIONARIES

I T IS NOT commonly known by the white people at large that a great number of colored people are against Mr. Washington. Being an educator and philanthropist, it is hard to conceive any reason why they should be opposed to him, but the fact remains that they are.

There are two distinct factions of the negro race, who might be classed as Progressives and Reactionaries, somewhat like the politicians. The Progressives, led by Booker T. Washington and with industrial education as the material idea, are good, active citizens; while the other class distinctly reactionary in every way, contend for more equal rights, privileges, and protection, which is all very logical, indeed, but they do not substantiate their demands with any concrete policies; depending largely on loud demands, and are too much given to the condemnation of the entire white race for the depredations of a few.

It is true, very true indeed, that the American negro does not receive all he is entitled to under the constitution. Volumes could be filled with the many injustices he has to suffer, and which are not right before God and man; yet when it is considered that other races in other countries are persecuted even more than the negro is in parts of the United States, there should be no reason why the American negro allows obvious prejudice to prevent his taking advantage of opportunities that surround him.

I have been called a "radical," perhaps I am, but for years I have felt constrained to deplore the negligence of the colored race in America, in not seizing the opportunity for monopolizing more of the many million acres of rich farm lands in the great northwest, where immigrants from the old world own many of acres of rich farm lands; while the millions of blacks, only a few hundred miles away, are as oblivious to it all as the heathen of Africa are to civilization.

In Iowa, for instance, where the number of farms total around two hundred and ten thousand, and include the richest land in the world, only thirty-seven are owned and operated by negroes, while South Dakota, Wisconsin, Minnesota, and North Dakota have many less. I would quote these facts to my father-in-law until I was darker in the face than I naturally am. He could offer no counter argument to them, but continued to vituperate the sins of the white people. He was a member in good standing of the reactionary faction of the negro race, the larger part of which are African M. E. ministers.

Since Booker T. Washington came into prominence they have held back and done what they could to impede and criticize his work, and cast little stones in his path of progress, while most of the younger members of the ministry are heart and soul in accord with him and are helping all they can. The older members are almost to a unit, with some exceptions, of course, against him and his industrial educational ideas.

A few years ago a professor in a colored university in Georgia wrote a book which had a tremendous sale. He claimed in his book that the public had become so over-enthused regarding Booker T. and industrial education, that the colored schools for literary training were almost forgotten, and, of course, were severely handicapped by a lack of funds. His was not criticism, but was intended to call attention of the public to the number of colored schools in dire need of funds, which on account of race prejudice in the south, must teach classics. This was true, although industrial education was the first means of lifting the ignorant masses into a state of good citizenship. Immediately following the publication of the volume referred to, thousands of anti-Booker T.'s proceeded to place the writer as representing their cause and formed all kinds of clubs in his honor, or gave their clubs his name. They pretended to feel and to have everyone else feel, that they had at last found a man who would lead them against Booker T. and industrial education.

They made a lot of noise for a while, which soon died out, however, as the author of the book was far too broad minded and intelligent in every way, to be a party to such a theory, much less, to lead a lot of reckless people, who never had and never would do anything for the uplifting of their race.

The Reverend and I could not in any way agree. He was so bitter against industrial education and the educator's name, that he lost all composure in trying to dodge the issue in our argument, and found himself up against a brick wall in attempting to belittle Mr. Washington's work. Most of the trouble with the elder was, that he was not an intelligent man, never read anything but negro papers, and was interested only in negro questions. He was born in Arkansas, but maintained false ideas about himself. He never admitted to having been born a slave, but he was nearly sixty years of age, and sixty years ago a negro born in Arkansas would have been born in slavery, unless his parents had purchased themselves. If this had been the case, as vain as he was, I felt sure he would have had much to say about it. He must have been born a slave, but of course had been young when freed. He had lived in Springfield, Missouri, after leaving Arkansas, and later moving to Iowa, where, at the age of twenty-seven years, he was ordained a minister and started to preach, which he had continued for thirty years or more. He never had any theological training. This was told me by my wife, and she added despairingly:

"Poor papa! He is just ignorant and hard-headed, and all his life has been associated with hard-headed negro preachers. He reads nothing but radical negro papers and wants everybody to regard him as being a brilliant man, and you might as well try to reason with two trees, or a brick wall, as to try to reason with him or Ethel. I'm so sorry papa is so ignorant. Mama has always tried to get him to study, but he would never do it. That's all."

We went up to the claims, taking the elder along. My sister had married and her husband was making hay on the claims.

I might have been more patient with the Reverend, if he had not been so full of pretense, when being plain and truthful would have been so much better and easier. I had quit talking to him about anything serious or anything that interested me, but would sit and listen to him talk of the big preachers, and the bishops, and the great negroes who had died years before. He seemed fond of talking of what they had done in the past and what more could be done in the future, if the white people were not so strongly banded against them. After this, his conversation would turn to pure gossip, such as women might indulge in. He talked about the women belonging to the churches of his district, whether they were living right or wrong, and could tell very funny stories about them.

In Dakota, like most parts of the west, people who have any money at all, carry no cash in the pocket, but bank their money and use checks. The people of the east and south, that is, the common people, seldom have a checking account, and, with the masses of the negroes, no account at all. During the summer Orlean had sent her father my checks with which to make purchases. The Reverend told me he checked altogether, but my wife had told me her father's ambition had always been to have a checking account, but had not been able to do so. I had to laugh over this, for it was no distinction whatever. We discussed the banking business and the elder tried to tell me that if a national bank went broke, the government paid all the depositors, while if it was a state bank, the depositors lost. As this was so far from correct, I explained the laws that governed national banks and state banks alike, as regards the depositors, in the event of insolvency. I did not mean to bring out such a storm but he flew into an accusation, exclaiming excitedly:

"That's just the way you are! You must have everything your way! I never saw such a contrary man! You won't believe anything!"

"But, Reverend," I remonstrated. "I have no 'way' in this. What I have quoted you is simply the law, the law governing national and state bank deposits, that you can read up on yourself, just the same as I have done. If I am wrong, I very humbly beg your pardon."

The poor old man was so chagrined he seemed hardly to know what to do, though this was but one of many awkward situations due to his ignorance of the most simple business matters. Another time he was trying to listen intelligently to a conversation relating to the development of the northwest, when I had occasion to speak of Jim Hill. Seeing he did not look enlightened, I repeated, this time referring to him as James J. Hill, of the Great Northern, and inquired if he had not heard of the pioneer builder.

"No, I never heard of him," he answered.

"Never heard of James J. Hill?" I exclaimed, in surprise.

"Why should I have heard of him," he said, answering my exclamation calmly.

"O, no reason at all," I concluded, and remained silent, but my face must have expressed my disgust at his ignorance, and he a public man for thirty years.

After this conversation I forced myself to remain quiet and listen to common gossip. Instead of being pleased to see us happy and Orlean contented, he would, whenever alone with her, discourage her in every way he could, sighing for sympathy, praising Claves and telling her how much he was doing for Ethel, and how much she, Orlean, was sacrificing for me.

The contest trial occurred while he was with us, and cost, to start with, an attorney's fee of fifty dollars, in addition to witnesses' expenses. I had bought a house in Megory and we moved it onto Orlean's claim. The Reverend helped with the moving, but he was so discouraging to have around. He dug up all the skeletons I left buried in M—pls and bared them to view, in deceitful ways.

We had decided not to visit Chicago that winter. The crop was fair, but prices were low on oats and corn, and my crops consisted mostly of those cereals. I tried to explain this to the Reverend when he talked of what we would have, Christmas, in Chicago.

"Now, don't let that worry you, my boy," he would say breezily. "I'll attend to that! I'll attend to that!"

"Attend to what?" I asked.

"Why, I'll send both of you a ticket."

"O, really, Reverend, I thank you ever so much, but I could not think of accepting it, and you must not urge it. We are not coming to Chicago, and I wish you would not talk of it so much with Orlean," I would almost plead with him. "She is a good girl and we are happy together. She wants to help me, but she's only a weak woman, and being so far away from colored people, she will naturally feel lonesome and want to visit home."

He paid no more attention to me than if I had never spoken. In fact, he talked more about Chicago than ever, saying a dozen times a day:

"Yes, children, I'll send you the money."

I finally became angry and told him I would not, under any circumstances whatever, accept such charity, and that what my money was invested in, represented a value of more than thirty thousand dollars, and how could I be expected to condescend to accept charity from him.

He had told me once that he never had as much as two hundred dollars at one time in his life. I did not want a row, but as far as I was concerned, I did not want anything from him, for I felt that he would throw it up to me the rest of his life. I was convinced that he was a vain creature, out for a show, and I fairly despised him for it.

At last he went home and Orlean and I got down to business, moving more of our goods onto the claim, and spending about one-third of the time there. We intended moving everything as soon as the corn was gathered. As Christmas drew near, her folks wrote they were looking for her to come home, the Reverend having told them that she was coming, and that he was going to send her the money for her to come. Her mother wrote about it in letter, saying she didn't think it was right. Just before Christmas, she wrote that maybe if she wrote Cousin Sam he would send her the money. Cousin Sam was a porter in a down town saloon. I felt so mortified that I swore I would never again have anything to do with her family. They never regarded my feelings nor our relations in the least, but wrote a letter every few days about who was coming to the house to see

Orlean Christmas, of who was going to have her at their homes for dinner when she came home, until the poor girl, with a child on the way, was as helpless as a baby, trying to be honest with all concerned. It had never been her lot to take the defensive.

My sister came down from her claim and took Orlean home with her. While she was in Tipp county a letter came from her father for her, and thinking it might be a matter needing immediate attention, I opened it and found a money order for eighteen dollars, sent from Cairo, with instructions when to start, and he would be home to meet her when she arrived, suggesting that I could come later.

I was about the maddest man in Megory when I was through reading the letter, fairly flying to the post office, enclosing the money order and all, with a curt little note telling what I had done; that Orlean was out on her claim and would be home in a few days, but that we were not coming to Chicago. I would have liked to tell him that I was running my own house, but did not do so. I was hauling shelled corn to a feeder in town, when Orlean came. She was driving a black horse, hitched to a little buggy I had purchased for her, and I met her on the road. I got out and kissed her fondly, then told what I had done. My love for her had been growing. She had been gone a week and I was so glad to see her and have her back with me. I took the corn on into town and when I returned home she had cleaned up the house, prepared a nice supper and had killed a chicken for the next day, which was Christmas. She then confessed that she had written her father that he could send the money.

"Now, dear," she said, as though a little frightened, "I'm so sorry, for I know papa's going to make a big row."

And he did, fairly burned the mail with scorching letters denouncing my action and threatening what he was liable to do about it, which was to come out and attend to me. I judged he did not get much sympathy, however, for a little while after Orlean had written him he cooled down and wrote that whatever Orlean and I agreed on was all right with him, though I knew nothing of what her letter contained.

The holidays passed without further event, excepting a letter from Mrs. Ewis, to my wife, in which she said she was glad that she had stayed in Dakota and stuck by her husband. The letter seemed a little strange, though I thought nothing of it at the time. A few months later I was to know what it meant, which was more than I could then have dreamed of. We were a lone colored couple, in a country miles from any of our kind, honest, hopeful and happy; we had no warning, nor if we had, would we have believed. Why, indeed, should any young couple feel that some person, especially one near and dear, should be planning to put asunder what God had joined together?

It was now the last of February and we expected our first-born in March. My wife had grown exceedingly fretful. Grandma was with us, having made proof on her homestead. Orlean kept worrying and wanting to go to her claim, talking so much about it, that I finally talked with some neighbor friends and they advised that it would be better to take her to the homestead, for if she continued to fret so much over wanting to be there, when the child was born, it might be injured in some way. When the weather became favorable, I wrapped her and grandma up comfortably, and sent them to the claim in the spring wagon, while I followed with a load of furniture, making the trip in a day and a half. We had close neighbors who said they would look after her while I went back after the stock. A lumber yard was selling out in Kirk, and I bought the coal shed, which was strongly built, being good for barns and granaries. Cutting it into two parts, I loaded one part onto two wagons and started the sixty miles to the claim. A thaw set in about the time I had the building as far as my homestead south of Megory. I decided to leave it there and tear down my old buildings and move them, instead. I received a letter from Orlean saying they were getting along nicely, excepting that the stove smoked considerably; and for me to be very careful with Red and not let him kick me. Red was a mule I had bought the summer before and was a holy terror for kicking.

My sister arrived that night from a visit to Kansas, and on hearing from Orlean that she was all right, I sent my sister on to her claim, and hiring more men, moved the balance of the building onto the old farm, tore down the old buildings, loaded them onto wagons, and finally got started again for Tipp county. That was on Saturday. The wind blew a gale, making me feel lonely and far from home. Sunday morning I started early out of Colone planning to get home that night, but the front axle broke and by the time we got another it was growing late. We started again and traveled about two miles, when the tongue broke, and by the time that was mended it was late in the afternoon. About six o'clock we pulled into Victor, tired and weary. The next day, when about five miles from home, we met one of the neighbors, who informed me that he had tried to get me over the phone all along the way; that my wife had been awfully sick and that the baby had been born, dead. It struck me like a hammer, and noting my frightened look, he spoke up quickly:

"But she's all right now. She had two doctors and didn't lack for attention."

On the way home I was so nervous that I could hardly wait for the horses to get there. I would not have been away at this time for anything in the world. I knew Orlean would forgive me, but we had not told her father. Orlean had told her mother and thought she would tell him. He made so much ado about everything, we hoped to avoid the tire of his burdensome letters, but now, with the baby born during my absence, and it dead, when we had so many plans for its future. It was to have been the first colored child born on the Little Crow, and we thought we were going to make history.

When I got to the claim I was weak in every way. My wife seemed none the worse, but my emotions were intense when I saw the little dead boy. Poor little fellow! As he lay stiff and cold I could see the image of myself in his features. My wife noticed my look and said:

"It is just like you, dear!"

That night we buried the baby on the west side of the draw. It should have been on the east, where the only trees in the township, four spreading willows, cast their shadows.

"Well, dear, we have each other," I comforted her as she cried.

Between sobs she tried to tell me how she had prayed for it to live, and since it had looked so much like me, she thought her heart would break.

When the child was born they had sent a telegram to her father which read:

"Baby born dead. Am well."

This was his first knowledge of it. We received a telegram that night that he was on the way and the next day he arrived, bringing Ethel with him. When he got out of the livery rig that brought them I could see Satan in his face. A chance had come to him at last. It seemed to say:

"Oh, now I'll fix you. Away when the child was born, eh?"

His very expression seemed jubilant. He had longed for some chance to get me and now it had arrived. He did not speak to me, but bounded into the room where my wife was, and she must have read the same thing in his expression, for, as he talked about it later, I learned the first thing she said was:

"Now, papa. You must not abuse Oscar. He loves me and is

kind and doing the best he can, but he is all tied up with debt."

He would tell this every few hours but I could see the evil of his heart in the expression of his eyes, leering at me, with hatred and malice in every look. He and Ethel turned loose in about an hour. From that time on, it was the same as being in the house with two human devils. They nearly raised the roof with their quarreling. Of the two, the Reverend was the worst, for he was cunning and deceitful, pretending in one sentence to love, and in the next taking a thrust at my emotions and home. I shall never forget his evil eyes.

Ethel would cry out in her ringing voice:

"You're practical! You're practical! You and your Booker T. Washington ideas!"

Then she would tear into a string of abusive words. One day, after the doctor had been to the house, he called me aside and said:

"Oscar, your wife is physically well enough, but is mentally sick. Something should be done so that she may be more quiet."

"Is she quite out of danger?" I asked.

He replied that she was. That night I told my wife of our conversation and the next day I left for Megory county.

CHAPTER XXXVIII

SANCTIMONIOUS HYPOCRISY

I WAS preparing to seed the biggest crop I had ever sown. With Orlean helping me, by bringing the dinner to the field and doing some chores, during the fall we had put the farm into winter wheat and I had rented the other Megory county farm. I hired a steam rig, to break two hundred acres of prairie on the Tipp county homesteads, for which I was to pay three dollars an acre and haul the coal from Colone, a distance of thirty-five miles, the track having been laid to that point on the extension west from Calias.

I intended to break one hundred acres with my horses and put it into flax. I had figured, that with a good crop, it would go a long way toward helping me get out of debt. I worked away feverishly, for I had gotten deeper into debt by helping my folks get the land in Tipp county.

After putting in fifteen acres of spring wheat, I hauled farm machinery to my sister's claim, and then began hauling coal from Colone. It was on Friday. I was driving two horses and two mules abreast, hitched to a wagon loaded with fifty hundred pounds of coal, and trailing another with thirty hundred pounds, when one of the mules got unruly, going down a hill, swerved to one side, and in less time than it takes to tell it, both wagons had turned turtle over a fifteen-foot embankment and I was under eight thousand pounds of coal, with both wagons upside down and the hind wagonbox splintered almost to kindling. That I was not hurt was due to the fact that the grade had been built but a few days previously, had not settled and the loose dirt had prevented a crash. I attempted to jump when I saw the oncoming disaster, but caught my foot in the brake rope which pulled me under the loads.

A day and a half was lost in getting the wreck cleared so I could proceed to my sister's claim, from where I had intended going home to my wife, fifteen miles away. I had left the Reverend in charge after he and Ethel had said about all the evil things words could express, and he, finding that I was inclined to be peaceful, had shown his hatred of me in every conceivable manner, until Orlean, who could never bear noise or quarreling, decided it would be better that I go away and perhaps he would quit. I did not get home that trip on account of the delay caused by the wreck, but sent my sister with a letter, stating that I would come home the next trip, and describing the accident.

I went back to Colone, and while eating supper someone told me three colored people were in Colone, and one of them was a sick woman. I could hardly believe what I heard. My appetite vanished and I arose from the table, paid the cashier and left the place, going to the hotel around the corner, and there sat my wife. I went to her side and whispered:

"Orlean, what in heaven's name are you doing here? And why did you come out in such weather."

She was still very sick and wheezed when she answered, trembling at the same time:

"You said I could go home until I got well."

"Yes, I know," I answered, controlling my excitement. "But to leave home in such weather is foolhardy."

It had been snowing all day and was slippery and cold outside.

"And, besides," I argued, "you should never have left home until I returned. Didn't you get my letter?" I inquired, looking at her with a puzzled expression.

"No," she replied, appearing bewildered. "But I saw Ollie hand something to papa."

I then recalled that I had addressed the letter to him.

"But," I went on, "I wrote you a letter last week that you should have received not later than Saturday."

"I— I— I never received it," she answered, and seemed frightened.

I could not understand what had taken place. I had left my wife two weeks before, feeling that I held her affections, and had thought only of the time we'd be settled at last, with her well again.

The Reverend had said so much about her going home that I had consented, but had stipulated that I would wait until she was better and would then see whether we could afford it or not.

Suddenly a horrible suspicion struck me with such force as almost to stagger me, but calming myself, I decided to talk to the elder. He came in about that time and looked very peculiar when he saw me.

The town was full of people that night and he had some difficulty in getting a room, but had finally succeeded in getting one in a small rooming house, and to it we now helped Orlean, who was anything but well.

As we carried her, I could hardly suppress the words that came to my lips, to say to him when we got into the room, but thought it best not to say anything. Ethel, who was sitting there when we entered, never deigned to speak to me, but her eyes conveyed the enmity within. The Reverend was saying many kind words, but I was convinced they were all pretense and that he was up to some dirty trick. I was further convinced that he not only was an arrant hypocrite, but an enemy of humanity as well, and utterly heartless. When he and Ethel had entered our home three weeks before, neither shed a tear nor showed any emotion whatever, and had not even referred to the death of the baby, but set up a quarrel that never ceased after I went away.

"Reverend," I said. "Will you and Ethel kindly leave the room for a few minutes? I would like to speak with Orlean alone."

They never deigned to move an inch, but finally the Reverend said:

"We'll not leave unless Orlean says so."

In that moment he appeared the most contemptible person I ever knew. My wife began crying and said she wanted to see her mother, that she was sick, and wanted to go home until she got well. I was angry all over and turned on the preacher, exclaiming hotly:

"Rev. McCraline, I left you in charge of my wife out of respect for you as her father, but," here I thundered in a terrible voice, "you have been up to some low-lived trick and if I thought you were trying to alienate my wife's affections, or had done so, I would stop this thing right here and sue you, if you were worth anything."

At this he flushed up and answered angrily

"I'm worth as much as you."

He was a poor hand at anything but quarreling, but knowing we'd make a scene, I said no more. It was a long night, Orlean was restless, and wheezed and coughed all through the night.

I have wondered since why I did not take the bull by the horns and settle the matter then, but guess it was for the sake of peace, that I've accepted the situation and remained quiet. I decided it would be best to let her go home without a big row, and when she had recovered, she could come home, and all would be well.

My wife had informed me that Claves kept up the house, paid for the groceries and half of the installments, while her father paid for the other half, but never bought anything to eat, nor sent any money home, only bringing eggs, butter, and chickens when he came into the city three or four times a year. But Claves' name was not on the contract for the home, only her father's name appearing. Her father was extremely vain and I had not pleased him because I was independent, and he did not like independent people. She also told me that her father always kept up a row when he was at home, but always charged it to everybody else.

The next morning, just before we started for the depot, I said:

"I'll step into the bank and get a check cashed and give Orlean some money. I haven't much, but I want her to have her own money."

"Never mind, my son, just never mind. I can get along," said the Reverend, keeping his head turned and appearing ill at ease, though I thought nothing of that at the time.

"I wouldn't think of such a thing!" I answered, protesting that he was not able to pay her way. "I wouldn't think of allowing her to accept it."

"Now! Now! Why do you go on so? Haven't I told you I have enough?" he answered in a tenor voice, trying to appear winsome.

Feeling that I knew his disposition, I said no more, but as we were passing the bank, I started to enter, saying to my wife:

"I am going to get you some money."

She caught me by the sleeve and cried excitedly "No! No!

No! Don't, because I have money." Hesitating a moment and repeating, "I have money."

"You have money?" I repeated, appearing to misunderstand her statement. "How did you get money?"

"Had a check cashed," she answered nervously.

"O, I see!" I said. "How much?"

"Fifty dollars," she answered, clinging to my arm.

"Good gracious, Orlean!" I exclaimed, near to fright. "We haven't got that much in the bank."

"Oh! Oh! I didn't want to," and then called to her father, who was just coming with the baggage:

"Papa! Papa! You give Oscar back that money. He hasn't got it. Oh! Oh! I didn't want to do this, but you said it would be all right, and that the cashier at the bank, where you got it cashed, called up the bank in Calias and said the check was all right. Oh! Oh!" she went on, beside herself with excitement, and holding her arms out tremblingly and repeating: "I didn't want to do this."

I can see the look in his face to this day. All the hypocrisy and pretense vanished, leaving him a weak, shame-faced creature, and looking from one side to the other stammered out:

"I didn't do it! I didn't do it! You— You— You know, you told her she should write a check for any money she needed and she did it, she did it."

Here again my desire for peace overruled my good judgment. Instead of stopping the matter then and there, I spoke up gravely, saying:

"I don't mind Orlean's going home. In fact, I want her to go home and to have anything to help her get well and please her, but I haven't the money to spare. Her sickness, with a doctor coming into the country twice daily, has been very expensive, and we just have not the money, that is all."

When he saw I was not going to put a stop to it, he took courage and spoke sneakingly:

"Well, the man in the bank at Carlin called up the bank of Calias, and they said the money was there."

"O," I said, "as far as that goes, I had five hundred dollars there last week, it has all been checked out, but some of the checks likely are still out."

I took twenty-five dollars of the money and gave Orlean twenty-five dollars. Her ticket was eighteen dollars. I went with them as far as Calias, to see how my account stood. I kissed Orlean good-bye before leaving the train at Calias, then I went directly to the bank and deposited the twenty-five dollars. The checks I had given had come in that morning, and even after depositing the twenty-five, I found my account was still overdrawn thirty dollars.

CHAPTER XXXIX

BEGINNING OF THE END

I WAITED to hear from my wife in Chicago but at the end of two weeks I had not heard from her, although I had written three letters, and a week later I journeyed to Colone and took a train for Chicago. When I called at the house the next day her mother admitted me, but did not offer to shake hands. She informed me Orlean was out, but that it was the first time she had been out, as she had been very sick since coming home. When I asked her why Orlean had not written, she said:

"I understand you have mistreated my child."

"Mistreated Orlean!" I exclaimed. Then, looking into her eyes, I asked slowly, "Did Orlean tell you that?"

"No," she answered, looking away, "but my husband did."

Gradually, I learned from her, that the Reverend had circulated a report that Orlean was at death's door when he came to her bedside; if he had not arrived when he did, she would have died, and when she was well enough to travel, he brought her home.

It was at last clear to me, as I sat with bowed head and feeling bewildered and unable to speak. I recalled the words of Miss Ankin eighteen months before, "the biggest rascal in the

Methodist church." I remembered the time I had called and saw him driving his wife, who was now sitting before me, and the rest of it. I saw all that he had done. He had abused this woman for thirty years, and here and now, out of spite and personal malice, because I had criticized the action of certain members of the race, and eulogized the work of Booker T. Washington, whom the elder, along with many of the older members of the ministry, hated and would not allow his name mentioned in his home, I was to lose my wife, to pay the penalty.

He had disliked me from the beginning, but there had been no way he could get even. He was "getting even," spiting me, securing my wife by coercion, and now spreading a report that I was mistreating her, in order to justify his action.

"Mrs. McCraline," I said, sneaking in a firm tone, "Do you believe this?"

Evading the direct question, she answered:

"You should never have placed yourself or Orlean in such a position." And then I understood. When Orlean had written her mother of the coming of the child, Mrs. McCraline had not written or told the Reverend about it.

I now understood, further, that she never told him anything, and never gave him any information if she could avoid it. What my wife had told me was proving itself, that is, that they got along with her father by avoiding any friction. He could not be reasoned with, but I could not believe any man would be mean enough to deliberately break up a home, and that the home of his daughter, for so petty a reason. It became clear to me that he ruled by making himself so disagreeable, that everyone near gave in to him, to have peace.

He had only that morning gone to his work. On hearing me, Ethel came downstairs and called up Claves. A few minutes later her mother called me, saying Claves wanted to talk to me.

When I took the receiver and called "hello," he answered like a crazy man. I said:

"What is the matter? I do not understand what you are talking about."

"What are you doing in my house, after what you said about me?" he shouted excitedly.

"Said about you?" I asked.

"Yes," he replied, "I hear you treated my wife like a dog, after I sent her out there to attend to your wife, called me all kinds of bad names, and said I was only a fifteen-cent jockey."

"Treated your wife ugly, and called you a jockey," here I came to and said to myself that here was some more of the elder's work, but I answered. Claves: "I haven't the faintest idea of what you are talking about. I treated your wife with the utmost courtesy while she was in Dakota, I never mentioned your name in any such terms as you refer to, and I am wholly at a loss to understand the condition of affairs I find here. I am confused over it all."

"Well," he answered, "suppose you come down to where I work and we will talk it over."

"I'll do that," I answered, and went down town where he worked on Wabash avenue.

One thing I had noticed about him was, that while he was ignorant, he was at least an honest, hard-working fellow, but was kept in fear by his wife and the elder. I saw after talking to him, that he, like Mrs. McCraline, did not believe a word of what the Reverend had told about my mistreating his daughter, and that he submitted to the elder, as the rest of the family did, for the sake of peace. But they were all trained and avoided saying anything about the elder.

During the conversation with Claves he told me he kept up the house, paid all the grocery bills, and half the payments. He had been advanced to a salary of eighteen dollars a week and seemed to be well liked by the management.

I went to a hotel run by colored people, and at about seven-thirty that evening, called up the house to see if Orlean had returned. She came to the phone but before we had said much, were accidentally cut off. Hearing her voice excited me, and I wanted to see her, so hung up the receiver and hurried to the house, some ten or twelve blocks away. When I rang the bell, Claves came to the door. Before he could let me enter, Ethel came running down the stairs, screaming as loudly as she could:

"Don't let him in! Don't let him in! You know what papa said! Don't you let him in," and continued screaming as loud as possible.

I heard my wife crying in the back room. Claves had his hat on and came outside, saying:

"For God's sake, Ethel, hush up! You'll have all the neighborhood out."

She continued to scream, and to stop her, he closed the door. We went together on State street and I took a few Scotch highballs and cocktails to try to forget it.

The next day being Sunday, Claves said he would try to get Ethel off to church and then I could slip in and see Orlean, but she refused to go and when I called up, about the time I thought she would be gone, she was on guard. My wife was at the phone and told me to come over and she would try to slip out, but when I called, Ethel had made her go to bed. It seemed that she ran the house and all in it, when the elder was away. Mrs. McCraline came outside, took me by the arm and led me over to Groveland park, near the lake. Here she unfolded a plan whereby I should find a room nearby, and she would slip Orlean over to it, but this proved as unsuccessful as the other attempt, to steal a march on Ethel. She held the fort and I did not get to see my wife but one hour during the four days I was in Chicago. That was on Tuesday following, after Claves had tried every trick and failed to get Ethel away. This time he succeeded by telling her I had left town, but when I had been in the house an hour, Ethel came and started screaming. I had to get out before she would stop.

The next day I called up and suggested to Orlean that I bring a doctor and leave her in his charge for I must return to Dakota. She consented and I went to a young negro doctor on State street and took him to the house, but when we arrived, Ethel would not admit us. The doctor and I had roomed together before I left Chicago, while he was attending the Northwestern Medical School, and we had always been good friends. He had been enthusiastic over my success in the west and it made me feel dreadfully embarrassed when we were refused admittance. When I called up the house later Ethel came to the phone, and said:

"How dare you bring a 'nigger doctor' to our house? Why, papa has never had a negro doctor in his house. Dr. Bryant is our doctor."

Dr. Bryant, a white doctor, is said to have the biggest practice among colored people, of any physician. That recalled to my mind some of the elder's declarations of a short time before. He had said on more than one occasion:

"I am sacrificing my life for this race," and would appear much affected.

After I returned home, my wife began writing nice letters, and so did Claves, who had done all a hen-pecked husband could do to help my wife and me. He wrote letters from the heart, declaring his intention to be more than a friend. He would be a brother. I received a letter from him, which read:

Chicago, Ill., May 30, 19——.

DEAR FRIEND DEVEREAUX:

Your kind and welcome letter was received a few days ago and the reason you did not receive my last letter sooner was because I left it for Ethel to mail, and she didn't do so. I am glad to hear you are getting your flax in good shape, and the prospects are fair for a good crop, and now I will tell you about Orlean. She seems happier of late than she has been at any time since she came home. Now, I don't know how you will feel, but I know it relieves my conscience, when I say that your wife loves you, and talks of you—to me—all the time.

Those papers and pamphlets you sent telling all about the display Nicholson brothers had on at the Omaha land show. She had opened it and when I came home she told me she could not wait because she was so anxious to hear about the Little Crow. She told me that Nicholson brothers were your best friends. I imagine they must be smart fellows for every paper in the batch you sent me had something about them in it. She took the money you sent her and bought some shoes and had some pictures made, so as to send you one. Mrs. Warner was over the next day, and said; "Where did you get the shoes?" and she answered, "My husband sent them to me."

Now, I hope you will not worry because she told me as soon as she was well enough she was going back to Dakota, and as for me, I intend to be more than a friend to you. I'm going to be a brother.

From your dear friend,
E. M. CLAVES.

My wife had written at the same time and used many "we" and "ours" in her letter, and I felt the trouble would soon be over and she would be at home.

That was the last letter I received from Claves, and when I heard from my wife again, it was altogether different. Instead of an endearing epistle, it was one of accusation, downright abusive. I made no complaint, nor did I write to Claves to inquire why he had ceased writing. I had always judged people by their convictions and in this I knew the cause.

CHAPTER XL

THE MENNONITES

DURING the first half of the sixteenth century, Menno Simons founded a denomination of Christians in Friesland, a province of the Netherlands. Many of these Mennonites settled in Northern Germany. This religious belief was opposed to military service and about the close of the American Revolution the Mennonites began emigrating, until more than fifty thousand of their number had found homes west of the Dneiper, near the Black Sea, in Southern Russia, around Odessa. These people were fanatical in their belief, rejected infant baptism and original sin, believing in baptism only on profession of faith, and were opposed to theological training.

In Russia, as in Germany, they led lives of great simplicity, both secularly and religiously and lived in separate communities.

The gently rolling lands, with a rich soil, responded readily to cultivation, and history proves the Germans always to have been good farmers. The Mennonites found peace and prosperity in southern Russia, until the Crimean war. Being opposed to military service, when Russia began levying heavy taxes on their lands and heavier toll from their families, by taking the strong young men to carry on the war, the Mennonites became dissatisfied under the Russian government, and left the country in great numbers, removing to America, and settling along the Jim river in South Dakota.

Among these settlers was a family by the name of Wesinberger, who had grown prosperous, their forefathers having gone to Russia among the first, although they were not Mennonites. Christopher the youngest son, was among those drawn to go to the war, but the Wesinbergers were properous, and paid the examining physician twelve hundred and fifty rubles (about one thousand dollars) to have Christopher "made sick" and pronounced unfit for service. With the approach of the Russian-Japanese War, when it was seen that Russia would be forced into war with Japan, the boys having married, and with sons of their own, who would have to "draw," the Wesinberger brothers sold their land and set sail for America. At the time the war broke out, John and Jacob were living on homesteads, in the county adjoining Tipp county on the north, Christopher having settled in western Canada.

It was while they were breaking prairie near my sister's homestead, that I became acquainted with the former, who, at that time owned a hundred and fifty head of cattle, seventy-five head of horses, hogs, and all kinds of farm machinery, besides a steam prairie breaking outfit and fifteen hundred acres of land between them.

During rainy days along in April, to pass the time away, I would visit them, and while sitting by the camp fire was told of what I have written above, but where they interested me most was when they discussed astronomy and meteorology. They could give the most complete description of the zodiacal heavens and the different constellations. It seems that astronomy had interested their ancestors before leaving Germany nearly one hundred and thirty years before, and it had been taught to each succeeding generation. They seemed to know the position of each planet, and on several occasions when the nights were clear, with a powerful telescope, they would try to show them to me, but as I knew little or nothing of astronomy, I understood but little of their discussions concerning the heliocentric longitude of all the planets, or the points at which they would appear if seen from the sun.

Before many months rolled around I had good reason to believe at least a part of what they tried to explain to me, and that was, that according to the planets we were nearing a certain Jupiter disturbance.

"And what does that mean?" I asked.

"That means," they explained, "It will be dry."

"Jupiter" said John, as he leisurely rolled a cigarette, "circumnavigates the sun once while the earth goes around it twelve times. In Russia Jupiter's position got between the sun and the constellation Pisces, Aries, Taurus and Gemini, it was invariably wet and cool and small grain crops were good, but as it passed on and got between the sun and the constellations Libra and Scorpio it was always followed by a minimum of rainfall and a maximum heat, which caused a severe drouth."

They had hoped it would be different in America, but explained further that when they had lived in Russia it commenced to get dry around St. Petersburg, Warsaw and all northern Russia a year or so before it did in southern Russia.

They had relatives living around Menno, in Hutchinson County, South Dakota, who had witnessed the disastrous drouth during Cleveland's administration. Jupiter was nearing the position it had then occupied and would, in sixty days, be at the same position it had been at that time.

While few people pay any attention to weather "dopsters," I did a little thinking and remembered it had been dry in southern Illinois at that time, and I began to feel somewhat uneasy.

According to their knowledge, if the same in southern America as it had been in southern Russia, it would begin to get dry about a year before the worst drouth, then a very dry year, the third year would begin to improve, and after the fourth year conditions would again become normal, but the concensus of their opinion was there would be a drouth.

CHAPTER XLI

THE DROUTH

CLOUDY and threatening day in May, there came an inch of rainfall. I had completed sowing two hundred and fifty acres of flax a few days before, and soon everything looked beautiful and green. I felt extremely hopeful.

During the six years I had been farming in Dakota, I had raised from fair to good crops every year. The seasons had been favorable, and if a good crop had not been raised, it was not the fault of the soil or from lack of rainfall. The previous year had not been as wet as others, but I had raised a fair crop, and at this time had four hundred and ten acres in crop and one hundred and ten acres rented out, from which I was to receive one third of the crop. I had come west with hopes of bettering my financial condition and had succeeded fairly well.

Around me at this time others had grown prosperous, land had advanced until some land adjoining Megory had brought one hundred dollars per acre, and land a few miles from town sold for fifty to eighty dollars per acre.

Before settling in the west I had read in real estate advertisements all about the wheat land that could be bought from ten to twenty-five dollars per acre, that would raise from twenty-five to forty bushels of wheat to the acre. While all this was quite possible I had never raised over twenty-five bushels per acre, and mostly harvested from ten to twenty. I had wondered, before I left Chicago, how, at a yield of thirty bushels per acre (and for the last seven or eight years prices had ranged from seventy cents to one dollar per bushel for wheat) the farmers could spend all the money. Of course, I had learned, in six years, that twenty-five to forty or fifty bushels per acre, while possible, was far from probable, and considerably above the average.

The average yield for all wheat raised in the United States is about fourteen bushels per acre, but crops had averaged from fair to good all over the northwest for some fifteen or sixteen years, with some exceptions, and the question I had heard asked years before, "Will the drouth come again?" was about forgotten.

During the three years previous to this time, poor people from the east, and around Megory and Calias as well, who were not able to pay the prices demanded for relinquishments and deeded lands in Megory, Tipp county, or the eastern states, had flocked by thousands to the western part of the state and taken free homesteads. At the beginning of this, my seventh season in Dakota, the agricultural report showed an exceedingly large number of acres had been seeded, and the same report which was issued June eighth, reported the condition of all growing crops to be up to the ten-year average and some above.

It was on Sunday. I had quit breaking prairie on account of the ground being too dry, and while going along the road, I noticed a field of spelt that looked peculiar. Going into the field, I dug my fingers into the soil, and found it dry. I could not understand how it had dried out so quickly; but thinking it would rain again in a few days, it had been but ten days since the rain, I thought no more about it. The following week, although it clouded up and appeared very threatening, the clouds passed and no rain fell. On Saturday I drove into Ritten, and on the way again noticed the peculiar appearance of the growing plants. It was the topic of discussion in the town, but no one seemed willing to admit that it was from the lack of moisture. The weather had been very hot all week and the wind seemed to blow continually from the south.

In past years, after about two days of south winds, we were almost sure to have rain. The fact that the wind had blown from the south for nearly two weeks and no rain had fallen caused everybody to be anxious. That night was cloudy, the thunder and lightning lasted for nearly two hours, but when I went to the door, I could see the stars, and the next day the heat was most intense.

The Wesinbergers had said the heavens would be ablaze with lightning and resound with peals of thunder but that they were only solstice storms, coming up in unusual directions, and that such storms were characteristic of a dry season. Furthermore, that heavy, abnormal rains would occur in scattered localities, at the same time, but they would be few and far apart.

June fifteenth I took my sister to Victor to make proof on her homestead, and from there drove to Megory, stopping in Calias to send my wife a telegram to the effect that I felt I was going to be sick and for her to draw a draft on the Bank of Calias, and come home. The telegram was not answered.

Next morning my sister left for Kansas, and that afternoon a heavy downpour of rain fell all over Megory county and as far west as Victor, but north of Ritten, where I had my flax crop, there was scarcely sufficient rain to lay the dust. On that day the hot winds set in and lasted for seven weeks, the wind blowing steadily from the south all the while.

I had never before, during the seven years, suffered to any

extent from the heat, but during that time I could not find a cool place. The wind never ceased during the night, but sounded its mournful tune without a pause. Then came a day when the small grain in Tipp county was beyond redemption, and rattled as leaves in November. The atmosphere became stifling, and the scent of burning plants sickening.

My flax on the sod, which was too small to be hurt at the beginning of the drouth, began to need rain, and reports in all daily papers told that the great heat wave and the drouth in many places were worse than in Tipp county. All over the western and northern part of the state, were localities where it had not rained that season. Potatoes, wheat, oats, flax, and corn, in the western part of the state, had not sprouted, and, it was said, in a part of Butte county, where seed had been sown four inches deep the year before, there had not been enough rain since to make it sprout.

The government had spent several million dollars damming the Belle Fourche river for the purpose of irrigation, and the previous autumn, when it had been completed, the water in it had been run onto the land, to see how it would work, and since had been dry. No snow had fallen in the mountains during the winter, and all the rivers were as dry as the roads; while all the way from the gulf, to Canada, the now protracted drouth was burning everything in its wake.

At Kansas City, where the treacherous Kaw empties its waters into the Missouri, and had for years wrought disaster with its notorious floods, drowning out two and sometimes three crops in a single spring, was nearly dry, and the crops were drying up throughout its valley.

I spent the Fourth of July in Victor, where the people shook their heads gravely and said, "Tipp county will never raise a crop." The crops had dried up in Tipp county the year before. I read that the railroad men who run from Kansas City to Dodge City reported that the pastures through Kansas were so dry along the route, that a louse could be seen crawling a half mile away. In parts of Iowa the farmers commenced to put their stock in pens and fed them hay from about the middle of June, there being no feed in the pastures. Through eastern Nebraska, western Iowa and southern Minnesota, the grasshoppers began to appear by the millions, and proceeded to head the small grain. To save it, the farmers cut and fed it to stock, in pens.

The markets were being overrun with thin cattle from the western ranges, where the grass had never started on account of lack of moisture. I watched my flax crop and early in July noticed it beginning to wilt, then millions of army worms began cutting it down. On the eleventh I left for Megory county, with my stock, to harvest the winter wheat there. It had been partially saved by the rain in June. The two hundred and eighty-five acres of flax was a brown, sickly-looking mess, and I was badly discouraged, for outside of my family trouble, I had borrowed my limit at the bank, and the flax seed, breaking, and other expenses, had amounted to eleven hundred dollars.

About this time the settlers all over the western highlands began to desert their claims. Newspapers reported Oklahoma burned to a crisp, and Kansas scorched, from Kansas City to the Colorado line. Homesteaders to the north and west of us began passing through the county, and their appearance presented a contrast to that of a few years before. Fine horses that marched bravely to the land of promise, drawing a prairie schooner, were returning east with heads hanging low from long, stringy necks, while their alkalied hoofs beat a slow tattoo, as they wearily dragged along, drawing, in many cases, a dilapidated wagon over which was stretched a tattered tarpaulin; while others drew rickety hacks or spring wagons, with dirty bedding and filthy looking utensils. These people had not made a dollar in the two years spent on their homesteads. At Pierre, it was said, seven hundred crossed the Missouri in a single day, headed east; while in the settlements they had left, the few remaining settlers went from one truck patch to another, digging up the potatoes that had been planted in the spring, for food.

One day I crossed the White river and went to visit the Wisenbergers, who lived seventeen miles to the north. On the way, out of forty-seven houses I passed, only one had an occupant. The land in that county is underlaid with a hardpan about four inches from the surface, and had not raised a crop for two years. The settlers had left the country to keep from starving. As I drove along the dusty road and gazed into the empty houses through the front doors that banged to and fro with a monotonous tone, from the force of the hot south winds, I felt lonely and faraway; the only living thing in sight being an occasional dog that had not left with his master, or had returned, but on seeing me, ran, with tucked tail, like a frightened coyote.

Merchants were being pressed by the wholesale houses. The recent years had been prosperous, and it is said prosperity breeds contempt and recklessness. The townspeople and many farmers had indulged lavishly in chug-chug cars. Bankers and wholesale houses, who had always criticised so much automobilism, were now making some wish they had never heard the exhaust of a motor. In addition to this the speculators were loaded to the guards, with lands carrying as heavy mortgage as could be had—which was large—for prosperity had caused loan companies to increase the amount of their loans. No one wanted to buy. Every one wanted to sell. The echo of the drouth seventeen years before and the disaster which followed, rang through the country and had the effect of causing prices to slump from five to fifteen dollars per acre less than a year before.

Now what made it worse for Tipp county was, that it had been opened when prosperity was at its zenith. The people were money mad. Reckless from the prosperity which had caused them to dispense with caution and good judgment, they were brought suddenly to a realization of a changed condition. The new settlers, all from eastern points, came into Tipp county, seeing Tipp county claims worth, not six dollars per acre, the price charged by the Government, but finding ready sales at prices ranging from twenty-five to forty-five dollars, and even fifty dollars per acre. They had spent money accordingly. And now, when the parched fields frowned, and old Jupiter Pluvius refused to speak, the community faced a genuine panic.

Came a day, sultry and stifling with excessive heat, when I drove back to the claims. Everywhere along the way were visible the effects of the drouth. Vegetation had withered, and the trails gave forth clouds of dust.

Late in the afternoon clouds appeared in the northwest and the earth trembled with the resounding peals of thunder. The lightning played dangerously near, and then, like the artillery of a mighty battle, the storm broke loose and the rain fell in torrents, filling the draws and ravines, and overflowing the creeks, which ran for days after. All over the north country the drouth was broken and plant life began anew.

My wheat threshed about eight hundred bushels, and when marketed, the money received was not sufficient to pay current expenses. Therefore, I could not afford the outlay of another trip to Chicago, but wrote many letters to Orlean, imploring her to return, but all in vain.

During the summer I had received many letters from people in Chicago and southern Illinois, denouncing the action of the Elder, in preventing my wife from returning home. The contents of these letters referred to the matter as an infamous outrage, and sympathized with me, by hoping my wife would have courage to stand up for the right. I rather anticipated, that with so much criticism of his action by the people belonging to the churches in his circuit, he would relent and let her return home; but he remained obstinate, the months continued to roll by, and my wife stayed on.

I had not written her concerning the drouth, which had so badly impaired crops. I knew her people read all the letters she received, and felt that with the knowledge in their possession that my crop had been cut short, along with the rest, would not help my standing. They would be sure to say to her, "I told you so." The last letter that I received from my wife, that year, was written early in the fall, in answer to a letter that I wrote her, and in which I had sent her some money, with which to buy some things for my grandmother. When Orlean had been in Dakota, she had been very fond of my grandmother, and had asked about her in every letter, whether the letter was kind or abusive, as regarded me. My wife's letter stated that she had received the money, and thanked me, also stated that she would get the things for "Grandma" that day. Neither grandmother nor I received the things.

I was so wrought up over it all, yet saw no place where I could get justice. In order to show the Reverend that he was being criticized by friends of the family, I gathered up some half dozen or more letters, including the last one from Claves and one from Mrs. Ewis, and sent them to him. The one from Mrs. Ewis related how he had written to her, just before he took my wife away, saying that she was in dire need, and wanted to borrow twenty-five dollars to bring her home. Needless to say, she had not sent it, nor assisted him in any other way, in helping to break up the home. As a result, she said, he had not spoken to her since.

I learned later that the letters I had sent had made him terribly angry. I received a letter from him, the contents of which were about the same as his conversation had been, excepting, that he did not profess any love for me, which at least was a relief; but, from the contents, I derived that he had expected his act to give him immortality, and expressed surprise that he should be criticized for coming to Dakota and saving the life of his child—as he put it—from the heartless man, that was killing her in his efforts to get rich.

He seemed to forget to mention any of the facts which had occurred during his last trip, namely; his many declarations of undying love for us; of how glad he was that we were doing so much toward the development of the great west; and his remarks that if he was twenty-five years younger it was where he would be. He also suggested that he would try to be transferred to the Omaha District, so that he might be nearer us.

CHAPTER XLII

A YEAR OF COINCIDENCES

ALTHOUGH the drouth had been broken all over the north, it lingered on, to the south. My parents wrote me from Kansas, that thousands of acres of wheat, sown early in the fall, had failed to sprout. It had been so dry. The ground was as dry as powder, and the winds were blowing the grain out of the sandy soil, which was drifting in great piles along the fences and in the road.

The government's final estimated yield of all crops was the smallest it had been for ten years. As a result, loan companies who had allowed interest to accumulate for one and two years, in the hope that the farmers and other investors would be able to sell, such having been the conditions of the past, now began to threaten foreclosure and money became hard to get.

From the south came reports that many counties in Oklahoma, that were loaded with debt, had defaulted for two years on the interest, and County warrants, that had always brought a premium, sold at a discount.

The rain that had followed the drouth, in the north, as the winter months set in, began to move south, and about Christmas came the heaviest snows the south had known for years. With the snows came low temperatures that lasted for weeks. As far south as Oklahoma city, zero weather gripped the country, and to the west the cattle left on the ranges froze to death by the thousands. A large part of those that lived—few were fit for the market, they were so thin—were sold to eastern speculators at gift prices, due to the fact that rough feed was not to be had.

The heavy snows that covered the entire country, from the Rocky Mountains to the Atlantic, and the bitter cold weather that followed, made shipping hazardous. Therefore, the rural districts suffered in every way. Snow continued to fall and the cold weather held forth, until it was to be seen, when warm weather arrived, the change would be sudden, and floods would result, such was the case.

It was a year of coincidences; the greatest drouth known for years, followed by the coldest winter and the heaviest snows, and these in turn by disastrous floods, will live long in memory.

To me the days were long, and the nights lonely. The late fall rains kept my flax growing until winter had set in, and snow fell before it was all harvested. All I could see of my crop was little white elevations over the field. There was no chance to get it threshed. My capital had all been exhausted, and it was a dismal prospect indeed. I used to sit there in my wife's lonely claim-house, with nothing else to occupy my mind but to live over the happy events connected with our courtship and marriage, and the sad events following her departure.

During my life on the Little Crow, I had looked forward joyfully to the time when I should be a husband and father, with a wife to love, and a home of my own. This had been so dominant in my mind, that when I thought it over, I could not clearly realize the present situation. I lived in a sort of stupor and my very existence seemed to be a dreadful nightmare. I would at times rouse myself, pinch the flesh, and move about, to see if it was my real self; and would try to shake off the loneliness which completely enveloped me. My head ached and my heart was wrung with agony.

I read a strange story, but its contents seemed so true to life. It related the incident of a criminal who had made an escape from a prison—not for freedom, but to get away for only an hour, that he might find a cat, or a dog, or something, that he could love.

It seems he had been an author, and by chance came upon a woman—during the time of his escape—who permitted him to love her, and during the short recess, to her he recited a poem entitled, "The right to love." The words of that poem burned my mind.

> *Love is only where is reply,*
> *I speak, you answer; There am I,*
> *And that is life everlasting.*
>
> *Love lives, to seek reply.*
> *I speak, no answer; Then I die,*
> *To seek reincarnation.*

As the cold days and long nights passed slowly by, and I cared for the stock and held down my wife's claim, the title of that story evolved in my mind, and I would repeat it until it seemed to drive me near insanity. I sought consolation in hope, and the winter days passed at last; but I continued to hope until I had grown to feel that when I saw my wife and called to her name, she would hear me and see the longing in my heart and soul; then would come the day of redemption.

CHAPTER XLIII

"AND SATAN CAME ALSO"

AME a day when the snow had disappeared; my threshing was done; I had money again, and to Chicago I journeyed. During the winter I had planned a way to get to see my wife, and took the first step toward carrying it out, immediately following my arrival in the city.

I went to a telephone and called up Mrs. Ewis. She recognized my voice and knew what I had come for. She said: "I am so glad I was near the phone when you called up, because your father-in-law is in the house this very minute." On hearing this I was taken aback, for it had not occurred to me that he might be in the city. As the realization that he was, became clear to me, I felt ill at ease, and asked how he came to be in the city at that time.

"Well," and from her tone I could see that she was also disturbed—"you see tomorrow is election and yesterday was Easter, so he came home to vote, and be here Easter, at the same time. Now, let me think a moment," she said nervously. Finally she called: "Oscar, I tell you what I will do. P. H. is sick and the Reverend has been here every day to see him." Here she paused again, then went on: "I will try to get him to go home, but he stays late. However, you call up in about an hour, and if he is still

273

here, I'll say 'this is the wrong number, see?' " "Yes," I said gratefully, and hung up the receiver.

I had by this time become so nervous that I trembled, and then went down into Custom House place—I had talked from the Polk Street station—and took a couple of drinks to try to get steady.

In an hour and a half I called up again and it was the "wrong number," so I went out south and called on a young railroad man and his wife, by the name of Lilis, who were friends of Orlean's and mine.

After expressing themselves as being puzzled as to why the Reverend should want to separate us, Mrs. Lilis told me of her. During the conversation Mrs. Lilis said: "After you left last year, I went over to see Orlean, and spoke at length of you, of how broken hearted you appeared to be, and that she should be in Dakota. Mrs. McCraline looked uncomfortable and tried to change the subject, but I said my mind, and watched Orlean. In the meantime I thought she would faint right there, she looked so miserable and unhappy. She has grown so fat, you know she was always so peaked before you married her. Everybody is wondering how her father can be so mean, and continue to keep her from returning home to you, but Mrs. Ewis can and will help you get her because she can do more with that family than anyone else. She and the Elder have been such close friends for the last fifteen years, and she should be able to manage him."

Then her mother said: "Oscar, I have known you all your life; I was raised up with your parents; knew all of your uncles; and know your family to have always been highly respected; but I cannot for my life see, why, if Orlean loves you, she lets her father keep her away from you. Now here is my Millie," she went on, turning her eyes to her daughter, "and Belle too, why, I could no more separate them from their husbands than I could fly—even if I was mean enough to want to."

"But why does he do it, Mama? The Reverend wants to break up the home of Orlean and Oscar," Mrs. Lilis put in, anxiously.

"Bless me, my child," her mother replied, "I have known N. J. McCraline for thirty years and he has been a rascal all the while. I am not surprised at anything that he would do."

"Well," said Mrs. Lilis, with a sigh of resignation, "it puzzles me."

I then told them about calling up Mrs. Ewis and what I had planned on doing. It was then about nine-thirty. As they had a phone, I called Mrs. Ewis again.

While talking, I had forgotten the signal, and remembered it only when I heard Mrs. Ewis calling frantically, from the other end of the wire, "This is the wrong number, Mister, this is the wrong number." With an exclamation, I hung up the receiver with a jerk.

Mrs. Ankin lived about two blocks east, so I went to her house from Mrs. Lilis'. On the street, the effect of what had passed, began to weaken me. I was almost overcome, but finally arrived at Mrs. Ankin's. Just before retiring, at eleven o'clock, I again called up Mrs. Ewis, and it was still the "wrong number." I went to bed and spent a restless night.

I awakened about five-thirty from a troubled sleep, jumped up, dressed, then went out and caught a car for the west side. I felt sure the Elder would go home during the night.

It is always very slow getting from the south to the west side in Chicago, on a surface car, and it was after seven o'clock when I arrived at the address, an apartment building, where Mrs. Ewis' husband held the position as janitor, and where they made their home, in the basement.

She was just coming from the grocery and greeted me with a cheerful "Good Morning," and "Do you know that rascal stayed here until twelve o'clock last night," she laughed. She called him "rascal" as a nickname. She took me into their quarters, invited me to a chair, sat down, and began to talk in a serious tone. "Now Oscar, I understand your circumstances thoroughly, and am going to help you and Orlean in every way I can. You understand Rev. McCraline has always been hard-headed, and the class of ministers he associates with are more hard-headed still. The Elder has never liked you because of your independence, and from the fact that you would not let him rule your house and submit to his ruling, as Claves does. Now Oscar, let me give you some advice. Maybe you are not acquainted with the circumstances, for if you had been, in the beginning, you might have avoided this trouble. What I am telling you is from experience, and I know it to be true. Don't ever criticize the preachers, to their faces, especially the older ones. They know their views and practices, in many instances, to be out of keeping with good morals, but they are not going to welcome any criticism of their acts. In fact, they will crucify criticism, and persecute those who have criticized them. Furthermore, you are fond of Booker T. Washington, and his ideas, and Rev. McCraline, like many other negro preachers, especially the older ones, hates him and everybody that openly approves of his ideas. His family admire the educator, and so do I, but we don't let on to him. Now I have a plan in mind, which I feel a most plausible one, and which I believe will work out best for you, Orlean, and myself. Before I mention it, I want to speak concerning the incident of last fall. When you sent him that bunch of letters, with mine in it, he fairly raised cain; as a result, the family quit speaking to me, and Orlean has not been over here for six months, until she and Ethel came a few days before Easter, to get the hats I have always given them. Now," she went on, seeming to become excited, "if I should invite Orlean over, the Elder would come along," which I knew to be true. "When you wrote me last summer in regard to taking her to a summer resort, so you could come and get her, I told Mary Arling about it. Now to be candid, Mrs. Arling and I are not the best of friends. You know she drinks a little too much, and I don't like that, but Mary Arling is a friend of yours, and a smart woman."

"Is that so?" I asked, showing interest, for I admired Mrs. Arling and her husband.

"Yes," Mrs. Ewis reassured me, "she is a friend of yours and you know all the McCraline family admire the Arlings, and Orlean goes there often." "Well, as I was saying," she went on, "last summer out at a picnic, Mrs. Arling got tipsy enough to speak her mind and she simply laid the family out about you. She told the Reverend right to his teeth that he was a dirty rascal, and knew it; always had been, and that it was a shame before God and man the way he was treating you. Yes, she said it," she reassured me when I appeared to doubt a little. "And she told me she wished you had asked her to take Orlean away; that she would not only have taken her away from Chicago, but would have carried her on back to Dakota where she wanted to be, instead of worrying her life away in Chicago, in fear of her father's wrath. So now, my plan is that you go over to her house, see? You know the address."

I knew the house. "Well," and she put it down on a piece of paper, "you go over there, and she will help you; and Oscar, for God's sake, she implored, with tears in her eyes, do be careful. I know Orlean loves you and you do her, but the Reverend has it in for you, and if he learned you were in the city, Orlean would not be allowed to leave the house. Now, she added, I will get him over here as soon as I can and you do your part. Good-bye."

I took a roundabout way in getting back to the south side, keeping out of the colored neighborhood as long as possible, by taking a Halsted street car south, got a transfer, and took a Thirty-fifth street car.

I was careful to avoid meeting anyone who might know me, but who might not be aware of my predicament, and who might thoughtlessly inform the McCralines.

I arrived at Mrs. Arlings without meeting anyone who knew me, however. They owned and occupied an elaborate flat at an address in the Thirty-seventh block on Wabash avenue. I rang the bell, which was answered by a young lady unknown to me, but who, I surmised, roomed at the house. She inquired the name, and when I had told her she let out an "O!" and invited me into the parlor. She hurried away to tell Mrs. Arling, who came immediately, and holding both hands out to me, said, "I am so glad you came at last, Oscar, I am so glad."

After we had said a few words concerning the weather, etc., I said in a serious tone, "Mrs. Arling, I am being persecuted on account of my ideas."

"I know it, Oscar, I know it," she repeated, nodding her head vigorously, and appeared eager.

I then related briefly the events of the past year, including the Reverend's trip to Dakota.

Raising her arms in a gesture, she said: "If you remember the day after you were married, when we had the family and you over to dinner, and you and Richard (her husband) talked on race matters that the Elder never joined. Well, when you had gone Richard said: 'Oscar and the Elder are not going to be friends long, for their views are too far apart.' When he brought Orlean home last year I said to Richard, 'Rev. McCraline is up to some trick.' Continuing, she went on to tell me, "You are aware how bitter most of the colored preachers are in regard to Booker T. Washington." "Yes," I assented. "Mrs. Ewis and I talked the matter over and she said the Reverend had it in for you from the beginning, that is, he wanted to crush your theories, and have you submissive, like Ethel's husband. He was more anxious to have you look up to him because you had something; but after he found out you were not going to, well, this is the result."

"Now, Oscar, whatever you suggest, if it is in my power to do so, I will carry it out, because I am sure Orlean loves you. She always seems so glad when I talk with her about you. She comes over often," she went on, "and we get to talking of you." Now before I tell you more, you must not feel that she does not care for you, because she allows her father to keep her away from you. Orlean is just simple, babylike and is easy to rule. She gets that from her mother, for you know Mary Ann is helpless." I nodded, and she continued. "As for the Reverend, he has raised them to obey him, and they do, to the letter; the family, with Claves thrown in, fear him, but as I was going to say: Orlean told me when I asked her why she did not go on back to you, 'Well, I don't know.' You know how she drags her speech. 'Oscar loves me, and we never had a quarrel. In fact, there is nothing wrong between us and Oscar would do anything to please me. The only thing I did not like, was, that Oscar thought more of his land and money than he did of me, and I wanted to be first.' "

"Isn't that deplorable," I put in, shaking my head sadly.

"Of course it is," she replied with a shrug, "why, that could be settled in fifteen minutes, if it were not for that old preacher. She always likes to talk of you and it seems to do her good."

"Now, my plan is," I started, with a determined expression, "to have you call her up, see?"

"Yes, yes," she answered anxiously.

"And invite her over on pretense of accompanying you to a matinee."

"Yes, yes," and then, her face seemed to brighten with an idea, and she said: "Why not go to a matinee?"

"Why yes," I assented. "I had not thought of that, then, "Why sure, fine and dandy. We will all go, yes, indeed," I replied, with good cheer.

She went to the phone and called up the number. In a few minutes she returned, wearing a jubilant expression, and cried: "I've fixed it, she is coming over and we will all go to a matinee. Won't it be fine?" she continued, jumping up and down, and clapping her hands joyfully, beside herself with enthusiasm, and I joined her.

Two hours later, Mrs. Hite—the young lady that answered the door when I came that morning—called from the look-out, where she had been watching while Mrs. Arling was dressing, and I, too nervous to sit still, was walking to and fro across the room—that Orlean was coming. We had been uneasy for fear the Elder might hear of my being in the city, before Orlean got away. I rushed to the window and saw my wife coming leisurely along the walk, entirely ignorant of the anxious eyes watching her from the second-story window. I could see, at the first glance, she had grown fleshy; she had begun before she left South Dakota. It was a bay window and we watched her until she had come up the steps and pulled the bell.

Mrs. Arling had told me my wife did not have any gentleman company. I had not felt she had, for, in the first place, she was not that kind of a woman, and if her father, by his ways, discouraged any men in coming to see her while she was single, he was sure to discourage any afterward. But Mrs. Arling had added: "I told her I was going to get her a beau, so you get behind the door, and when she comes in I will tell her that I have found the beau."

I obeyed, and after a little Orlean walked into the room,

smiling and catching her breath, from the exertion of coming up the steps. I stepped behind her and covered her eyes with my hands. Mrs. Arling chirped, "That is your beau, so you see I have kept my word, and there he is." I withdrew my hands and my wife turned and exclaimed "Oh!" and sank weakly into a chair.

We had returned from the theatre, where we witnessed a character play with a moral, A Romance of the Under World. We had tickets for an evening performance to see Robert Mantell in Richelieu. Mrs. Arling ushered us into her sitting room, closed the door, and left us to ourselves.

I took my wife by the hand; led her to a rocker; sat down and drew her down on my knee, and began with: "Now, dear, let us talk it over."

I knew about what to expect, and was not mistaken. She began to tell me of the "wrongs" I had done her, and the like. I calculated this would last about an hour, then she would begin to relent, and she did. After I had listened so patiently without interrupting her, but before I felt quite satisfied, she wanted to go to the phone and call up the house to tell the folks that I was in town.

"Don't do that, dear," I implored. "I don't want them to know, that is, just yet." The reason I was uneasy and wanted her to wait awhile was, that I felt her father would go to call on Mrs. Ewis about eight o'clock and it was now only seven. But she seemed restless and ill at ease, and persisted that she should call up mother, and let her know, so I consented, reluctantly. Then as she was on the way to the phone I called her and said: "Now, Orlean there are two things a woman cannot be at the same time, and that is, a wife to her husband and a daughter to her father. She must sacrifice one or the other."

"I know it," she replied, and appeared to be confused and hesitant, but knowing she would never be at ease until she had called up, I said "Go ahead," and she did.

I shall not soon forget the expression on her face, then the look of weak appeal that she turned on me, when her father's deep voice rang through the phone in answer to her "Hello." The next instant she appeared to sway and then leaned against the wall trembling as she answered, "Oh! Pa-pa, ah," and seeming to have no control of her voice. She now appeared frightened, while Mrs. Arling and Mrs. Hite stood near, holding their breath and looked discouraged. She finally managed to get it out, but hardly above a whisper, "Oscar is here."

"Well," he answered, and his voice could be heard distinctly by those standing near. "Well," he seemed to roar in a commanding way, "Why don't you bring him to the house?"

What passed after that I do not clearly remember, but I have read lots of instances of where people lost their heads, where, if they would have had presence of mind, they might have saved their army, won some great victory or done something else as notorious, but in this I may be classed as one of the unfortunates who simply lost his head. That is how it was described later, but speaking for myself, when I heard the voice of the man who had secured my wife by coercion and kept her away from me a year; which had caused me to suffer, and turned my existence into a veritable nightmare, the things that passed through my mind during the few moments thereafter are sad to describe.

I heard his voice say again, "Why don't you bring him to the house?" But I could only seem to see her being torn from me, while he, a massive brute, stood over lecturing me, for what he termed, "my sins," but what were merely the ideas of a free American citizen. How could I listen to a lecture from a person with his reputation. This formed in my mind and added to the increasing but suppressed anger. I could see other years passing with nothing to remember my wife by, but the little songs she had sung so often while we were together in Dakota.

Roses, roses, roses bring memory of you, dear,
Roses so sweet and endearing,
Roses with dew of the morn;
You were fresh for a day then you faded away.
Red roses bring memories of you.

The next moment I had taken the receiver from her hand, and called, "Hello, Rev. McCraline," in a savage tone. When he had answered, I continued in a more savage voice, "You ask my wife why she did not bring me to the house?"

"Yes," he answered. His voice had changed from the commanding tone, and now appeared a little solicitous. "Yes, why don't you come to the house?" I seemed to hear it as an insult. I did not seem to understand what he meant, although I understood the words clearly. They seemed, however, to say; "Come to the house, and I will take your wife, and then kick you into the street."

I answered, with anger burning my voice, "I don't want to come to your house, because the last time I was there, I was kicked out. Do you hear? Kicked out."

"Well, I did not do it." Now, I had looked for him to say that very thing. I felt sure that he had put Ethel up to the evil doing of a year before, and now claimed to know nothing about it, which was like him. It made me, already crazed with anger, more furious, and I screamed over the phone, "I know you didn't, and I knew that was what you would say, but I know you left orders for it to be done."

"Where is Orlean?" he put in, his voice returning to authoritative tone.

"She is here with me," I yelled, and hung the receiver up viciously.

It was only then I realized that Mrs. Arling and Mrs. Hite

had hold of each arm and had been shouting in my ears all this while, "Oscar, Mr. Devereaux, Oscar, don't! don't! don't!" and in the meantime fear seemed to have set my wife in a state of terror. She now turned on me, in tones that did not appear natural. The words I cannot, to this day, believe, but I had become calm and now plead with her, on my knees, and with tears; but her eyes saw me not, and her ears seemed deaf to entreaty. She raved like a crazy woman and declared she hated me. Of a sudden, some one rang the bell viciously, and Mrs. Arling commanded me to go up the stairs. I retreated against my will. She opened the door, and in walked the Reverend.

Orlean ran to him and fell into his arms and cried: "Papa, I do not know what I would do if it were not for you," and kissed him—she had not kissed me. After a pause, I went up to him. As I approached he turned and looked at me, with a dreadful sneer in his face, which seemed to say, "So I have caught you. Tried to steal a march on me, eh?" And the eyes, they were the same, the eyes of a pig, expressionless.

Feeling strange, but composed, I advanced to where he stood, laid my hands upon his shoulder, looked into his face and said slowly, "Rev. McCraline, don't take my wife"—paused, then went on, "why could you not leave us for a day. We were happy, not an hour ago." Here my stare must have burned, my look into his face was so intense, and he looked away, but without emotion. "And now I ask you, for the sake of humanity, and in justice to mankind, don't take my wife."

Not answering me, he said to my wife: "Do you want your papa?"

"Yes, yes," she said and leaned on him. Then she looked into his face and said: "He insulted you."

"Yes yes, dear," he answered. "He has done that right along, but you step outside and Papa will tend to him."

She still clung to him and said: "He has made you suffer."

He bowed his head, and feigned to suffer. I stood looking on mechanically. He repeated, "Run outside, dear," and he stood holding the door open, then, realization seemed to come to her, she turned and threw herself into Mrs. Arling's arms, weakly, and broke into mournful sobs. Her father drew her gently from the embrace and with her face in her hands, and still sobbing, she passed out. He followed and through the open door I caught a glimpse of Claves on the sidewalk below, the man who had written—not a year before, "I am going to be a brother, and help you."

The next moment the door closed softly behind them. That was the last time I saw my wife.

THE END

Epilogue

The Givens Foundation for African American Literature

YOU HAVE to know where you came from to understand where you are going. This familiar expression of the value of history is at the heart of the Givens Foundation for African American Literature. Our mission is to promote historical and contemporary black literature. This partnership with Washington Square Press to republish out-of-print African American classics helps accomplish the goal of keeping literature and its lessons alive.

The Givens Foundation is inspired by and draws its mission from the Archie Givens, Sr., Collection of African American Literature. Housed at the University of Minnesota's Elmer L. Andersen Library, the collection includes over nine thousand books, pamphlets, manuscripts, letters, and ephemera representing more than two centuries of African American cultural accomplishment. Many of these items are signed, rare, and first-edition volumes. Each year hundreds of books, ranging from novels, plays, poems, short stories, and autobiographies to nonfiction and scholarly titles, join the collection and enhance its portrayal of the African American experience.

While we protect these historical artifacts for future generations in a secure environment, we also strive to keep their content circulating, so that contemporary audiences can learn from their timeless messages. The Givens Foundation actively celebrates and promotes African American literature and history. Our public programs, readings, conferences, and exhibits build on the collection and increase public awareness of African American writers. Using themes such as the Harlem Renaissance and the Black Arts Movement, we also create online lesson plans and teacher-training seminars for educators seeking African American literary resources for the classroom.

The Givens Collection Classics series is an exciting new venture because it unveils powerful stories and expressions from over a century ago. We believe that our past informs and shapes both our present and future. And it is our profound hope that a new generation of readers will discover these books and gain a deeper understanding of our multifaceted American history, and an increased ability to appreciate the texture of the lives that lie ahead of us.

—*Archie Givens, Jr.*

President

Givens Foundation for African American Literature

www.givens.org
7151 York Avenue South
Minneapolis, MN 55435
(952) 831-2555